COMBAT: CLOSE-UP

Each time we rolled over and over, locked in a death embrace, more sand got into my eyes, nose, and mouth. We each had an arm around the other's neck. I held his wrist that clawed at my face, keeping it from extracting my eyes.

The VC was stronger than I could have imagined for his size. My own strength seemed nonexistent . . . just enough to hang on. The greasy, rotten clothing and putrid stench of body odor, mixed with my fear of not finding the necessary energy reserves, made my stomach begin to retch.

I also had a fear of one of his comrades coming up and blowing the back of my head out. . . .

"THE QUINTESSENTIAL COMBAT AUTOBIOGRAPHY"

—National Catholic Review

BOOK YOUR PLACE ON OUR WEBSITE AND MAKE THE READING CONNECTION!

We've created a customized website just for our very special readers, where you can get the inside scoop on everything that's going on with Zebra, Pinnacle and Kensington books.

When you come online, you'll have the exciting opportunity to:

- View covers of upcoming books

- Read sample chapters

- Learn about our future publishing schedule (listed by publication month *and author*)

- Find out when your favorite authors will be visiting a city near you

- Search for and order backlist books from our online catalog

- Check out author bios and background information

- Send e-mail to your favorite authors

- Meet the Kensington staff online

- Join us in weekly chats with authors, readers and other guests

- Get writing guidelines

- AND MUCH MORE!

Visit our website at
http://www.kensingtonbooks.com

GREEN KNIGHT, RED MOURNING

RICHARD E. OGDEN

PINNACLE BOOKS
Kensington Publishing Corp.
http://www.kensingtonbooks.com

Dedicated to the 2.8 million Americans who served in Vietnam.

Be proud; it wasn't your mistake. With the social consciousness concerning humanity that was prevalent in the sixties and seventies, any war for any reason, justifiable or not, would have been unconscionable.... Our country was not proud of itself; therefore it was unwilling, if not crippled, in showing us any pride or compassion.... Be proud you served and grateful you survived. You know more about life than anyone else around you.

A special thank you to Beth, who pushed and insisted that I read; to Patricia Chapman, who insisted that I write; to Maureen Wilkinson, Greg Hill, Jane Stewart, and Martin George; to my parents, Dell and Jack, who gave me the courage and will to survive in a "rough" world; to J.A.S.; and to the great John D. McDonald.

R.E.O.

CHAPTER ONE

The company commander was a tall, lean Naval Academy graduate from Austin, Texas, who spoke with a soft twang influenced most of the time by a wad of chewing tobacco.

"I regret I can't wish you boys a good morning. Your squad leaders informed you earlier this morning that our listening post was hit last night, and as a result we have two dead Marines; two KIAs. As I see it, one of them killed the other."

Confusion and anxiety rushed up and down the ranks. A small Marine at the end of the first rank raised his hand and was called on.

"Sir, how was it possible? They were buddies, the best of friends."

"We all know that, don't we?" the captain answered. "One of them killed the other just as though he pulled a K-Bar and sliced his throat where he slept."

His voice and temperament changed back and forth

7

radically with each sentence like an evangelist at the pulpit. His young tanned skin stretched over high cheekbones and a wide jaw. He had piercing brown eyes accented by a dark, thin brush of eyebrows that revealed perhaps a drop or two of Indian blood. He scanned every member of the congregation and looked each of them right in the eye—the juvenile delinquents, the honor students, the junior high school dropouts, the choirboys, the muggers, the cowards, the Blacks, the Chicanos, the Orientals, the Marxists, the Catholics, the Jews, the leaders, and the shitbirds. The cross section of his company was a cross section of every Marine outfit.

"Either Edwards or Holmes was supposed to be awake on watch but went to sleep, allowing the Vietcong to get to them. Their remains were found at the listening post. The enemy was not only giving us an object lesson on what happens to the man who goes to sleep on watch, but something far more reaching. Something that can destroy everything we've learned in training: courage and morale. If we allow them to tamper with our brains and souls, we will be ineffective in our role here. I am going to use this incident as an object lesson of my own, since we've already paid a heavy price for it. We are new here in Vietnam, and things are much different than we expected. I know most of you are barely out of Algebra One and Two, figuratively speaking. We've made mistakes, but we'll learn. Your job is to engage and destroy the enemy, and my job is to keep you alive. It's also my job to write your mother and tell her you won't be coming home. My primary purpose right now is to impress upon you that we are in the middle of a real war. The enemy means business, and so do we. Thanks to the Vietcong last night, I think I've found the ultimate solution. I guarantee no one will fall asleep on watch or take their duties lightly after what you experience this morning."

Each squad filed off from the formation and followed the captain around to the rear of the CP tent. No one spoke. The seriousness of the situation began to penetrate and register on their faces.

Two corpsmen (medics) stood solemnly, adjacent to a large mound lying on a canvas covered with a shelter half. The perimeter of the exposed canvas was saturated with blood. Tiny drops of blood slowly dripped off onto the ground, refusing to be absorbed by the fine dust, and formed tiny wine-colored beads of perfect symmetry that rolled across the powder into the giant crater of a nearby footprint.

The sight and the metallic, pungent odor of human blood was already changing the color and the stomachs of the onlooking troops. The corpsmen pulled back the bloody shroud and dropped it in the dust. A synchronized gasp of horror and a spontaneous rush of nausea swept the paralyzed, captive audience. Some immediately turned away, pushing through the crowd to hide their weakness and embarrassment, while others in the rear pushed forward to see what was creating the fervor. Most held their ground and stared, immobilized, in shock.

Somehow the bodies of the two Marines had been meshed together, integrated into one single mound of horrifying flesh and bone as if they had been quartered and dropped into a blender with the setting on "coarse chop." It was first thought by the corpsmen that the heads had been severed and were missing; but after closer examination, they discovered the presence of broken teeth and fragments of jawbone. The skulls had been smashed and pulverized. The eyes had been extracted intact and were scattered on top of the mound. They stared out in all directions, one set blue and the other brown, giving the hideous mass a lifelike appearance, as if it could slide off the canvas in any direction, either to escape or to attack. The large bones of the bodies—the femures, tibias, and pelvises—were completely filleted of flesh, cracked and pulled apart, revealing the bone marrow. The hearts, livers, and genitals were left intact and were on display.

"What madness compels a human to such diabolical butchery? What is its disguise—survival, politics, religion?" the captain reflected.

The sick and shocked did not hear him, lost momentarily in the horror and the confusion of the incident. There was the irony surrounding the two casualties, even in contemporary times of diminished social unrest. They were unique only for the reason that they had been very good friends and they had inadvertently killed one another. They would be buried together, but in separate places; one box in New Mexico and the other in Michigan; one black and the other white.

A small white-faced Marine sagged on an ammo box against a tree. He hung his head and wiped the slime of an erupted breakfast off his lapel with a handful of grass.

The corpsman kneeled down. "You all right, pardner?"

"No, I'm not all right. I'm not going to be sick any more, but I don't think I can handle it. I mean this war, this place . . ."

"You'll be all right. We all will. I think the captain was right in showing us the bodies. I'm sure it was a hard decision. He wanted to impress upon all of us the fact that this isn't another training maneuver or war game. It didn't seem like a war was going on here in this lush, beautiful community. Last night proved there is."

"Doc, you're older and you know a lot. What kind of a human or animal stalks around here and can do something like this?"

"I know it's hard to believe. They're men like you and me, with families and dreams."

The little one stood up in a rage. "You're out of your goddamn mind. You're crazy!" He stomped away.

Doc sat down on the ammo box, rested his elbows on his knees, chin in hand, and looked after the pathetic little Marine. He mumbled into his folded hands: "The Vietnam War welcomes you to Algebra One and Two."

The early rise of the demon sun had not yet sucked the much-relished residual moisture from the air or devoured the pleasantness of the morning. The silence of mourning replaced the symphony of crickets, frogs, and beautiful, nocturnal feathered spirits that haunt

11

the night.

Defensive positions are the same in every war. Through the centuries the materials change; sandbags replace logs and stones, the strains of concertina wire replace thorn bushes. But the trench lines are the same, the men are the same, and the reasons are the same.

CHAPTER TWO

On November 10, 1945, in the tiny seacoast town of Bellingham in northwest Washington, another unimportant statistic was recorded.

I always envied the few kids I knew who were born on Halloween. It was a special, if not classic, date. I missed it by eleven days. I had mixed emotions regarding the irony surrounding my own shred of uniqueness. Due to my introversion—which is a kinder word for just plain backwardness—and the Marine Corps' intense passion for celebration, I was ready to keep my secret under wraps forever. I was born on the 170th birthday of the Marine Corps.

We were a divorced family living in North Seattle when I was four years old. A combination of prolonged months of commercial fishing in Alaskan waters and other phantom jobs, plus the peculiarities of temperament between the older city-wise man and the younger backwoods woman frayed the fabric of family unity

13

beyond repair. My mother remarried, and a desperate plan was put into motion. We decided to load up the Model A Ford with kin and courage and flee to the country, away from the ghetto of auto courts, rats, bedbugs, and unscrupulous landlords.

The change of worlds was exciting. Our tiny parcel of land at the end of a very long gravel road left us in the middle of nowhere. The land was lush, clean, and green. It was thickly carpeted with fern and well-guarded with thick, heavy alders. There were so many things for a four-year-old to explore, uproot, chew on, and get lost in, it was mind-boggling. We lived in a tent until our poor excuse of a house was built. It was a two-room, tar-paper shack constructed of used lumber collected from a construction job where my stepdad worked; someone's old barn was transformed into our little house at the end of the road. Laura Ingalls Wilder would have been delighted. The rats and bedbugs we left behind in Seattle would pass in review and weep for us.

My mother was seven months pregnant but insisted on climbing up to the roof to help finish laying it down before the winter weather came. We planted an enormous garden filled with anything that could be grown and consumed. Nearly everything grown, foraged, or hunted was canned in preparation for the long cold winter. There were plenty of deer, pheasants, and grouse in the surrounding woods. The population of our modest farm seemed to grow daily with chickens, ducks, turkeys, and rabbits. Pens, hutches, and coops sprang like a zoological ghetto to keep them from the garden. The work load increased when frost began to lay on the hardiest of garden vegetables, the pumpkin. My chores included anything I could be trained to do at such a young age. I carried wood to the house or fetched water from the nearby creek under close supervision. I never fell in or got wet . . . much.

The first year, the little house was without lights, water, or a sewer. Before sundown, coal-oil lanterns were lit. When the winter of 1950 finally came, it was the worst in years. The tar-paper mansion held up remarkably well against the driving blizzards. It offered very little resistance; the wind whipped through the knotholes and cracks. The tar paper was expensive; we substituted cardboard for insulation. My brother and I slept in cardboard boxes lined with newspapers. Below us, under the floorboards, huddled the hounds and other livestock. Baby turkeys and newborn chicks were brought into the house and put in a makeshift brooder next to the wood stove. Turkeys were very hard to raise in their early stages; they died easily in the slightest draft, but when they were grown, they could sit in the trees in the wintertime during a blizzard without a problem. For years to come, in the winter months there was always someone in the intensive-care ward next to the stove.

Our most insufferable, uncelebrated convenience was the very little house at the end of the road without its folklore mail-order catalog. My most unsavory memory of it was when I accidentally dropped a flashlight down the hole and was ordered to retrieve it. Never underestimate the genius of a six-year-old.

When my brother and I were older, we converted the chicken coop into a bunkhouse. We were delighted with it. We had our own place, and the chickens didn't seem to mind; they weren't giving up much. We didn't realize until we started school that we were going to be subjected to a different kind of burden. Not everyone seemed wealthy, but we were below the poverty-line poor. We went barefoot all summer so there would be money for boots in the winter. We were treated like we had some kind of scourge, or leprosy. We did not understand.

I was an educational contradiction. I was a poor student, but never missed a day of school. I excelled in the classes that consumed my interest, like music and art, and failed at those I found boring, which I later regretted. I needed school for its social life. It was still limited, but it was a diversion from the hard, never-ending chores on the farm. I had grown to hate the chores, the poor excuse for a home, and everything else. I had little reward other than something to eat and a place to sleep.

I enjoyed sports, even though I was too small to be very competitive. I was overjoyed to suit up, sit on the bench, and be a part of the fraternity. The little things pleased me, but the chores and the family's lack of understanding intervened.

By the time I was sixteen, the confrontations with my mother had become more frequent and more intense, almost to the point of violence; she was tiny, endurably strong, and very stubborn, and I was getting more and more frustrated. My stepdad understood my problems;

I guess he understood all our problems. He tried to keep the peace and to mediate the best he could. One day at the highest point of my restlessness and frustration, I was surprised when my mother agreed I should enlist. I chose the Marine Corps because I liked their song.

CHAPTER THREE

At 10:00 A.M., April 10, 1965, with a command from the bridge, Second Battalion, Third Marine Division, climbed over the side of the four-story-high assault ship. We headed down the debarkation nets that went taut and slack with each roll of the great ship. The nets stretched to the waiting landing craft hugged against the ship like debris, bouncing and straining against the tide and the breeze.

It was a bright sunny morning. The sea was more black than blue, accented with wind-lashed whitecaps. We hung three abreast in mid-air in the net. We looked down at the tiny buffeted target on the surface and waited for the net to go taut with the next roll of the ship. We scrambled down like spiders clinging to a communal web under siege, refusing to be popped off by the increased gusts of wind or washed off by the sea now beginning to dash up between the hull of the ship and the LCPs. We were carrying about forty pounds of gear each. Men had fallen off in training and had been crushed under milder circumstances.

Grinning Charlie, to my right, was still grinning, and Red, to my left, was expressionless. He licked the salt from his cheeks, waiting for another wave. One of the secrets to getting down safely was staying abreast to balance out the net and not letting anyone get ahead of the others. At the right time, I gave the signal. We scrambled down the rest of the way. When the landing craft was considered full we were jammed in tight, life jacket to life jacket. It was like any other training maneuver we had endured hundreds of times before, but the three bold letters of WAR stood out in a gray haze on the bulletin board of my mind, which was already cluttered with diesel exhaust fumes and the oncoming twinges of seasickness. One of the reasons I joined the Corps was to stay out of the Navy, because I was chronically seasick every time we went fishing as a kid. I did not know the Marine Corps was part of the Navy—the worst part!

Before we made the long haul from San Diego to Yokohama, I had been a reasonably respected and trusted leader. I was the smallest and the youngest at seventeen. I was doing well until seasickness dropped me to my knees and I became almost totally delirious for the entire trip. I was incapable of taking care of myself, let alone commanding a fire team. Members of the fire team had to carry me back and forth from cot to chow. Left under a ladder or stairwell during the day, I sometimes lay in my own puke, unable to get to the rail. I couldn't go below and lie in the cots during the day. I was in a minor running conflict with two of the squad leaders of the platoon. Now that I was incapacitated, they were unforgiving. I was relieved of my fire team.

At one point, it seemed I had recovered; I had developed stronger, though still less than adequate, sea legs. On a fire watch down in one of the compartments in violent seas, I had a relapse and passed out where a seabag and some valuable equipment, including a rifle, were stolen. I nearly got into a fight with one of the squad leaders when he kept calling me a shitbird during the investigation. I told him what he could do with himself in very explicit language. It even startled me, the believer, who carried a small New Testament tucked away in the web of my helmet. My whole world was falling apart. I was found guilty of dereliction of duty at an Office Hours proceeding. I wasn't busted since I had an unblemished service record, but I spent a week in the hot filthy bilges stripping paint. It was a less-than-adequate remedial exercise for seasickness.

Everything I had worked for in the last couple of years was shot away. I'd always felt that the self-confidence I painstakingly laminated together was like tiny shreds of courage the thickness of veneer. No matter how small the triumphs were, I was building something . . . somebody I wanted to be . . . someone I could have more pride in. But from then on, the troops reacted a little differently around me—not cold, but cool. My own fire team was less than warm, and when snide remarks surfaced from others behind my back like platoon pussy, a dissident, and a shitbird, I didn't blame the team. My reputation was at its lowest ebb. Grinning Charlie was the exception. He patted me on the back reassuringly.

"Don't let them kid you. Those assholes are just as fucking scared as anybody!" He was one of the older privates in the platoon, and elected to remain a private.

We continued to circle in a wide berth around the mother ship, waiting for the entire battalion to debark, join up, organize, and assault the beach in waves. I doubt if anyone got any sleep the night before. Most of the troops lay around in their racks, quiet and sullen, thinking and wondering. Others, not thinking or contemplating any less, showed more exuberance by burning up nervous tension sharpening and re-sharpening bayonets and shaving each other in tests of their ability. They stripped down weapons, reassembled them time and time again, polished rounds of ammo, counted hand grenades, and many tried to get more than the regular allotment of ammunition and hand grenades. No one seemed to be afraid of what could happen tomorrow. They were high on anxiety and excitement, like Olympians eager to be tested after years of bone-crushing agony in training, sacrifice, and discipline.

We had been living literally on top of each other in the hold of the ship for nearly a month. Racks or bunks were stacked eight high. Heavy seas, undue harassment by Naval Personnel, bad food, endless drills, endless inspections, rough seas, seasickness, and more rough seas caused nerves and tempers to fray to their last thread. Everyone was more than ready, and God help anyone who opposed us on the beach. Even after lights-out the locker-room antics continued, with self-confirmed cowards listening to self-confirmed heroes brag about how psychotic and volatile they were going to be tomorrow. I lay in my rack with two darning needles in my wooly brain busily working on all the tangled fabric, trying to construct some kind of an emotional pattern. But when some of the more arduous knots and confused snarls were worked free, a chilling thought would tug on the strands, seizing them up again. The thought of killing someone terrified the hell out of me.

The lip of the monster popped. Its great jaw slammed down to the white, hot Vietnamese beach and spewed out hundreds of green, screaming and yelling moronic organisms programmed and primed for trouble. With the race of diesel engines, the traditional primal cry of an attack battalion, the momentary confusion of finding one's prospective unit and getting into proper order on line, to advance on a single command was nearly impossible. A mile-long line of men at five-yard intervals can advance inland in a matter of seconds if unopposed. Unless someone fell, there was no way to tell if we were drawing hostile fire.

We came ashore several miles north of Danang in the area technically known as Red Beach, characterized by white sand dunes and scrub pine trees, and intense heat. The surrounding area was referred to as the I Corps; Elephant Valley to the indigents, and Phu

Young Province to the map makers of old. All this information we were painstakingly supplied with didn't mean a damn thing. We, the subordinates, were lost any time we left the ship in any country.

We lay in our firing positions at the crest of the searing hot sand dunes competing for lungs full of almost-useless hot air. From time to time we caught our breath. The awesome gripping sound of absolutely nothing grabbed one's head as though it were trapped in the clutches of a fist. We were told we could expect a "hot" beach in the military sense of the word (bullets). Sweat dripped into the mechanisms of our immaculate, freshly oiled weapons, safeties off and fingers laid heavy on the triggers, while blood pounded back and forth from one ear to the other. Salt-irritated eyes scanned the lower sand dunes; shrubbery danced like a fantasy in the intenseness of the heat waves—and after long agonizing minutes of nothing but silence, the slow, withdrawing relief from the intense pressure was frustrating and demoralizing. It was like being the victim of an unfunny hoax. Would we have been elated had there been machine guns waiting for us? Fear is healthy and stimulating, but risking your life looking for trouble is not.

Silence was broken somewhere down the line like a rock shattering a window pane.

"I see something."

The needles in the built-in human survival mechanism jumped back to red again; pivoting eyeballs locked up; the entire respiratory system froze. Without the slightest warning the wind began to blow, carrying sand and creating a foglike mist over the ground. Nothing could be trusted, animate or inanimate, with the combination of blowing sand and heat waves. Everything danced. Without taking my eyes from the front, I popped open the breech of the M-79 and felt for the butt end of the shell, like I had done so many times before, to make sure I hadn't forgotten to put in a shell. I had inherited the M-79 grenade launcher from Morales, who had taken over my fire team. I was almost totally unfamiliar with it. It resembled the twenty-millimeter sawed-off shotgun, and looked similar to a tear-gas gun. It throws out a shell three hundred meters with the explosiveness of a hand grenade. It gives a man one hell of a throwing arm.

A small, dark, squiggling mass appeared on the crest of a sand dune about three hundred yards away. It grew to be the unstable outline of a man, then another, and another. The enemy was advancing down the barrels of the entire battalion. A battalion-sized ambush in broad daylight in open terrain was hard to believe. Speculations and explanations began to filter up and down the line. "It must be a Bonsai attack!" More figures appeared over the horizon. They were growing into a small mob heading in a straight line toward Hotel Company and our platoon. They opened up with machine guns! . . . No! It was the turbo engine on a chopper gunship flying in the background. The mob kept growing bigger and getting closer. The word was passed down the line to hold our fire. Every rifleman and machine-gun crew had a single individual as a target. I kept re-estimating the range and re-adjusting the rear sights. Again, the word came down to hold our fire. They were about two hundred yards away. There were three dozen in a very loose group about platoon size. They didn't seem to be very disciplined, and didn't practice the five-yard interval between each man. A good-sized mortar neatly placed would nearly wipe them out. Once more the word was passed. The tiny nerves under my left eye began to twitch. My hands began to shake. I looked around to see if anyone was watching me. Grinning Charlie had no grin for the first time since I'd known him. Trudeau, the squad leader, was breathing heavy with clenched teeth and open mouth. Red blinked hard and frequently to keep salt-filled perspiration from burning his eyes.

"It's the press corps!"

Immediately the machine guns they carried on their shoulders began to look more like cameras, and the mortar baseplates and ammo boxes began to look more like sound equipment. There wasn't a weapon among the whole group. We remained rigid in our firing positions, exhausted and dumbfounded. It was literally an invasion of the press. They greeted us with smiles and hellos. The logos on the cameras read ABC, CBS, and NBC. The assault on Red Beach had turned into a television special!

"Where's the war, for crissakes?" a Marine yelled.

"Walter Crankcase here?"

"I thought I saw Huntley and Brinkley over there somewhere, and Mike Wallace, too!"

"It's not Wallace, but it looks like Roger Mudd!"

"I prefer Eric Sevareid, myself!"

"Shut up, you guys," Trudeau yelled. "Stay in your positions and watch your front!"

A reporter with a very dark tan, clad in a Hawaiian shirt, shorts, and sandals, came over and stuck a mike up to my mouth. A cameraman went down on his knees and moved in close, racked and focused.

"How do you like the Vietnam war so far, son?"

I stammered and stuttered.

"Look into the camera now and say hello to Mom. She may catch the six o'clock news."

I looked into the lens that kept moving in and out. I could see myself reflected in the glass. I gave a weak sheepish hello and a terrified grin.

Charlie was up grinning for the still photographers. Red had attracted another network. Nellis, on the other end of the squad, was busy scribbling something in a reporter's notebook, probably something to his dad in Chicago.

When the camera was turned off, I asked a reporter where the fighting was going on.

"There's fighting going on everywhere, but it's at night. The farmers till the rice fields during the day and pick up weapons at night. Nothing ever happens during the day around here." That was all too obvious.

I didn't understand, but I thanked him. The word was passed not to talk to reporters.

"Don't tell them anything!" Charlie yelled up the line.

"Tell the colonel to relax. His secret mission has been uncovered. It's six o'clock news now."

We had somehow survived our first beachhead and

human-wave assault. The press party had been hastily terminated by the irate colonel and his staff. He suffered the humiliation, while we thought it was hilarious.

When we calmed down from our precombat jitters, we weren't anticipating the hot trek across Elephant Valley to the mountains. The one-hundred-degree heat and gusting furnacelike air was a little more tolerable when we learned that a six-bi, "troop truck" convoy was going to pick us up. No one complained about the bone-crushing nontorsion air ride, the bronchial-clogging iron-rich dust, or the teenage drivers cursed with "Indie" phobia. The only fear I had of trucks were antitank mines capable of throwing a Volkswagon three stories into the air.

The mountains, saddlebacks, and gullies surrounding Elephant Valley were remarkably familiar; not unlike Camp Pendleton, only much greener. The convoy had moved more than a mile across the valley; and still the sugar-white sand dunes, although diminished in size and sprinkled sparsely with green, dominated the terrain. Farther on, patches of grass and low-lying shrubs began to appear along the tiny elevated road. We noticed some mounds in the area. They were sculptured and looked like large blisters of sand. They were meticulously manicured and preserved from the hot breezes that blew across the valley. We learned later that they were individual peasant graves maintained for generations without the benefit of granite.

We continued. Foliage of a more practical vein

appeared, vast colored carpets of rice paddies, each with its own perimeter of dikes. To the north of the sea of rice lay a large green island of banana trees, coconut palms, and an occasional grass hut. A life of another kind began to appear. Farmers looked up, unconcerned, then went back to their backbreaking work of planting rice seedlings in the decaying mud. I wondered if what the reporter had said was true about night and day.

The convoy arrived at the end of the road at the base of what no longer looked like low-lying foothills, but very steep mountains. Somehow, they'd quadrupled in size since we left the beach. The trucks formed a defensive circle, like a wagon train waiting for Indians, so we could dismount safely. Parts of the convoy veered off. The other companies had their own areas of responsibility, and eventually we would all be tied together along the top of the ridge, forming a battalion defensive line.

The heat was even more than we had endured before. In the beginning, the rugged, rock-strewn trail was wide enough for a column of twos, and the company angled up and along the slithering trail like a great menacing worm invading virgin territory. During the first hour, the first heat exhaustion casualties began to appear. This most harassing casualty occurs when all the salt is pumped out of the body and the built-in cooling system goes haywire. A deathlike weakness comes. And in the midst of one hundred degrees plus, a chill comes that cripples like a heavy strain of flu virus. The skin becomes pale and clammy, and the man is unable to perspire.

The heat and the terrain could be measured in the faces of the men whose guts were beginning to fray. The seasickness had left me a few pounds lighter, but not as weak as I thought I might be. I was doing very well. In boot camp, my size and frailty had been used against me. The drill instructors were determined to wash me out; but not being very bright, I pledged myself to the task of making myself physically perfect. I would never give up and consider myself physically inferior, because I had some control over it, unlike the weakness between the ears. To our amazement, months of undaunted, personal harassment, along with the overall boot camp program, shaped me into one of the strongest men in the platoon. After extensive testing I was surpassed by only one man who was huge, all hair and teeth. I wished there was something they could have done to prepare me better socially and emotionally.

More agonizing bodies began to give up and sit down on the trail. Some pushed further until their legs and minds gave out. They fell on their faces without even trying to break their fall. I grinned inside like a Cheshire cat, eardrum to eardrum. What's the matter, Momma's boys? Die, you helpless, unmerciful bastards!

Usually, I helped as many as I could to make the rest of the march—but not this time. The innocent were going to pay along with the guilty. Their labels— "shitbird," "misfit," "pussy"—did not sit very well. I found myself enjoying the climb after a surge of mental vengeance, almost as though I had some kind of telekinetic powers that heightened their agony. I felt a lot better.

The worm and the trail disappeared into heavy brush in the near-vertical side of the mountain. We grabbed at rocks, roots, and brush that many times gave way from too much use. I was summoned to the front of the column because I carried a machete. We slashed through the jungle. We rested and peered up at a great, towering, forbidden mountain. Up until now, it had protected religious myths and the secrets of the ancient high priests. It was glutted with treasures protected by prehistoric monsters, King Kong, and a tribe of beautiful people: women with beautiful hair, perfectly plucked eyebrows, and theatrical rouge. We were going to conquer this mountain today without John Hall and his native guide.

Using our final reserves of blood, sweat, and spit, we finally caught up with the late-afternoon sun. We had left the jungle behind littered with casualties and jumping corpsmen. We covered the last few yards on hands and knees. Those who were first to stand on the summit did not rejoice or congratulate each other, but I'm sure there was a touch of Sir Hillary in all of us. Our faces and clothes were starched dry with white crystals of salt. Body fluid and energy never existed. I felt sorry for the troops who were still climbing to the top at dusk. We had survived our second encounter of the day, the terrain.

CHAPTER FOUR

We survived and recouped from the ordeal up the side of the forbidden mountain, but we found no prehistoric monsters or treasure. Our only reward . . . it was over. The price was exhaustion, dehydration, and sunburn.

Tiny pieces of real estate were assigned in two-man lots along the irregular ridge-line that doglegged in and out, up and down. The summit seemed to have a grade to it, as though an ancient road had been carved all along the top. On one side of the ridge our defensive positions would face the sea and Elephant Valley. The sun set on rugged mountainous jungle bordering Laos to the west. On the south tip of our peninsula in the sky, a huge ravine lay. It was a natural pass through the mountains, and both companies set up machine-gun positions lacing together each other's field of fire. We were able to cover every square foot of the terrain without firing in each other's direction. Once on the ridge, it was easy to see why we were here. A few miles to the southeast lay Danang Field, where Skyhawks and Phantoms lifted off and landed night and day. The division was systematically populating the high ground throughout the Danang area in an attempt to curb the traffic of guerillas and equipment crossing Elephant Valley and entering the suburbs of Danang.

The clank of the entrenching tools attempting to penetrate the chastity of the sacred mountain sounded more like a Water and Power crew trying to penetrate Second Avenue downtown. No one was surprised when our tools bounced off the mountain like rubber mallets, or when we were told to move our positions several yards to the north, to spread out to cover more territory and start over again by Caswell, the platoon sergeant. He was a big, heavy, ex-drill instructor whose mind still wandered around the recruiting depot in San Diego. He had little or no consciousness of today's contemporary corps.

The grenadier is the odd man in the squad, and tactically shares a firing position with the squad leader behind the squad and the forward defensive positions. I would be living in a four-by-five hole in the ground with "Chicken Foot" Trudeau. He was vicariously named by the comedic underground within the platoon because of his skinny legs and a disturbing birdlike walk. Living in the same hole with him was going to be an interesting domestic experience. We had been at odds the moment he arrived in the division, ousted from a lush guard-duty assignment in Spain and thrown into a dirty, despicable infantry outfit training to go overseas. He was designated squad leader because of his time in grade and rank.

The squad was a mockery in the field and training. He was incapable of taking advice. I was not the most competent leader, but at least I had knowledge of the fundamentals. His egomania and insensitivity got him into hot water. The troops refused to listen to him but would listen to me, which put me in hot water. The pressure was on him, and he attempted to conceal his insecurities by yelling and screaming all the time. My own insecurities were covered over and hidden with more insecurity, which just barely worked for me. I did not give in to his micropolitics. He probed the chain of men for its weak links and pitted one against the other. He promoted the ambitious into allied positions and demoted anyone who threatened his security and conscience.

I was too young and naive to roll with the punches. I went from second in command to last in command. The rat pack, as they so mercifully called themselves, were not intimidated. Grinning Charlie, Red, Nellis (sometimes labeled "Richard III"), and Campbell (sometimes justly called "The Horn") had nothing approaching undaunted loyalty to me, but they were my friends. They were considered by the NCOs as a rare species of shitbird, and incorrigible. They were more like an adaptation of the Bowery Boys: too bright to get into real trouble, and too ambitionless to be intimidated with promotions. There was a single, silver thread of solidarity that bound us together. I had once loaned them bail money to get out of the Tijuana jail. During the days of my seasickness and disciplinary problems aboard ship, Trudeau managed to slip a wedge between us. I did not blame them for not wanting to chip paint in the hot bilge. It would have taken the grin out of anyone's fun. Temperatures had been cool ever since.

I sheltered our newly acquired parcel of land with a poncho and some sticks. Now, in the luxury of shade, I sat and tried to figure out how to extract nearly a hundred cubic feet of earth hard enough to dull a jack hammer. I thought of the virtues of no longer being a team leader. I didn't have to baby-sit anyone else twenty-four hours a day, and with the pressure off, I could relax. Relax, be cool, do my job, stay out of trouble—and perhaps Chicken Foot would get off my back. There was a good chance we would all be in a tough spot one of these days. There must be a war going on somewhere around here.

I etched out the perimeter of the hole with a stick right down to the centimeter. I was not about to make a hole any larger than regulation specified. I had joined the symphony of picking, scraping, and clanking when The Foot arrived. He threw himself down in the shade in my makeshift cabana, sweaty and tired from his motherly squad-leader duties. "Ogden, this whole mountain is nothing but a fucking rock. There isn't anything resembling dirt in any one of these positions."

"I just can't believe it. You mean this rock is nothing but a dirtless mountain? I'm glad to hear no one else has any dirt either. It wouldn't be fair if you and I were the only ones without dirt. Without dirt, the Marine Corps isn't the Marine Corps. There can't be a war without dirt. Maybe we can requisition some dirt. We can have it flown in by dirt-carrying helicopters and dropped right here." I purposely rattled on mindlessly to see if I could break the tension between us.

"Ogden, shut up and keep digging!"

"Yes, Corporal. Corporal, if you want your own room with a private bath, you'll have to give me about six months."

"Don't worry, I'll do my share. The lieutenant wants one man to dig, the other to stand watch, then trade off."

I went back to work. For the moment, we seemed to be getting along. He wasn't bitchy. He was still an NCO. But I was curious to know what went on behind those little brown eyes showcased in a lean, small-boned, almost feminine-looking face accented with a little bird nose and a less-than-predominant chin and jaw. He was frail in stature and didn't fit the description of a fighter, but probably could be dangerous; his eyes took on an occasional psychotic glare when enraged. He had learned English in high school and spoke without a trace of a French accent. He had a particularly fine-tuned ear for phonetics and had picked up Vietnamese in language school quickly. When he stuttered slightly it was another tip-off he was on the warpath. He was a classic example of a French Canadian from Quebec.

A heavy work day ended without a whistle. The dinner hour was announced without a bell. Before too long, the ridge line was permeated with the aroma of an all-too-familiar but welcome cuisine of beans and meatballs, beans and franks, ham and lima beans, instant coffee, or whatever else luck had bestowed. C-ration mealtime was always an interesting and creative phenomenon. An amusing array of unissued spices, sauces, and other exotic condiments awakened and titillated a dormant palate.

After the meal, I was about to take a pull on a canteen and wash down the grease when the second squad leader showed up passing the word again to conserve water. I took two pulls instead of the required half-dozen or more. J. P. Jason was a Texan in the classical sense. He thought everything was bigger and better in the Lone Star State, of course. They all bragged about it like it was a democratic capitalistic entity all by itself, a sovereignty within the United States, equal to the rest of the world on every front.

The only thing impressive about Tex was his big gut hanging from an average-to-lean frame. He seemed physically old for a man in his mid-twenties. The muscle seemed to have lost its elasticity, and everything hung. He had receding sandy hair; two little smoke-blue marbles pasted in deep, narrow slits; a pointed, almost abstract, impression of a nose; and a mouth larger than normal and fitted with so many perfect teeth it resembled the grill of an old Buick.

"Well, how are you and shitbird getting along here, Trudeau?"

I could have gone all week without that remark. He had to keep pushing, and Trudeau wasn't about to do me any favors. Jason and I had locked horns aboard ship. In the old days, he would have been the one to tie a rope around one leg and throw me overboard to be dragged behind the ship until I washed innocent or drowned. I fantasized grabbing him by his skinny, Texas-turkey neck, throwing him on his back on the ground, squeezing until his eyes popped, and making him promise to leave me alone. My fantasy ended, and I was still glaring into the tiny, smoke-blue marbles. I would never understand myself. Why was I so hollow and inept? Make-believe men have make-believe guts, and the thought of jail scared the hell out of me.

I grabbed my helmet and walked away to the edge of the ridge to be alone. I threw the helmet to the ground and sat on it. I drew up my knees, wrapped my arms around them, resting my chin on my knees, and looked out across Elephant Valley to the sea. I wondered where the elephants were. In the first moments of peace and quiet I had had all day, it was difficult to turn my mind off and indulge in the beauty before me.

The land we had invaded and trekked across was more beautiful and exotic than any place I had ever seen before. The meticulously cultivated floor of the valley began at the lower foothills and stretched to the sea. Toward the sea the floor was broken up by vast, sugary sand lakes and dunes. The valley floor was a spectacle of colored tapestry: vast sectors of tiny, irregularly shaped rice paddies fitting perfectly against their neighbors. They were divided neatly and manicured by small canals, hedgerows, or small mud dikes. Each paddy had its own hue of brown or yellow or any shade in between. A breeze gusted in off the water and circled the half-moon shape of the valley while each tiny rice stalk waved in one direction and then in the other in unison, giving an inadvertent but practical art form a gentle sense of motion.

The mountains and foothills grew larger as they stretched north, extending to the northern tip of the valley and then dropping straight down to the beach.

At its most northern point, the valley appeared as though it might have been a giant cove the land had reclaimed over millions of years. To the other side the valley was open, devoid of hills and mountains, lushly covered with a carpet of jungle and elephant grass. I assumed that many villages and hamlets thrived beneath its green canopy.

Several ships listed peacefully in the harbor, including the one besieged by the scourge of my own dread personal disease, seasickness and insolence. Danang, the most fortified air base in the history of modern warfare lay to the southwest, rarely seen but often heard. Often the ancient peacefulness of the valley would be disrupted by the clap of thunder from the Skyhawks and Phantoms igniting their booster rockets and accelerating like a missile to a near-vertical flight pattern, then leveling off toward North Vietnam with a payload of volatile mail, paid for by the good citizens of Tacoma, Toledo, and Tallahassee. They barely cleared the mountains to the north. The residue of the afterburners in a space-age war trickled down onto the valley floor, settling upon a medieval castlelike fortress that stood at the north end of the valley. It was a monument to the other wars, a symbol of defeat, and its presence was awesome—like an unexplained time warp with strange silver ships flying overhead.

The standard of native human existence in the valley had risen modestly and painstakingly above Neanderthal stages within the last ten thousand years. A cobblestone road led from the castle, inching across the valley, giving the appearance and accenting the centuries of European influence. At any moment, a troop of mounted armored knights would appear, horses' hooves clattering on the cobblestones and echoing through the valley in search of ancient adventure.

The long nights were dull and uneventful except for an occasional barrage of illumination flares from artillery batteries up the valley. Illumination flares drifted slowly on the warm night air currents suspended from tiny linen parachutes. If enough were dropped simultaneously, the entire valley would experience a premature sunrise. Sunburned eyes and necks strained then to see a sign of life or any movement at all. Each man fantasized hordes of enemy guerillas coming across the rice paddies.

We had scratched and hammered at our fighting holes for nearly a week, and C-rations were cut back to two meals a day. The water rations had been cut in half without an explanation. Sunburn turned to deep, dark brown; layers of fatty tissue were replaced by hard muscle; and blisters matured into hard protective callouses. Conditions were worse than on an Alabama chain gang.

The water rations were cut again. Lips began to

crack, along with tempers. Work was finally cut back to early morning and early evening to conserve body fluids. We sat all day watching choppers flying out of the air base. Why couldn't they fly over and kick out a few cans of water? More military bungling and red tape was going to cost us more misery than we already had. No one ever dreamed it was going to take weeks of hard labor to construct fighting positions on the ridge line.

CHAPTER FIVE

The dry blistering days passed like decades. A patrol was sent out into the mountains to find a small stream or some source of water, but found nothing. Dehydration started to set in, and all work was curtailed. The savers and the hoarders began sharing with the careless. The Foot and I had half a canteen between us. We sat around in the hot shade watching the clock, and every thirty minutes we took a canteen capful of water. Several times a day a chopper was sighted heading in our direction. All eyes would lock onto it. Hearts stopped, and leathery tongues began to moisten. The engines ground out a dull moan and the blades chopped the hot air as it continued toward the ridge, turning away at the last moment to another heading as though we were the subject of a great tease. The great and honorable warring knights of the West were being defeated by peasantry because someone forgot the drinking water. There must be a great proverb or limerick there, somewhere.

A squad leader's meeting was called and the world's greatest drill instructor never got up from the shade in his lean-to. He gave whatever instructions he had to pass on like a great sultan; only the peeled grapes and a young black servant with a large fan were missing. We wondered what his highness was going to do for a fighting hole if the need should arise—probably wait for the lieutenant to dig one for him.

While The Foot was away absorbing motherly knowledge, I entertained myself by playing with a large black beetle that had carelessly fallen into the hole, inadvertently caught up in an unexpected adventure on its long odyssey of exploration. It had a large horn on its head, so it was safe to assume it was a rhinocerous beetle. I made it perform impossible feats of mountain climbing. Up the sheer rock face of El Capitan, then on to the Devil's Tower. It was free-climbing without the benefit of rigging or pitons, climbing on sheer nerve, looking for hand- and foot-holds. I marveled at its endurance. I wondered if it was bad tempered and nearsighted, and if it lowered its horn and charged other creatures in the bush. Kids in the Philippines strung them and sold them in the streets like candy. I've seen the ad before: Hard and crunchy on the outside, creamy, rich and smooth on the inside. Melts in your mouth, not in your hand.

The Foot jumped into the hole, causing an earth tremor, and my hero fell off the south slope of Mt. Everest, landed on his back on a glacier, and slid to the bottom. I put him back on his trail of adventure into the bushes, disgruntled and indignant.

"What's the earth-shattering news, Corporal?"

He quickly began tearing through his pack. "Rifle inspection!"

"You're kidding! We're slowly dying of thirst like a lost brigade of Legionnaires, and he wants a rifle inspection?"

"That's right. He figures because the work has stopped, we should be able to do other things; and a rifle inspection seems to be his first plan. We are going up one at a time. You're first!"

"Me? The platoon shitbird? I get it. You send me up there and find out how bad he's gonna grind me up—and you know he will. And you can warn everyone. Right?"

He didn't answer. He started breaking down his M-14.

"Give me your forty-five. I'll clean it. That's the least I can do. I like the idea of using it to check the lines instead of this thing."

This would be interesting. Everyone knew these rifle inspections were always rigged. Somebody has to burn, no matter how clean the weapons are. I just happened to be popping out all over the popularity charts these days.

"Here, I'm trusting you with this." He threw me his barrel assembly. "Clean it!"

"Now, Corporal, that's not fair."

"Who said anything has to be fair?"

I grinned. "But Corporal, I'm not to be trusted."

"Do you think I'm gonna sit here and clean all these

weapons while you play around with bugs? You're crazy. Get busy!"

I walked across the perimeter with an immaculate forty-five on my hip and felt like I was headed for the OK Corral. We had even taken apart the magazine and dusted out the holster. I scanned the other positions as I walked by. Every weapon was now reduced to little pieces while tiny brushes, cloths, swabs, toothbrushes, and any other imaginable tools of the trade were being reluctantly applied.

There was a time in my military career when any kind of an inspection was a piece of cake—I was spit and polish right down to the last screw on a butt plate, and my service record book was proof perfect in proficiency and conduct. This didn't sit very well with new NCOs coming into the company. It was cause for contempt. They didn't care for perfect subordinates when they themselves were untrained, inept; and only rank, not merit, gave them positions of leadership.

Corporal Sheldon, the third squad leader, and I had been two of thirteen men picked out of the company to perform in the Marine Corps' squad competition. We were a perfectly tuned thirteen-man squad competing with other squads throughout the Marine Corp. It was a grueling thirty days of training and competition in every phase of combat tactics and proficiency. We outclassed all the other companies. We swept the battalion with no problem at all. We missed representing the First Marine Division and traveling to Virginia for the final challenge for the top squad in the Marine Corps, but lost by only a few points. We were honored by the battalion with thirty days leave. When the battalion began to reform to go overseas, Sheldon was promoted to corporal and the squad leader. He kept his mouth shut and stayed cool. But not me. I was the bright boy, and challenged injustice and incompetence at every turn. They plucked the feathers out of the primal bird one by one. I was now the principal jester in a court of clowns and fools.

I didn't know how Caswell was going to conduct this mockery of readiness and efficiency. I decided to go formal all the way, and stood in front of the lean-to at attention.

"Private First Class Ogden reporting as ordered." I pulled out the forty-five, pulled back the slide, ejected the magazine into my left hand, and waited. He continued to lay on his back in the shade and watched me in silence.

I was unnerved by him. He had punched troops while they stood at attention in formation, especially the smaller ones, but he hadn't hit or gone after me yet. I wondered how I had avoided his wrath so far. I was overdue. I wasn't sure why the lieutenant had let him get away with so much. Either he didn't know or he didn't care.

Caswell should have been a movie star. He had one of those faces too perfect to be born with, painstakingly built by Beverly Hills plastic surgeons. Perfect dark hair, perfect dark eyes, perfect nose, perfect square jaw, perfect teeth, perfect nails, perfect clothes, and perfect gear to clean, just like the psycho who knows he's perfectly sane but must wash his hands vigorously every two minutes of the day. Even "Rock" would be envious. He was tall, lean, fit, and well over six feet, with a stride familiarized by "The Duke." He would have been great bullying young actors and actresses around, intimidating new insecure directors, and making outrageous demands to producers and networks.

He sat up and reached. I placed the weapon in his hand and held my breath. He kept it much too long and went over it like a baboon mother looking for a flea. He barked loud and clear. "This thing looks like shit!" He handed it back. I holstered it. "Go back to your position, crud, and clean it. Then I want to see it again."

I turned and headed back to the position, thoroughly convinced he was mad in the clinical sense. I was totally fed up. The games crazies play were becoming a bore. Jail didn't seem so frightening. At least, they didn't send you back to the same outfit when you were released.

Trudeau had put himself in a precarious position when he cleaned the forty-five. No matter how immaculate he made it, we both had known I was going to get burned. I was stuck in the middle, the loser. Maybe Trudeau would sweat and have a little sympathy.

I handed the forty-five back to its adopted caretaker. I couldn't resist the temptation. "You're a crud, Corporal. This thing's a piece of shit!"

He looked at me, shook his head slowly, and

suppressed dialogue unbecoming a motherly NCO.

I grinned with anticipation. "I told him you cleaned it for me."

He jumped to his feet, feathers ruffled. "Stop fucking around. You know what could happen if he finds out what we're doing."

"I have a fair idea, Corporal. I'm already in the middle of it with no way out. I've been there a lot lately. Maybe I should tell him. You and your friend Tex over there have dealt me some pretty crummy cards."

He felt the mental armhole pressure and squirmed a little. His fingers fumbled trying to get the barrel assembly out of the pistol.

"I'll tell you, Corporal; I'm going to give it to you up front. I'm going to play my final role in this Mickey Mouse Club right to the hilt. But things better change around here. If we don't start playing together, we're going to get screwed, every last one of us. Imagine taking orders in combat from that idiot."

He looked at me. It was the first time since I'd known him that he didn't have anything to say. He just fumbled with the pieces of the pistol. He wiped the sweat from his brow. He blew for the last time into the barrel and handed it to me. "I've got to see how the rest of the squad's doing."

He started to climb out of the hole and I stopped him. "Relax, Corporal. Maybe he'll get bored with me."

He smiled. "I hope so. The Mickey Mouse Club is starting to bore me to tears."

* * *

Caswell's nostrils and eyebrows flared. He growled through clenched teeth. "You fucking shitbird. Go back to your squad leader and tell him I want you back here with an entrenching tool. You're going to dig me a four-by-four, and I don't care how long it takes you."

Well, that answered a few questions. I was sentenced to weeks of hard labor for nothing. The fear of jail nearly dissipated entirely. I wanted to put my foot in his perfectly miserable face and break it. It was still a fantasy. No guts! I walked back to the position. I was getting catcalls from the platoon. They must have overheard Caswell's profane diatribe.

"Hey Ogden, you can borrow my entrenching tool!"

"Tell me, how does it feel to be the biggest shitbird in the crotch, you gutless wonder?"

"Why don't you get seasick?"

The sound of a chopper diverted their attention. It changed course.

I stood alone on the patch of ground where my punitive inquisition was to take place. There was no breeze, no shade; only a swarm of flies. My head throbbed; my lungs and stomach ached with rage. My eyes were fixed on the spot, but I saw nothing but a blur. My entrenching tool hung from a limp arm. I was on the edge. The burn of a breaker circuit had been forthcoming. I had endured my emotional incarceration for so long that the iron bars began to bulge and give way under the stress. The rivets began to pop. I raised the entrenching tool slowly over my head. Gristle and cartilage snapped and popped in the shoulders. I came crashing down on all my enemies like a ceremonial samurai. I was smashing and whacking the unwilling soil. Muscle and gut tightened with each burst of energy. I was swinging faster and faster, out of control. A psychotic, epileptic animal in full frenzy, head pounding and eyes nearly swollen shut with sweat. The more it hurt, the more I accelerated. I was consumed with vicarious anguish, physical for mental. Through a fog of froth and fit in a delirious state almost below the level of consciousness, I felt an acidlike pain in my hands. My knees were numb from falling down and getting up. I began to wind down like a ridiculous dime-store toy. I collapsed in the dust and lay there. No appreciable depth had materialized from the precision craftsmanship, only dust.

I looked around me through one partially unimpaired eye to see if anyone had caught my overzealous contribution to the safety of our platoon sergeant. I was on a gentle slope from the main perimeter. No one had. Had anyone seen me, they would have hastily summoned the corpsman, who would have sprung a net and carried me off to the nearest infirmary. I sat up. I felt embarrassed and foolish, but I was calm. The trauma had passed. Pain in heart was transferred to pain in hand. Large blisters had developed under the tough, calloused skin and had burst. They were grim-looking meat hooks. It was time to see the corpsman and add malingering to a long list of transgressions.

I headed to the lean-to, shaky but in better spirits. I could hardly wait to tell him the sad news. I was no longer a healthy indentured servant. In a bemused, clear voice, I startled him out of a little catnap.

"Sergeant Caswell, I've got a problem. I'm going to see the corpsman." I held my hands up. One was bleeding.

He came on with a fiendish growl and the usual facial contortions and gnashing of teeth. This time there was a new ingredient in the kabuki act: he slobbered on himself.

"Get back to work! You're not going to see any goddamn corpsman. I'm going to work you until the meat comes off your goddamn bones."

Now was the time for all young men to come to their own aid. I yelled so loud the entire Elephant Valley could hear me. "You're not doing anything to me, asshole!"

I wasn't scared of anything. I loved the sound of the word as it rolled off my lips. Especially the phonetics and the accent on "ol." I loved the expression on his face; as though I had kicked him in the groin and the pain hadn't caught up to the brain yet. I loved the whole world. It was a wonderful place to be! I was back in it and among the living again, if for just one triumphant moment.

He sprang to his feet, too quick and agile for a man of his size. The huge paw missed me, and I stumbled back. It slashed through the air with the size and heft of a tree trunk. The uneven, sloping ground was against me. Its unevenness made him seem more massive than he was and made the difference between us an absurdity, as though I were on my knees before him. I was never in proper balance. I took one impressive swing, but it only managed to throw me the rest of the way off balance and down into the gravel and dust.

You asked for it, stupid. The least you can do is participate. He'll only send your head into the next Vietnamese county. Maybe I should be groveling around in the gravel looking for a perfectly round, smooth stone. Meanwhile, the Philistine with the finesse of a dinosaur mentally measured the distance between me and a size thirteen, triple-E boot. The enormous kick was close enough to knock the dust off my utility jacket, and missed my rib cage by the thickness of the fabric.

I rolled again and got up onto my feet before he could regain his balance for another strike. Without giving it the slightest thought, and with lightning precision as though I had been doing it all my life, I drew my forty-five and pulled back the slide, let it go home, and aimed it between two perfect eyes. Nothing I could have done physically would have frozen his action so quickly. It was like using a high-speed shutter, freezing the freight train in frame. The immaculate forty-five glistening in the sun rendered me a moment of freedom from a world gone mad.

I rose to my feet. "You miserable son of a bitch, if you ever touch me or anybody else in this platoon, I'll blow your fucking head off!"

Fear and uncertainty began to surge again. My gun hand shook, and I supported it with the other.

He had no expression. His hands rose slowly over his head. He knew I could flip at any second and empty a seven-round magazine in five seconds. Irony had also made a fool of him. I was so preoccupied with him that

I hadn't remembered to reload the magazine. I would go to jail knowing I had brought the house down with a broken straight, the ultimate bluff.

He slowed backed up the hill to give me room. His head turned, eyeing the perimeter. I followed. Every man in the outfit was watching this incredible drama unfold. It was right out of the pages of a bad novel, but could we tag it with a cheap happy ending?

The body's built-in anesthesia, "numbness," began to lift, and salty sweat poured into the open contusions. My arms holding the weapon so purposefully and rigidly began to ache. My mind began to whirl like a carousel. I was having second thoughts about the stupid stunt I had pulled. My whole future life turned before me. Jail, court-martial, jail, court-martial, and maybe even a firing squad.

Jason stepped in like Marshall Dillon. "Okay, Ogden, put it away!"

Gee, Marshall, you just got here in the nick of time, or I would have blown him away for sure. You probably saved me from hanging!

I holstered the weapon. I looked both Caswell and Jason in the eye and scanned the perimeter myself. "I'm gonna see the corpsman now." I took off toward the CP tent.

Caswell began yelling and screaming. "You god-damn son of a bitch, I'm gonna have you court-martialed. You son of a bitch!" He took his forty-five out and shook it at me. He looked at it and realized the mistake, and put it away. He continued to yell and rave as his spellbound platoon looked on.

The iodine brought tears to my eyes as he bandaged my hands. I told the corpsman my bizarre, impossible story.

"It sounds like a clear-cut case of maltreatment to me."

"Are you sure, Doc?"

"Of course, you understand there will probably be some kind of a hearing to unravel some of the legal ramifications, witnesses, and evidence. It looks like a stand-off. It would be easier to settle out of court, so to speak."

"I'll settle out of court. Loan me a forty-five shell. I left mine back at the ranch."

He grinned. "Now don't be rash, my friend. You've already had an eventful afternoon. I'l snip this off. There you go. Come back tomorrow and let me check it."

"Thanks, Doc. You certainly know how to turn a bad day into a good one. With your know-it-all, see-it-all bedside manner, you'd make one hell of a witch doctor."

He gave me a puzzled smile.

When I got to the hatchway of the tent, Caswell was stomping by. I'd give anything to hear his side of the story. What irony: one homicidal maniac tattling on another. The words of the doc had given me some emotional footing. In fact, I felt rather good. I looked at the sterile white cheesecloth. I had handled some very hot potatoes today.

I headed back slowly to the OK Corral and wondered how the rest of the hands would react to a natural-born gun slinger.

"Freeze, Ogden!" I recognized the sharp, nasal resonance of the company executive officer, First Lieutenant Bailey. He was short, thick, and as amusing as a fifty-gallon barrel of crude oil. He also had a funny walk that led the underground comedy writers to nickname him "Baby Hughie." He overreacted to everything. He probably had his forty-five aimed between my shoulder blades, or perhaps the whole squad on line. When Caswell told him the whole horrifying story, he had probably had to sit down to keep from fainting. I was confused about where to put my hands. Caswell had looked rather stupid with them over his head. With my hands bandaged, hitting the ground, rolling, and getting the drop on him was definitely out; but Steve McQueen could probably have pulled it off.

Where's Marshall Dillon when I need him? What strange, childlike reveries pass through our almost-grownup minds in the presence of adversity.

He stepped up behind me. "Drop your pistol belt and turn around." I was almost disappointed; he had no gun and he was alone. "Private Ogden, you threatened the life of a fellow Marine in a combat situation."

"Sir, our fellow Marine was trying to kick my sides in."

"Shut up! I'm going to see they throw the book at you." Not very original material for a college man. "Go to your squad leader and tell him I want all of your weapons; knife, every grenade, and all your ammo. I want them left at my tent right away!"

If I were so dangerous, why didn't he arrest me, tie me up, and gag me so I wouldn't froth at the mouth? After all, I could be working up some heinous plot to knock over Caswell in the still of the night. If I had such a plan, I'm sure someone would see that I had an entire truckload of weapons at my disposal if I needed them.

I headed across the perimeter toward the position, mouth so dry there was no room for the growth of a large, useless tongue. As I walked into the area, heads popped up everywhere from their holes like little prairie dogs. Someone began to clap, then another. Cheers went up. I was being applauded and not jeered. I didn't know what to do. I grinned like a fool and waved like a politician. The squad leaders were frantic. They yelled for everyone to shut up.

Trudeau and Jason were at the position. I sat down in the shade and grabbed the canteen.

"What in the fuck are you trying to pull, Ogden, a mutiny? You'll wind up in Portsmouth for the rest of your life."

"Just trying to survive, Corporal Jason, just trying to survive," I said smugly. I turned to The Foot. "Tell him the story, Corporal."

"I didn't know you were going to pull a dumb-ass stunt like that."

"To tell you the truth, neither did I. I kinda got pushed into it."

All hell broke loose within the perimeter. Jason yelled. "Ogden, you have started a goddamn mutiny!"

I grinned at both of them and we stood up. I must admit the idea was very appealing.

A much more important moment was happening. Somehow, a chopper had got in close to the ridge without anyone seeing it, and from its belly swung a net full of very precious cargo. Water cans!

When they were dispersed, we had all the water we could possibly drink. I was cordially invited to a house party at Charlie's, and all the "good old boys" were there. I was the toast of the town. The first anti-hero of the war for First Platoon, Hotel Company. We drank until our bellies were bloated while each one of them congratulated me and recreated his own version of what had happened.

With the day's soap opera and the critical arrival of water, morale was so high that the squad leaders did everything they could to keep the lid on. Everyone was jubilant. For all of us, a very important and unexplained crisis had passed.

I still had a personal crisis to face, though—at least a general court-martial. The more I thought about it, the less credence I gave to the doc's comments. Eddie Slovik had never thought for a moment he would be shot for desertion in World War Two.

CHAPTER SIX

"Saddle up! We're moving out!" the squad leaders yelled.

I had just finished breakfast and stepped out on the patio to stretch. The Foot had made it back from the squad leaders' meeting in a hurry.

"What's up, Corporal? Where are all the king's men headed now? Did they call off the war for lack of participation?" I asked as the rest of the squad gathered around.

"The battalion CP is moving and setting up on the other side of the hill. We're gonna provide a perimeter for them. Golf Company is gonna fill in here. The battalion's geared for hot chow! Get your asses in gear and be ready to move out!" Everyone cheered and moved back to their positions.

"Is there any word about yesterday?" I asked as we started to tear the roof off our summer home and packed up.

"The lieutenant said you would report directly to the captain when we get to the battalion area. Caswell didn't say a thing during the briefing. I don't know what to tell you."

I continued to pack the few pieces of gear I had left. The scourge of my uncertain fate settled on top of a hastily prepared cold breakfast like a rock. I wondered what poor fool at company headquarters would be carrying my material burden down the mountain. I wondered why the lieutenant hadn't jumped down my throat before this. Maybe he thought Caswell was a lunatic also. The captain must be going to handle it. I decided to keep my mouth shut and not discuss it with anyone. I would do exactly what I was told. I would be a good clown in this traveling circus.

We slid and stumbled down the mountainside we had so painstakingly clawed our way up. I felt foolish and naked without my weapons. I had to be the only combat soldier in the whole of South Asia armed with only a fork and spoon.

By the time we were halfway down the mountain, the sun had burned off the morning dampness and chill. It began to cook us in a boundless laser oven. A few troops again felt the effects of heat exhaustion, but not as badly as when we'd climbed up. Following the trail of footholds, I kept from careening down the slope by holding onto branches and bushes. Some men never adapt to rough terrain no matter how hard they train. Red had given up. He was sitting down in the middle of the trail, close to passing out. His round, fat, freckled face was nearly as red as the tuft of curly hair that hung down under the lip of his helmet. When I got to him, he was puffing too hard and his skin was dry.

"How are you feeling, Red?"

He snorted through a rubbery, flat, no-cartilage nose pulverized by too many left jabs in the amateur light-heavyweight division. "Fuck this motherfucking corps, and fuck Vietnam!"

"We've still got ten rounds to go, and you told me you always go the distance. I'll get the doc to give you a couple of salt tablets and you'll be all right. In the meantime, give me your pack. I'm traveling pretty damn light."

I helped him wiggle out of it. Charlie and Nellis slid to a stop, and threw the pack on top of mine and tied it down. Charlie stood by with a grin.

"At least you're good for something: a damn pack mule. Here, let me put my rifle up there, too. It's getting too heavy for me." He laid it up there for a moment. "Nellis, why don't you give him our pack, too?" He laughed and took off down the trail.

Ten minutes later, I realized I had bitten off more than I could chew. I was having trouble shifting the weight back and forth on two numb shoulders with two useless paws. The weight was riding high and the pack straps were digging deep. The pain and pinching became unbearable. I stopped alongside the trail to figure out what to do besides quit. A moment later, Caswell was behind me.

"Move out, Ogden!" I had been wondering when and how he would start something. "Move out, Ogden!" I ignored him. He leaned over close to the back of my neck and hissed through locked jaws. "You son of a bitch, I'm gonna put you out on point on a combat patrol without any weapons."

It was this idiotic statement, so uncreative and childish, that clued me in solidly that there was a gross lack of any appreciable intelligence. He sounded like something out of the mouth of a cartoon character in a twenty-five-year-old combat comic book.

"Move out, shitbird!" He gave me a good shove from behind.

I staggered forward with forty pounds of extra weight tied around my neck. My center of gravity was lost. In seconds I was careening helplessly down the mountainside. I landed on my back on a pile of rocks, racking a knee. I hoped it was broken in a dozen places. The only thing that saved me was the fact that I landed belly-up on the rocks, and the packs absorbed the impact. I tried to get up, but the packs were wedged in the rocks and I was totally helpless.

Caswell started down the bank as Lieutenant Bailey rushed up. "Knock it off, Caswell. Get back to your platoon!" Maybe Bailey thought Caswell was coming down to finish me off. Maybe he was. The lieutenant climbed down the bank. "Are you all right, Ogden?" Bailey turned and yelled to the troops congregating on the trail above. "Keep it moving. Get a corpsman here. We've got a man down!" I tried to get up. "Don't move until the doc gets here. You may have broken something!"

The doc lost his footing and slid on his butt down the bank. "What are you doing here, boy, trying to take a

60

shortcut? Where does it hurt?"

"I banged up my left knee, Doc."

He grabbed the ankle and moved the knee back and forth gently. "How does that feel? Is there any sharp pain? Let's get you up. See if you can walk on it. You're in one hell of a tangled mess here! What in the hell are you doing carrying two packs? What do you think you are—a damn billy goat?"

I put some weight on it, and leaned on his shoulder and whispered. "I think our case is looking a little better, Doc. The plaintiff just attempted to kill the defendant in the presence of a key witness. If I keep hanging around you, I'll be talking like a lawyer."

"If you keep getting into trouble like this you're going to need it, too. How does it feel?"

"Just awful, Doc," I whispered and grinned. "Do you think you can get me a stretcher to make it look good?"

Lieutenant O'Connor stood at the top of the bank. "What happened, Ogden?"

"I tripped and lost my balance, sir."

"Are you gonna be able to make it?"

"Yes, sir, I think so."

O'Connor turned to Trudeau. "Get a couple of men and make sure that gear gets down to the battalion area."

I favored the knee as much aś possible, especially when Bailey was near. With a boost from the doc, I was put on the trail heading down toward some hot chow. I felt pretty good with forty pounds of weight off my back and the smell of reprieve in the air. Two acts of maltreatment. One witnessed by the XO, who probably would have hanged me just on hearsay yesterday, but was now on my side.

The battalion command post was nestled in a canyon at the foot of the mountains. It was about a half-mile to the south from where our defensive positions were. From a distance, it took on the appearance of a traveling circus. The column moved past tanks deployed outside the mouth of the canyon. Once we were inside the hastily erected canvas housing project, we made good use of the city's public water supply, which consisted of a water buffalo, a strange animal that looked like a giant oil drum on two wheels. The company was deployed in a huge semicircle at the mouth of the canyon. Each platoon was tied in with a tank. Company headquarters set up mid-ground between the perimeter and the battalion area. To our amazement, we spent the rest of the afternoon digging into soft ground. We were all thinking of fresh food, instead of something that had been packed away in cans for ten or twelve years. No one was greatly surprised when the hot meals and showers turned out to be a rumor, a mistake, or a hoax.

Captain Martin was on the radio to the battalion when I approached. I waited for him to sign off, then reported. He returned the salute. "At ease, Ogden."

He seemed very young and a little on the frail side to be running a Marine company. But he was an impressive leader. He exuded an air of confidence and spoke well when addressing troops.

I remembered Lieutenant O'Connor's first introduction to the platoon. He was so terrified, he could hardly speak. He stuttered, stammered, hemmed, and hawed. He was a tall, gangly Irishman with red hair. Somebody immediately tagged him "Muldoon." During training he overcame his insecurities and became a good, confident platoon leader, but the name "Muldoon" was too cute to drop. They started calling Red "Little Muldoon," but he was quick to put a stop to it. We all agreed that the leadership of the other platoon leaders was rather questionable.

I liked and respected Captain Martin. I was embarrassed to be coming up again in front of him for yet another disciplinary problem. I also felt like a live chicken looking into a hot frying pan.

He took off his helmet. He sat down on a pile of C-ration cases, folded his hands, looked down at the ground, and took in a deep breath. He looked up at me rather strangely while still holding his breath. I took in my own breath and held it.

"Were you blowing off steam up there?"

"Yes, sir, I was."

"How are your hands?"

"They're fine, sir."

"Go back to your platoon and keep your nose clean."

I was stunned! It was obvious something else was on his mind. He had changed it at the last moment. I was speechless and didn't move. He put on his helmet and turned around. "Move it, Marine!" I saluted smartly. I did an about-face, forgetting all about a return salute. I started back toward the squad position as fast as I could.

"Ogden," he yelled.

I put on the brakes, slid, and nearly fell down. He was pointing to the ground next to him.

"You forgot your gear."

I rushed back and flung the M-79 on my shoulder. I threw the bandoliers of rounds around my neck, gathered up the K-Bar killing knife, and put the hand grenades on my belt. I lumbered away like a new recruit who had been issued his first set of toys and couldn't wait to play with them.

We spent two days in the battalion area, then were relieved by another company and climbed back to our summer homes on the ridge line. We sent out squad-sized recognizance patrols throughout the valley. We were briefed that the farmers were indeed farmers during the day and were playing games at night. The weeks of intense patrol were tedious and exhausting. The excitement of our very first combat patrol had given way to a dull, hot, tiring routine. Our morale seemed to decline in direct proportion to the increase in physical fitness, stamina, and adaptability to climate and terrain. Through miles of deep rice paddies, shifting sands, and vertical hills and mountains, we found no evidence of any weapons and no acts of overt aggression or open hostility. But we still looked upon the indigenous population with contempt and suspicion. The farmers continued on with their daily lives as though we didn't exist. We had specific orders not to enter the village under any circumstances. In our speculations and fantasies, we knew the village hosted several battalions of Vietcong and hundreds of

Vietcong sympathizers. The war machine was laboring under a stagnant and poignant silence. The climb from the valley floor to the top of the ridge line after each patrol had become nothing but a mere inconvenience.

Only the sound of sand shifting underfoot, the squeak of shifting gear, or the occasional clank of a canteen broke the ominous stillness of the valley floor. Salt and saliva had formed around the corners of our mouths and hardened. The sun had scorched our bodies for what seemed like thousands of hours and had turned our exposed skins a deep, rich brown. The only relief from a robotlike motor reflex was to move forward and take a pull from a canteen to keep the sides of the throat from collapsing in the middle and adhering together. The water was at least eighty-five degrees cool, a lot cooler than the ambient air surrounding us. Not even the tiniest leaf or spider's web clinging to a bush moved in the stillness of the stagnant hot air.

Jason broke in on our numbed senses. "Pass the word up to the point to veer to the right toward that grass hut; we'll take a break."

Corporal Jason looked back at me. "Goddamn it, Ogden, it's hot! This has to be the hottest fucking day since we landed."

I didn't want to waste any energy replying. Tex, The Foot, and I seemed to be getting along a little better. I was assigned to Tex's squad for a patrol because his own grenadier had suffered a sprained ankle. Lucky guy!

The squad was spread out over a lot of territory

because of the openness of the terrain and the lack of cover. I looked back over my shoulder. The last man was just coming over a small sandy knoll. His image was distorted like a mirage drifting in and out of the heat waves, like a ghost. To be able to sit down in the shade for a few minutes would be as welcome as tumbling into a Cascade mountain stream.

The next instant, I froze in stride and breath. My eardrums snapped with the crack of automatic weapons fire. All ten of the highly conditioned and programmed computers hit the deck simultaneously with muscles flexed to their capacity. Blood and adrenalin accelerated, triggering the most primitive of survival mechanisms. Eyeballs focused and refocused on the periphery of the jungle that surrounded Le Mai Village approximately five hundred yards from the left flank. The volume and intensity of automatic weapons fire was unimaginable. The valley had been so extremely quiet since our occupation; I'm certain everyone imagined hordes of armed enemy would come rushing out of the jungle toward our position any second.

Jason began yelling orders up and down the line. "Keep down!" "Keep your positions!" "Lock and load!" He didn't realize it, but everyone had been shoving magazines into their rifles, and bolts were already going home.

Jason and I were laying belly down behind a low sandy knoll. The squad was stretched out on either side of us on line. I flipped over on my back and broke open my pop gun. I fumbled for a round, shoved it in the breech, and slammed it closed. I rolled over and began to work with the front sight blade. We were edgy as hell. Our minds worked flawlessly from subconscious reflex. There was no evidence of any incoming rounds, but it would have been hard to confirm because of the soft sand. The firing was loud enough to cover the sound of any rounds breaking the air over our heads. Only a hit would let us know for sure.

Jason reached the company commander on the radio. "We are under fire, sir. It's coming from the village. I have no casualties." The radio cracked and buzzed, but was audible.

"Get your squad back here as soon as possible, Jason. Hotel Actual, out."

"Roger, sir."

"Ogden, pass the word we are going home. The rear guard is now the point."

We were literally frying where we lay, but the thought of just staying alive banished all thoughts of discomfort of the day. We got up and moved out in a quick crouch. No one took his eyes off the tree line until we were well out of range.

When we got back to the company, we learned that our anxiety and near heatstroke was due to a Golf Company patrol that had broken the rules and jumped a Vietcong inside the village. They'd blown away a sixteen-year-old kid carrying a Thompson submachine gun after he gunned down their squad leader.

One tended to forget that every member of a squad carrying an M-14 had commandeered an illegal selector switch that made the M-14 optional, semiautomatic or fully automatic. Extreme overkill was flagrant with this much fire power in the hands of the overzealous. Only three members of the squad were issued this automatic switch. Each squad had virtually nine or ten machine guns, a fully automatic weapon resting on every trigger finger. We had never experienced that kind of fire power in training. Who could stand up to that much fire superiority? Ever since the battalion had hit the beach in March, there'd been feverish bragging and betting on what company, platoon, or individual would score the first kill. Golf Company cancelled all bets when one of their own went down. The young Vietcong was torn to shreds.

It was ten o'clock in the evening when Red scrambled over to our position. He was excited. "Hey Oggie, we've finally got a station speaking American!"

He rushed back to his position and I followed quickly. Nellis had tried for weeks to tune in the armed forces station overseas on a tiny radio, the size of a pack of cigarettes. This evening, he had inadvertently laid the radio down on the comp wire that stretched from the battalion to each company, and the huge network of wire, thousands of yards long, acted as an aerial. But it was not an armed forces station. It was the eeriest and most bizarre broadcast we had ever heard.

A soothing, provocative voice said, "I want to give a special hello this evening to the Marines in Hotel Company on top of Hill 853."

Everyone immediately moved in closer to hear. "That's us! She's talking about us!"

Nellis began to laugh. "I know who it is now. It's

Peking Polly. Yeah, my cousin's in the Navy, and he told me about her. She's like Tokyo Rose!"

"She sounds so sexy, I could go down on her in a minute."

"Shut up, Red, and listen!"

She said we were sitting in dark, cold foxholes when we could be at home with our friends and loved ones. We agreed with that. She said members of the National Liberation Front, whoever they were, crawled up the side of the mountain, stole our boots and equipment, scared us to death, and we could be heard crying in the night.

Such ridiculous commentary broke us all up with jeers and laughter. The whole broadcast was saturated with farcical, ludicrous statements. Originating from Peking meant it was traveling around the globe. We were in the midst of international intrigue. We were where the action was, and it made us feel important.

We adopted the show as regular late-night entertainment for awhile. Before long, though, we walked away, either bored or amused by the same silly rhetoric. We fantasized about the mystic Oriental beauty with the mouth of an angel. We had lewd thoughts about an enemy who was specializing in outrageous propaganda and who attacked our masculinity. Maybe she was a defected exchange student from Cincinnati or Seattle. She spoke impeccable English.

CHAPTER SEVEN

I was not surprised when word came down we were going to assault the village in the morning. It would be a company-sized predawn assault sweeping the entire length of the village. Trudeau delivered a skimpy combat order taken at a hastily gathered squad leaders' meeting.

"We'll leave at 0400. We'll be in position on line along the trail on the west side of the village. We'll sweep toward the sea. We'll take prisoners if possible. They'll be herded back to the rear to a designated staging area until after the operation. We'll carry packs with one meal. A green star cluster will signal attack. A med-evac L.Z. will be designated by yellow smoke. The lieutenant wants every man to break down his magazines, pull out the old rounds, and clean them to cut down on the chance of malfunctions. Are there any questions?"

No one spoke.

"This is going to be a surprise attack. Like it or not, I want socks around the canteens so they don't rattle, and dog tags taped if they aren't already. No talking or bullshitting around. Oh, another thing. This is a search-by-fire operation. We will open fire on the green star cluster. Ogden, the lieutenant designated you to stay with him to spot M-79 rounds. Okay, everybody back to your positions and turn to while we still have daylight left."

That doesn't make sense, I thought. I'm the least qualified of the three men in the platoon at firing the M-79. I had fired it once in training just to get the feel of it. I thought about the search-by-fire routine. It would be like turning loose a massive lawn mower on a hamlet built of bamboo and grass.

I rested on my knees in the predawn darkness. We were drenched, and shivered from the dew that hung heavy in the towering elephant grass around us. It was a long, tedious battle to get into our final positions.

My body began to shake more from the chill and excitement. I remembered my first duck-hunting expedition, sitting in a blind in the darkness, waiting for daylight and a flock of mallards. It felt much the same, but I couldn't remember the knot in my stomach.

The minutes dragged on. A cock crowed. Then another. The darkness began to give way to shadows that formed recognizable objects. The terrain began to appear ever so slightly like a very slow developer solution breaking down the chemical and allowing the hidden image to be exposed on a print. The silence of the moment was heightened by the pungent sweet and sour scent of the primitive existence. It was different from the scent of stagnant, fermenting rice paddies. I began to pray for comfort. I hoped nothing would happen today that I would regret.

Lieutenant O'Connor and Trudeau were on each side of me as the hand signals for everyone to get up on their feet were given. The flare popped over the village, piercing the senses and signaling the dawning of the war we had so painstakingly anticipated. A wave of men in green stepped through the concealing hedgerows and moved cautiously across the fields toward the village. The order to commence firing was given. Automatic weapons began to chatter up and down the lines, spewing out hot glowing chaser rounds that disappeared into the shadows.

I stayed behind the advancing platoon with Lieutenant O'Connor as he barked orders to keep the interval, stay on line, and keep firing. He yelled at the members of the weapons platoon attached to our squad that rocket teams were only to fire on solid structures. An M-60 crew was in front of us barely keeping up the pace. The gunner had the M-60 slung from his shoulder and was firing from the hip. The assistant gunner fed a belt of ammo into the breech. The gunner was slightly bigger than me, but each burst of the gun sent him back two or three steps. At the end of each burst, the crew would run forward to catch up with the line.

The M-60 is a heavy weapon designed to be mounted on a tripod or on a vehicle. The gun crew enjoyed what they called "John Wayning it." It gave them more mobility and more power to the platoon during an assault. The rocket teams on the line waited patiently for an appropriate target and a command. The gunner carried the stove-pipelike apparatus on his shoulders. His assistant, heavily laden with a pack board carrying the rocket rounds, guided the tail section of the rocket launcher that held the rocket.

I could see many bamboo huts shrouded and camouflaged by banana palms as I looked through the blue haze of burning powder and hot gun oil. There were many trails worn smooth by decades of bare feet. They led from the village down to the rice-paddy dikes holding in the water that submerged the cultivated land and surrounded the village.

The second platoon rocket team cut loose with a screaming round. It went deep into the village and detonated, sending tiny streaming particles of white phosphorus in all directions. We were now just a few yards short of entering the village, and there was a lull in the firing. The troops extracted empty magazines and replaced them with full ones.

I scanned up and down the line intensely, trying to take in everything. The awesome, unforgettable sight and sound of our first combat assignment was exhilarating almost to the point of hysterical excitement. Frustration and anxiety were exuded like sweat from the pores. In the frenzy of the moment, we had forgotten what damage, death, and agony we could incur or had incurred. We only knew we were getting paid to do a job.

After the company entered the village, the pace and

firing slowed down considerably. Then an unexpected horror stopped the entire line of troops cold. Pungee sticks! Thousands of them. Some were partially camouflaged, while others were in the open. They were needle-sharp bamboo stakes tempered hard as iron by heat and sometimes dipped in dung. Their presence triggered another terrifying thought: booby traps! Yells of caution and discovery ran up and down the lines like a panic. Orders to watch for trip wires were called out. Sheldon's squad found a pungee trap. It was a neat little hole about the size of a shoe box, with pungee stakes in the bottom and a well-camouflaged layer over the top. If hit right, the stake would jab all the way through the sole of the boot and into the bone of the foot. The lieutenant and squad leader continued to bark orders to keep the interval and the line moving.

"Ogden! See the temple, the thing with the red tiles on the roof? Hit it!"

"Yes, sir!" I estimated the range to be about three hundred yards. I lifted the rear sight, locked it into place, and slid the yardage marker all the way to the top. I lined up the rear blade and front sight blade with the target. I took in a deep breath. My forearm shook. I was afraid of missing! I needed to do something right for a change. With the barrel stretched almost straight up in the air, I pulled the trigger. The round leaving the barrel sounded like a plug being extracted from a thermos bottle. I waited for what seemed like forever to see where it would hit. To my astonishment, it blew several large tiles from the corner of the roof.

"Good hit, Ogden," the lieutenant said with mild

amusement. "That weapon is not heavy enough to do any damage on that heavy a structure. We'll concentrate on the huts."

I couldn't believe it. I just couldn't miss. The secret was not only aiming the weapon, but also calculating the yards to the target.

I moved up the line with the rest of the troops. The lieutenant ran over to the rocket teams to give them instructions. We moved deeper into the village. The going was getting tough. We stayed off the trails to avoid the booby traps. We fought and clawed through the heavy hedgerows that dissected the village. I wondered why we weren't receiving any incoming fire.

Trudeau yelled from the right side of the line. "Lieutenant, we've got bunkers over here!"

"Clean them out," came the reply.

The assault wave broke up slightly and took on the appearance of a search-and-destroy mission. Corporal Jason came crashing through a hedgerow from the left flank. "Spread it out, you guys! Mortars will get you all. Move it out!"

At that moment, a dog raced from a hut that smoldered with white phosphorus. The dog, a German shepherd, headed in my direction at top speed. It immediately disappeared into a hole a few yards in front of me. It was a strange sight to see—a domestic animal acting like a wild cornered beast in the presence of humans. It was the first sign of life all morning.

"Throw a hand grenade in that hole!" Jason yelled. "Pop one in and let's get out of here!"

The first sign of life, I thought again. I stopped in my

tracks. My mind raced. We hadn't seen or heard a soul all morning. It could mean they had fled during the night or early morning. Or had they? I took a closer look around me. Spread out everywhere in the sun to dry was food: peanuts, potatoes, beans, and rice. There was laundry hanging near the huts. Some were children's pants and shirts. My imagination was racing again. There wasn't any hostile fire this morning. Pets were staying behind instead of running away with their owners. It didn't make sense. Then it hit me: they were underground! Grown men with weapons did not hide in holes waiting for the enemy to poke a rifle or a grenade into it, but defenseless noncombatants might. I let out a yell. "They're underground, all of them!"

"You're goddamn right, they're underground," Jason yelled back. "Throw a hand grenade in there, goddamn it, and let's go!"

"I can't! They're underground!" I yelled irrationally. "Where there's a dog, there's kids! Don't you see?" I pleaded. "We're blowing them up and burying them at the same time, without giving them a chance. Women, kids, babies, for crissake!"

Jason tore a hand grenade off his belt, pulled the pin, and threw it in. He gave me a sickening cliché: "Ogden, war is hell! I'm going to run you up for disobeying an order and for cowardice in the face of the enemy. What are you standing around for? Move it!"

The grenade blew with a dull thud that shook the ground underfoot. My mind was dazed and confused. My stomach was sick. I ran over to the hut and snatched a tiny pair of trousers from the clothesline. I ran back and threw them in his face. He caught them and looked at them with a total lack of concern. He still didn't understand.

"There's your goddamn enemy. You kill 'em all!"

He grit his teeth. "I'm warning you, Ogden!" He looked down at the muzzle of his rifle, then back to me.

I looked at the muzzle also, then we locked eyeballs. "If you're thinking what I think you're thinking," I said, "you'd better pull the trigger." I was ashamed for the lack of a better cliché.

He quickly relaxed. "You're under stress. You've had a bad time of it lately."

He still hadn't figured it out. Maybe he had, and didn't care. I propped open my grenade launcher, extracted the shell, and walked away. I didn't know who or what was around me. I was embroiled in an undercurrent of outrage and despair. I didn't fire the weapon again that day.

There were tears of rage, fear, and confusion for the next few minutes. Maybe I'm wrong, maybe I'm just overreacting. I knew for sure a perfectly harmless pet had been wasted. The morning's feelings of excitement and exhilaration seemed distant and unreal. I knew unequivocally that I didn't want to be there. We didn't belong there; and if we did, there had to be another alternative. We didn't know what we were doing. The fun was over!

The operation had taken on an even more fragmented posture; more search and probe by sight instead of mow-them-down tactics. The word was passed down to conserve ammo with no looting or unnecessary destruction. I'm sure that looting never crossed anyone's mind. Perhaps they had a few dollers in piasters. We could possibly go for a chicken or a duck, feathers and all.

I was still moving on line adjacent to the machine gun crew when the ground gave way—or what I thought was the ground crumbled beneath my feet. I was seized with panic. I flailed my arms like a goose, and with quick, spasmodic twists of the body, I attempted to become lighter than air. I fell, but the angle of the pungee stake was slightly off. In the midst of my wild gyrations, I had managed to do something right. It gouged through the soft leather of the arch of my boot but managed to miss the fleshy part of my instep. I pulled my foot from the trap and pried the nasty little stake from the canvas of my boot. There were several other stakes in the pit. I pulled all the sod away and broke the sticks with the butt of my weapon. The incident served a good purpose: it woke me sharply out of a morose stupor of guilt and confusion. It made me recognize the continuing hazardous situation and focused my senses on walking around fifty to sixty pounds lighter.

The machine gun crew opened up on another bamboo hut about thirty yards in front of us. The gunner never let up until his finger became cramped. The wall of the structure quivered and vibrated during the tempest of hot lead and splintered bamboo. I watched the wall of the hut partially disintegrate. For some reason, my entire concentration was on the hut. It was just another hut like all the rest behind us, but I sensed a strange feeling. My entire body felt like it had taken a low-voltage charge. It gave my body a tingling, buzzing sensation, especially the scalp. I was experiencing some kind of a deep, low-level extrasensory perception I had never experienced before. My pulse raced and kept time with the machine gun. My wide, unblinking eyes still focused on the smoldering hut. There was something about it. I had no meaningful thought.

I yelled, "Cease fire! Cease fire!" I ran back and forth up and down the firing line. No one seemed to believe or hear the command until I started shrieking, "Cease fire! Cease fire!" I had literally taken over control of the troops in my immediate vicinity, those who were within hearing distance.

I hadn't become disoriented. My eyes were still glued on the hut. My commands finally registered. I had no business taking over Lieutenant O'Connor's command. He stood there locked in amazement. The men turned and observed my wild antics as though I had flipped out.

I quickly shoved my grenade launcher at the assistant machine gunner, turned, and moved out at a dead run toward the hut. I was running on instinct and fear at top speed. I took my forty-five from my holster, and by the time I had pulled back the slide, I had covered the distance. In full stride, I hurled my body to the ground, landing heavily on my belly and chest. I wiggled and slithered quickly on knees and elbows toward the open doorway. I quickly pushed the forty-five around the corner of the doorsill. Even though I was functioning with mindless instinct or insanity, I still had the presence of mind to be careful. The rest of the men were confused at the present situation but acted instinctively. They dropped to their bellies and took up firing positions.

With my face shoved tightly up against the pole that reinforced the door, I inched around to see what was inside. I could feel the blood bang on the sides of my head with each pulsebeat. I stopped breathing; it had become a nuisance that impaired my hearing. I let one eye adjust to the darkness. I scanned the room, trying to penetrate the shadows. Nothing moved, nothing happened. I inched in closer. My eyes began to dilate and adjust. I crawled in slowly, like an unwanted reptile.

The body of a woman or a girl lay on the floor in the middle of the hut. Her back was to me. Her head was tucked down and her knees drawn up in the fetal position. My eyes adjusted with the help of the tiny, thin rays of sunlight filtering through the thatched walls.

Continued discoveries were more startling. Another girl lay on the smooth, almost polished, earthen floor. She was facing the other woman with her knees drawn up, also. Together, the two bodies formed a near circle. To my astonishment, within the circle were a number of babies. They were no older than eighteen months. They were also huddled together on their sides with their knees drawn up like little unborn fetuses. I knew they were all dead. One, two, three, four. There were five. Their mothers or guardians had tried to protect them with their own bodies. In a corner on the opposite side of the hut lay a little red mongrel dog. He was stretched out on his belly with his head resting on his paws. He was alive! He watched me and growled deep in his throat.

"How did you survive this, fellow?" I asked.

Out of the corner of my eye, I caught a movement and jumped. The body closest and with its back to me had turned around and looked me right in the eye. She straightened out her legs, rolled over, and sat up with no sign of pain. A little baby stirred and looked around. The girl sat up. I was crazy with excitement. I couldn't believe my eyes. The entire nursery began to stir. I realized I was still pointing my forty-five, and quickly holstered it. I moved in closer, and knelt down and looked them over for wounds. There wasn't a scratch on any of them. What kind of miracle kept babies motionless without a whimper, spared them from the onslaught of machine-gun fire, and had compelled me to act in such a bizarre, irrational manner? I'd seen nothing. I'd heard nothing consciously—or had I?

I turned and ran out of the hut. I was overcome with joy to near embarrassment at the discovery, and was pleased to know that I wasn't a candidate for a net. I yelled and waved for the men to move in. I ran back into the hut, and within moments the whole squad was crowding around the door.

"Look at this." I picked up one of the babies. "Now one of them has a scratch. A whole damn nursery!"

"You musta heard them, huh, Oggie?" Nellis asked.

"I must have," I lied.

Trudeau pushed everyone back outside. "Okay, back out. We've still got a job to do!"

Each woman picked up a baby. Trudeau, Nellis, and I filed out, each carrying a baby. They started crying and fussing. We sat the family down, if that's what it was, under the shade of a breadfruit tree just outside the hut. The females were all young girls of child-bearing age, but it was inconceivable that they were the mothers of all these babies. Perhaps it was a day-care center. They sat together on the ground in a little huddle. The little red dog stood guard.

Through the yards and little plots of vegetables the troops were still advancing, slowly but deadly. An occasional rocket zipped through the trees and detonated. At this point, we didn't know what to do. Trudeau gave an order for the first squad to quit bunching up and spread out. Nellis asked if it was okay to give our tiny prisoners some water. Canteen cups and candy bars appeared.

Trudeau slapped me lightly on the back. "Ogden, go get the lieutenant. Nellis, go get the doc."

The lieutenant and radio operator were already on their way to the scene. When the lieutenant arrived, the doc had one of the little ones on his lap. The lieutenant crouched down and scanned our catch of tiny prisoners of war already covered with chocolate. He winced and shook his head. "How are they, Doc?"

"They're just fine, Lieutenant. They're not even scared anymore."

The lieutenant gave Jason some orders to spread out the squad and stay put. He summoned Morales, the radio operator. The lieutenant spoke to the captain and explained the situation. It took about five minutes of passing the word up and down the line to get the rest of the company to cease fire.

A bluish-white fog of sulfur and smoke lay undisturbed over the silent village. The search-and-destroy mission had been reduced to search only. The spot where the babies were found was designated a refugee area. The third squad remained behind and the rest of the platoon continued to sweep through the area. The remainder of the morning was tedious, and the air hummed with millions of flies. We no longer felt the village was a threat, but we proceeded with caution. Most of our attention and concern had shifted from the huts and structures to the tunnels and holes. Trudeau used both his French and Vietnamese to coax the hideaways to the surface. Hunting for people burrowed under the ground was a strange treasure hunt, but now and then our patience was rewarded.

We lay on our bellies near the hole, listening for signs of life. Trudeau spoke gently into the hole while we held our breaths and listened. The silence was broken by a tiny, muffled voice deep within.

"Somebody's in there, Corporal," I said with excitement.

We both grinned. It was like fishing; some bit and some didn't. I'm sure everyone was grateful there was an alternative to our earlier tactics.

I'm sure we all entertained the thought of the silence

at the bottom of a black pit, terrified, surrounded by snakes, bugs, and rodents. Your babies cling to you as machine guns and rockets devastate everything you've loved and owned above the ground. The sound of strange voices and boots above your head, then the mysterious appearance of a tiny, white-hot flame that sputters and rolls closer, giving off a sulphur vapor that completely chokes off the air.

"She's coming out," Trudeau said, and we moved back.

The head of a woman appeared. She was a little older than the others, and she was covered from head to foot with dirt. She shaded her eyes from the pain of the sun. Clutching her breast like a tiny monkey was a six-month-old baby. It didn't seem to inconvenience the little one in the least when her mother left the dark cool hole and crawled into the bright hot sunshine. Her breakfast continued right on without a hitch.

Lieutenant O'Connor designated Red to escort the women and children back to Corporal Jason at the staging area. The third squad was now up to its elbows in women, young kids, and babies. The sight of Jason bouncing a three-month-old baby on his knee made me want to confront him and paraphrase his earlier statement, but I thought better of it. I thought all of us had learned a painful lesson. For us, war was not cut and dried as it was for our predecessors. We had one hell of a responsibility.

We found that cutting some bamboo sticks and probing the least-worn paths for unwanted little surprises enabled us to move through the village with greater ease.

Someone had given the word to hold up. We stopped and listened. There was a low moaning sound coming from the other side of a high, thick hedgerow. We approached cautiously. It was a very old woman rocking an old man in her arms, and both were in a near-skeletal state. As she moaned, tears rolled down her wrinkled face past a mouth full of black betel-nut stained lips and teeth. They wore black pajamalike clothing. The old man's pant legs were rolled up above his knees to keep them from getting wet when he worked in the rice paddies. On his right leg was a makeshift bandage or tourniquet. He must have been hurt by a stray round or piece of shrapnel while trying to save their hut. It lay in ruins. Lieutenant O'Connor removed the makeshift bandage. A round had gone through the calf and out the other side. The old man was unconscious, either from shock or perhaps a stroke.

I couldn't get over how ancient and pathetic they appeared. Anyone their age back home would have been in their nineties. The average lifespan in Vietnam is only thirty years. How could these people survive for so long in such a primitive life style?

They were both ravaged with arthritis and other bone-related diseases. Their knuckles and joints were swollen and deformed. Even without the wound, their suffering must have been intolerable. Betel nut, a mild narcotic, offered little comfort.

Lieutenant O'Connor took the old man's arm and felt for a pulse. The woman resisted and pushed his arm away, but finally gave in.

"Trudeau, send a man back for the doc, quick. The old man still has a pulse!"

I picked up a conical straw hat and began to fan them. I felt helpless, and derived very little pleasure from the knowledge that they were miserable before we came. We had sent in a 3.5-inch white phosphorus rocket that had burned and blown everything they owned to dust.

"How can these gooks live like this?" the assistant gunner asked. "I thought Asia had a rather sophisticated culture, but the people are more primitive than those we came across in Malaysia or in the jungles of the Philippines. I thought the niggers in Africa were the only ones in this squalor."

I knew that I was not a student of this planet's cultural theme; but if I had had an answer for him, I would have chosen not to discuss the subject on his level. The labels "gooks" and "niggers" didn't roll off my tongue very well.

Around mid-afternoon, the village was considered secured. We had rounded up and accounted for about four hundred people. A few were still hidden, and some were hidden forever. The exact count of the missing would take some time, preferably after we were gone.

The assault on Le Mai was a gross error. It was the first actual assault by Americans in Vietnam, an order that came directly from President Johnson. The day's event set a precedent for most American combatants.

There are millions of innocent people caught in the middle of war, and it is our responsibility to protect them and gain their confidence in order to deal with the Vietcong effectively. It was a good theory, and sometimes it worked. In the case of Le Mai, it worked. The division helped rebuild it, immediately setting up a hospital and a school and delivering much-needed supplies, making life as tolerable for the people as it could be after being squeezed by the Vietcong.

It is unfortunate that we could not have helped all of the villages. To my knowledge, never again was a village arbitrarily stepped on unless its people insisted on harboring Vietcong.

CHAPTER EIGHT

The Ca De River runs peacefully down out of the mountain and flows past Le Mai Village and onto the South China Sea. It was more like a creek, and not navigable in many places. It was a main Vietcong arterial from the mountains to Elephant Valley.

Le Mai Village had been considered a major Vietcong supply center before it was stomped on by the Third Battalion. To the east, in the mountainous jungle, another tiny village lay nestled on the river. Recon teams learned the village was under Vietcong control. With Le Mai Village under marine control, the Vietcong could no longer move freely in the area to supply themselves. They recruited inhabitants of the village to make the hazardous trek down the mountain past the patrols and ambushes to get supplies. The pressure and the danger became too great, and the people began to refuse. The Vietcong applied more pressure with torture and extortion. The request was granted to relocate the villagers to a safe area. The new location would serve two purposes: it would protect the villagers, forcing the Vietcong back into the mountains to look for another source of supply; and it would cut their mobility and freedom to forage and recruit.

It was 0430, and another chilly morning was coming to life. We were standing outside a column of amtracks near Le Mai receiving our final orders. We were baffled, and mumbled among ourselves. A combat patrol going up a mountain pass in a column of amtracks was a novel, if not crazy, idea. But when it was explained, it appeared to make sense and seemed to fit the operation—at least in theory. We were not to engage the enemy. We would attempt to get the villagers out of their grasp. Tracked, armored bread-boxes big enough to carry nearly two squads gave us protection from snipers and ambushers.

The mouths of the great monsters dropped open in unison and we walked up the ramp and down into the belly. We packed in our benches and found something sturdy to hang onto. We knew it was going to be a rough ride.

We were used to driving out of the mouth of a ship and plunging off the ramp into the open sea. In a rough sea, they sometimes completely submerged for a moment or two then came bobbing back to the surface, venting out their exhaust system like a young great whale. The tracks turned, continuously treading water, and kept the craft from sinking while we headed toward the nearest beach. Each time one of these unlikely sea creatures grabbed hold of the bottom and dragged itself up on the beach, it seemed like a miracle.

The engines began to whine and the cables went taut as the huge gate swung upward like the power gate of a commercial truck. The crew chief sealed the door and switched on a tiny red lamp. Only the coxswain and crew chief could actually see where we were going. Their seats and controls were up forward, on stanchions, and their heads stuck out of hatches in the overhead when the craft was not totally buttoned up. They wore helmets, with communication systems in them similar to a pilot's. The crew chief manned a thirty-caliber machine gun mounted topside. The engines whined under greater strain, and the coxswain slammed the machine into gear. It jolted forward like it had no transmission, only "go" and "stop," and no in-between. We jiggled and bounced inside the belly of this manmade dinosaur. We could barely see each other in the dim red shadows. The steel-footed monster bucked, pivoted, and swayed, crunching over rock and clawing through marsh as the strange, steel wormlike column angled its way up the gorge. Trudeau and Charlie sat on either side of me, and Lieutenant O'Connor, Morales, and Campbell straddled the bench running down the center.

I could barely hear myself over the roar of the engines. "Lieutenant, sir, whose idea was it to use amtracks to evacuate the village?"

"Mine."

The rest of us looked at each other quickly as though our own leader, Muldoon, didn't have the quality to dream up such a hare-brained idea, much less sell it to the battalion commander. His voice held an edge of reluctance, as though he didn't care to discuss such an urgent plan with peons—or maybe it was plain modesty.

He explained: "The steep mountain jungle terrain makes it impossible to evacuate people by helicopter, and to bring the whole village down the trail would invite every sniper and ambush artist in the country down on us. Can you imagine running into an ambush with a bunch of women and children? Their lives would be in jeopardy, as well as the lives of every man here. We'll load all the inhabitants in tractors and send them down the gorge. We'll take to the trail on foot. An evacuation like this in broad daylight will probably draw some enemy—"

Blam!!!

It sounded like someone had hit the outside of the tractor with a brick. The crew chief opened up with a machine gun. It was incoming enemy small-arms fire bouncing off the skin of the craft. The skin was not thick enough to withstand an armor-piercing bullet. Lieutenant O'Connor jumped up and braced himself, holding onto the overhead. He got to the phone near the coxswain and found out the others were also drawing small-arms fire. The word was to keep on moving. We looked around at each other and hung on. Our machine gun kept blazing. The almost-useless air-conditioning was working overtime, but we could hardly notice it. The tension wrung the sweat from our bodies, and it flowed freely.

Another round slammed into the side. Each time we

were hit, the head snapped, the lungs froze, the bowels turned to ice water. We knew that if one of these rounds found its way through the skin of the craft, more than one of us would get hurt.

I turned to Trudeau. "If they have any mortars or rockets, even little ones, we're screwed."

He didn't say anything. He gritted his teeth, sweat, and hung on.

The crew chief yelled down for some more ammo. Charlie bent down under the bench and dragged out an ammo can. He popped it open and handed it to him. He helped him feed the belt into the gun. It continued to cook. I had visions of running out of ammo and fuel while hundreds of Vietcong swarmed over us and dropped hand grenades down the hatches. In each man's face there was a contortion of tension and anticipation of a hit that might rip through the side, shatter into tiny fragments, and volley around the inside of the compartment.

Someone up forward yelled out, "Let's stop and get the hell out of here!" I agreed in my mind immediately. O'Connor told him to shut up and sit down. I closed my eyes, hung on, and continued to sweat.

Charlie turned from the machine gun and yelled at me. "Give me more ammo. He doesn't see anything out there; we're just spraying the area."

I reached down, popped open the metal box, dragged out a dangling belt of ammo, and handed it to him. The platoon clown with big, bushy eyebrows and an infectious grin was doing a good job. I was proud of him. He fed the ammo into the breech. He waved for another belt. I dropped it over his shoulder and around his neck. It was our first time in a combat situation, and our fate was in the hands of a coxswain and a crew chief. We were as helpless as blind rats at the bottom of a well. I knew that popping open the ammo cans was only a small contribution, but it kept me from feeling helpless.

The heat in the rolling sauna was no longer taken for granted. My eyes began to burn and swell from the briny perspiration trickling down from under my helmet, and the river continued to flow down the middle of my back into my shorts.

A volley of rounds slammed into the outside. A violent shiver momentarily raced up and down my back as I flexed to pop open another ammo can. We continued to pitch, roll, and bang our way to our destination. The tension and pensiveness gave way to a more wide-eyed, elusive expression on the faces of the men. I knew none of us would be able to handle a hell of a lot more of this.

The coxswain reached down and tapped O'Connor on the shoulder. O'Connor quickly put his head up near the hatch, hoping for some information. He patted the coxswain on the back and turned around.

"All right, men, listen up! Make sure you have all your gear. The minute the gate drops, we'll get out of here and tie in with the rest of the platoon."

At that moment the craft hit something and nosed up, nearly knocking the lieutenant down on us. It slammed down again hard on its belly. The engines raced and screamed, but we were no longer moving.

The coxswain frantically slammed the vehicle in and out of gear and quickly moved the jockey stick that controlled the vehicle's every movement. The engines screamed in and out of gear. His inaudible lips worked feverishly at the mike in front of his mouth. We had bottomed out on some rock. The engine of the tractor couldn't get any traction forward or in reverse. The noise was still at a tremendous level, but we were motionless. Another round bounced off the overhead. Panic set in. We were trapped!

Some of the men got out of their seats, screaming and yelling. "We're sitting ducks. Let's get the fuck out of here!" The rest of us were probably too scared to move or yell. Breathing had become more difficult.

O'Connor yelled and shoved the men back down to their seats to maintain order. "Goddamn it, listen up! We're all right. Sit down and shut up! Keep your heads!"

At that instant, something slammed into the rear of the vehicle like an explosion. It knocked O'Connor back against the bulkhead and everyone else back into their seats. He quickly recovered and found something to hang onto. We were hit from behind again by another amtrack in the convoy and knocked free. We were rocking and pitching forward on our own again. A round of cheers went up. It was the longest thirty-minute ride any of us would ever experience.

The gate popped and had hardly begun to drop when we scrambled out. The cool, damp morning hit us like a welcome icy blizzard. The intake into the lungs was like the first breath at birth.

We tramped around in the jungle in typical confusion. We finally got on line and swept to within one hundred yards of the village, anticipating snipers every inch of the way.

A Vietnamese interpreter was assigned to first squad. His name was Nugent Cao Tai. He was above-average height for a Vietnamese and was dressed in perfectly tailored and starched tiger-striped utilities with a black beret. He seemed too young for the job, but spoke better English than anyone else in the squad—or in the company, for that matter. He was a startling contrast to the Vietnamese villagers and the Vietnamese army we had come across.

The first squad was assigned to get into the village and inform the people. Our own interpreter, "The Foot," had proven a success, but even a Vietnamese organizing and mobilizing an entire village was going to have a difficult job.

We entered the village cautiously. The village was considerably smaller than Le Mai. It nestled on the bank of the tiny river and was protected by towering, exotic, floral-covered hillsides. It was a beautiful lost Shangri-La.

Portions of the jungle high on the hillside gave way to neatly cultivated terraces. It was peaceful and quiet. The intense tranquility gave way to nervousness. The sound of one's own heavy, labored breathing did not fit in with this scheme of beauty.

We assumed that the villagers would be desperately trying to evade the jaws of the Vietcong terrorism. We anticipated a pushing, shoving, unruly mob trying to evacuate—but the village appeared to be already cleared. There wasn't a sign of life anywhere.

We spotted the probable cause. In the center of a tiny courtyard, we discovered the body of a man about forty years old, clad only in a pair of shorts. The body lay chest-down in an enormous pool of blood. The bloodless face with liquid, staring eyes gazed up into the morning sunrise. The eyes were still clear, and seemed to be staring in wonder. The head had been severed cleanly above the collarbone, leaving the entire neck with the head. To see your first death was shocking, but to see a human head totally separated was horrifying.

For a moment we were speechless, unable to move, strangely entranced by the horror that lay at our feet. Blood has a strange metallic smell like tarnished brass when exposed to air; it jells, contracts, and turns black. There were tiny, diminishing furls of steam rising out of the severed esophagus and trachea of the torso.

Trudeau began to unstrap his poncho that was folded and tied to his cartridge belt. His eyes squinted and his forehead wrinkled as though in deep pain. "Jesus Christ!" There was a strong undertone of "why?" in his words. We covered the body with the poncho.

The interpreter spoke in perfect English. "This is a Vietcong execution. By the signs, it happened a few moments ago. He was probably a village leader or chief. To defy the Vietcong means a sure death. The alternatives to the people are traumatic. To leave their homes and ancestors behind and break with ancient binds to the land would be sacrilege. They would suffer the loss of dignity and hope."

We began to search the village for more casualties or for anyone at all. Trudeau and the interpreter began to speak in Vietnamese, asking the people to come out from hiding and telling them we were there to take them to a safe place. Their voices echoed strongly from mountain to mountain. We stood motionless, listening and watching for any sign of life. The strange Vietnamese dialogue echoed off the hillsides for about ten minutes.

Charlie and I stood in the shade of a hut. He fumbled for a pack of cigarettes, put one in his mouth, and was about to light it. The cigarette got away from him as he pointed and yelled. "There they come! Across the river!"

We looked through the grove of banana palms that grew on the river bank. On the opposite bank, a slow progression of people entered the water, coming in our direction out of the jungle. There were men, women, and children of all ages. They walked with heads down as if in mourning. The water was about knee high, and the mothers lifted the little ones and carried them across.

Leading the forlorn procession was a very old man carrying a young boy of nine or ten. The child was very limp in his arms, either sick or dead. They drew near the courtyard, and I could see tears streaming down the face of the old man. The woman directly behind was being helped by two young girls. Probably the mother, she was also crying.

The old man stopped in front of Trudeau and the interpreter. The rest of the group gathered around. Charlie and I approached the sad procession. The old man was speaking rapidly. The little boy's chest was a mass of meat and blood. Someone had cut the skin and then peeled it away in long strips, literally skinning him alive.

The interpreter relayed to us what had happened. The old man was the father of the dead man and the grandfather of the little boy. The villagers had been forced to watch the torture of the child and the anguish of the father, who was held and made to observe closely and listen to the screams of the boy. Then they cut off the father's head in the presence of the mother and forced her to hold it.

"Tell them to get their belongings. We are getting out of here," Trudeau said. He turned to Campbell, who was on the radio. "Tell the lieutenant we are almost ready to roll."

He quizzed the old man, who told him that the Vietcong had left about fifteen minutes ago, headed east back into the higher mountains.

The interpreter told the people to get their belongings and anything they could carry. The villagers dispersed in all directions, except for the old man and woman. He continued to speak. He said he wanted to remain behind to bury his son and grandson. He would never leave the village, no matter what happened. Someone had to stay behind to take care of the village.

"They'll come back and kill him for sure," I said.

He said he would rather die with his family and

ancestors than in a strange place.

I could hear the amtrack engines start to hum and grind further down the canyon. The exodus had commenced. The remainder of their broken lives began to pile up in the courtyard: material things with little intrinsic value; things that could easily be replaced but that had much-needed sentimental and esthetic value to these people who were being torn from mental and spiritual sustenance. There was an endless array of baskets of all sizes filled with everything imaginable. Crude pack boards, poles, grass mats, chickens, ducks, calves, goats, and piglets.

The amtracks pulled up behind the village and dropped their gates like huge hungry beasts. We helped carry their gear, but they were reluctant to enter the jaws of the beast. We coaxed them, then showed them by example that there was no danger. The old were more reluctant to leave than the young. It registered sharply in the faces of the old women who chattered feverishly, probably cursing the Vietcong—and us, for that matter. Some just went along with the excitement of boarding the vehicle, nursing naked babies and cradling lambs and piglets. One old lady in her conical straw hat clutched a great white goose as though it were the last of her family.

We loaded as much gear topside as we could possibly tie down. We packed the inside of the vehicle with as many humans and creatures as it could hold.

Trudeau walked over to me as I heaved another basket of rice up to Charlie. He handed me a puppy about eight weeks old.

"This has got to be the strangest Marine Corps combat assignment of all time—juggling ducklings, puppies and babies. What am I going to do with this?" I asked.

"I don't know. Find its mother, or it's gonna be left behind."

The puppy was cute and alert, his big brown eyes and needle-sharp teeth that found a finger to chew on.

"It's sure a fuzzy little thing," I said. I looked around for a place to put it.

Charlie, arms spread out as if to envelope the whole mourning scene, said, "Gentlemen, how does it feel to be contemporary Noahs with your little steel arks?"

"Why don't you jump down here and take a whiff inside of one of these little arks? Then tell me what you think, Noah."

"Where's your spirit, Oggie?"

I paused. "I've got a handful of it," I said. "This dog just pissed all over me!"

He laughed and nearly fell off the amtrack.

Our experience this morning would never be forgotten. Helping and protecting these people who were caught between two hard spots had enlightened our spirits.

The captain gave the word to move out. The amtracks looked like huge piles of mechanized rubbish, pivoting and bucking down the trail, grinding up over tree stumps and fresh earth that they had gouged out coming up from the river banks.

CHAPTER NINE

Military buildup around Danang was evident day by day. We watched Uncle Sam's warships sail in and out of the harbor. The early rumors of going home within weeks gave way to new rumors of an extension for as much as one year. Total control of the Elephant Valley was crucial to the protection of Danang Air Base. The taking of Le Mai Village, the control of the Ca De River, and the use of the French castle to the north end of the valley as a tactical observatory was further restricting the Vietcong's mobility and easy access to the supplies. In retaliation they blew bridges along the main supply route from Danang that led to the castle.

The vast, complex irrigation system of the valley was facilitated by numerous bridges which were crucial to the local population and the resupply of the Third Marine Regiment. The road was cluttered daily with supply trucks, civilian bases, bicycles, scooters, and numbers of pedestrians coming and going from the marketplace.

With so many Americans present, tiny vendors and shops sprang up along the roadway. They were always on the move with their little baskets and carts. Some of the more industrious sellers even climbed to the top of the ridge line to sell to the troops in the foxholes, right under the noses of the unsuspecting—or lenient—leadership.

It seemed like everyone was selling Coca Cola, and even the tiny kids who could only carry one or two bottles were out trying to make a buck. Tiger Beer, crudely brewed in the village, and loaves of French bread, were the next biggest sellers. They were a delectable relief from C-rations. It sometimes became a nuisance when overzealous little kids attempted to follow us on patrols. The rear guard had to continuously shoo them away.

It seemed as though we had established a good rapport with the people of this sector. And why not? Commerce and trade was indeed a universal language. The Americans had become captured victims of consumerism, supply and demand, the root of capitalism, the sinister, cultural, polluting system these Vietnamese were supposedly fighting against. Who cares about all that while sucking on a popsicle on a combat patrol in one-hundred-ten-degree heat in enemy and bug-infested Southeast Asia?

Our next assignment was to ensure that the main arterial between town and village, supply ship and troop concentration, was kept from being interrupted. Iron Bridge Ridge was probably named by some classroom lieutenant carrying a map case three times practical size—but at least it had more of a creative ring than Monkey Mountain, or some of the others. I preferred native names for things and places. A name like Iron Bridge Ridge could have been anywhere in the world—even along the banks of the Snohomish River in Snohomish County, where hardy, overdressed, overenthusiastic anglers braving the sleet-filled Northwesterly, possessed less intelligence than the highly prized steelhead that lurked in the dark, swirling pools.

The ridge was a tiny island populated by palm trees and low, impossible brush. It rose from the ebb and flow of a golden sea of rice that covered thousands of acres in all directions. The tiny microdot of uncultivated land was divided by a deep, stagnant slough on which sat a bridge built by a nineteenth-century French genius with an oversized erector set. It was strong and wide enough for a tank and a hundred more years of bare feet, if the Vietcong didn't blow it first. The rusty angle-iron, worn beams, and rivets had already survived several of their attempts. All traffic, vehicle and pedestrian, would have to check through Hotel Company for the time being.

The captain assigned platoon areas, long stretches of real estate around the island that seemed like a beach front. Palm trees and a never-ending stream of vendors and pretty girls to admire made the area seem like an envious place to be.

Speculation on luxurious Iron Bridge Ridge was quickly laid to rest when a complex network of trench lines had to be dug with bunkers every twenty yards.

The whole island would become a series of rat paths and burrows with weeks of gophering and filling sandbags. Sandbags were issued to each platoon in one-hundred-pound lots, along with axes, picks, and long-handled shovels. The shovels were reverently referred to as "Ethiopian back-hoes."

The trench lines were three-feet wide and about waist deep. Three layers of sandbags were stacked up on the outsides of the parapet, which would give a rifleman a good firing position. I would need a box to stand on just to look over it. The bunkers were six by six, and shoulder-deep with edges also lined with sandbags laid overlapping each other like bricks and spaced to allow portholes on three sides.

The biggest and most beautiful palm trees came crashing down in all directions, falling prey to hordes of self-ordained lumberjacks, most of whom did not know or care to know how to fell a tree properly as long as it tumbled from the sky into their clutches. I guess the enthusiasm could be attributed to the first-time syndrome. Knocking your first huge tree out of the sky can be paralleled with knocking your first mallard down or catching your first rainbow trout. I never quite understood the fervor and zealousness that surrounded the building of bunkers and diggings of trench lines. It was very mundane and unexciting work except for the tiny ceremonial celebration when two squads would meet, and only six inches of earth remained to link the two projects. Larger commemorations were celebrated when platoon projects came together. If such nonsense were allowed to get out of hand, I could see the ultimate trench-tying ceremony: a command chopper landing, with Secretary of Defense McNamara and General Walt stepping out, carrying bottles of champagne and wielding golden Ethiopian back-hoes.

It took the entire weapons platoon to carry and lift each log they put on top of their bunkers. Each log was twelve feet long and eighteen inches thick, which made more than formidable roof. They squabbled among themselves like they were in competition or they knew something that we didn't, like the Vietcong had B-52 bombers or they had taken over the Seventh Fleet and were wielding twelve-inch naval guns.

We watched them build their pyramids in the sun. They relished their achievements with the same idiotic pride that motivated their smallest men to carry the biggest, heaviest, and most cumbersome weapons. We were all glad we were not part of their idiotic circus. We would be considered underachievers.

I was glad our platoon was a little lazy and didn't see the need or compulsion to show how strong or brainless we could be. Our projects met practical minimum requirements. Whether they were suffering from lack of leadership or some other peculiarity, weapons platoons were still a necessary evil. If they had had Caswell, they would have pushed him into a well-needed straight jacket a long time ago.

Concertina wire circled the entire ridge, two sections high, looking like huge tunnels of hair coming off a hot curler before brushing. In front of each squad's field of fire on the other side of the defense line, small anti-personnel mines called claymores were set strategically, one per squad. These remained above the surface, and when detonated electrically, blew thousands of tiny, diced steel fragments in a one-hundred-sixty degree front. Their firing patterns overlapped the entire perimeter. They were un-booby-trapped each morning and brought in, and were set out each evening; they were also booby-trapped to blow if not disarmed in proper sequence. Empty C-ration cans with a pebble inside were tied to the concertina wire. They swung freely in the breeze and sometimes sounded off with the least amount of disturbance.

Sheldon, the third squad leader, wasn't quite satisfied with our defensive setup. He scrounged a fifty-five-gallon oil drum and some plastic explosives from engineers who were studying the bridge. He decided to devise an anti-personnel mine of his own creation. Taking two pounds of plastics which had the consistency of modeling clay, he fastened it to the bottom of the barrel on the inside. We dig the barrel into the side of the ridge below the concertina wire. When completely dug in, the mouth of the barrel pointed out across the paddies like a giant cannon. He crawled in the mouth of the cannon and placed electrical blasting caps with two lead wires. He strung the wires back up the hill to his position and tied them off, then we commenced to scrounge for Coke bottles. We roamed the entire island scavenging empty throwaways from the rest of the company. Coke bottles are ideal: extremely thick, with a heavy base; and when broken, they can be very effective in a blast. We were enthusiastic as sadistic fiends breaking up bottles and filling our cannon to the brim. Crude but ingenious. When detonated, it could conceivably cover the entire platoon area.

Sheldon grinned with a set of teeth big enough to pearl-handle a forty-five. "If them motha fuckas come after me, they gonna get glass in they ass."

"Amen, brother," a Richard Pryor fan yelled.

Later, I began to wonder and worry about all the fortifications and precautions. Next to the castle, this was the most perfectly fortified and strategic spot in the entire valley. I just couldn't imagine the enemy getting close enough to need anti-personnel mines. We were slightly elevated, and there were thousands of yards of open space with just rice stalks for cover. Even at night, eighty-ones and artillery could send up illuminations. It would be suicidal even to get close to this place; they would have to come by the thousands. The more I thought about it, the more ridiculous it sounded. We'd probably never see anyone.

After the construction on the island had been completed, the furor of activity during the day dwindled to playing cards and throwing the football around. There were numerous farmers peacefully attending their rice crops every day. I was amazed how they worked from sunup to sundown in extreme heat without taking a break. Unlike Mexico, there didn't seem to be a siesta. If they were resting or taking shifts, we were unaware of it. We were preoccupied with looking for little antidotes to escape the boredom of hot, tropical afternoons.

Ed and I shared the responsibility of one of the

bunkers. Fifty-fifty watch night and day; we could break it up any way we liked. Ed was from my old fire team, one of the original members of the squad back at Pendleton. He was tall, but very frail, and timid. He had huge brown eyes like those of a lemur, and little chipmunk teeth, and tiny wiry hands. His helmet and uniform were always too big for him, and he looked like a squirrel monkey in green. He managed to do everything wrong and jumped nervously when anyone called his name. In training, the NCOs gave up on him and considered him just another shitbird. We got along well. He was unintentionally funny. It was like having Don Knotts around.

When I became fire-team leader, my quest for perfection was relentless. The night before inspections we would stay up until the wee hours of the morning trying to get him ready. I had to do practically everything for him, but somehow we always managed to make it; he would pass.

One day he told me that he appreciated my helping him a lot, and asked me if I could care to go on liberty with him. He lived in San Diego, which was only a couple of hours away. He said he could probably fix me up with a girlfriend for the weekend. I thought it was a good idea. If nothing came of it, we could scoot across to Tijuana.

It was during liberty that I discovered I was dealing with two different human beings. He was a fine dresser with above-average taste. He drove his mother's Chevy Malibu as though it were a formula car. But the most astonishing trait of this dual character was that, despite his inadequacies, he had an inexhaustible, voracious appetite for women. This was why the underground nicknamed him "The Horn."

He was not just another mouth, but a man of action. During the course of a better weekend, he introduced me to two or three different girls. He didn't have great taste, but his string of sun bunnies were tanned, soft, and giggly. We frolicked in the sun and surf of San Diego's Mission Bay. At last, the endless nights of midnight classes in the fine art of spit shines were paying off.

I asked him why he'd joined the Marine Corps. I thought he should have joined another branch of the service, since he was born right in the middle of the naval community. He said it was a drunken dare. His buddies said he wouldn't last a week. They were almost correct.

I admired his guts in carrying it through. But, like some other people, he just couldn't adjust to the Marine Corps way of doing things. Most people end up with severe disciplinary problems; but with his mild temperament and my patience, he just barely climbed the hurdles.

When he was off on liberty, though, there were no holes barred, and the sky was the limit. He did not need help from anyone. The tables were turned. I needed help with the women.

CHAPTER TEN

To break the monotony, I decided to take a tour of the area. I hadn't been away from my position for a number of days. I walked over a grassy knoll toward the CP area. The ground leveled off and was bare. It was the center of the island, and to my right was an old French blockhouse. It was green and black from generations of moss. The west wall was knocked down and part of the roof was caved in. It was obviously constructed for the same reason: to protect the bridge from the same type of political factions. Only the names had changed.

Toward the west end of the island they had managed to move in a four-deuce artillery piece. I started down the other side of the knoll. The CP bunker jumped up at me like a brand new supermarket that had been constructed across the street when you go away on vacation, and you wonder how they could have built it so quickly. It was quite an awesome structure for this tiny island. It was about five times longer than any other bunkers, with walls three- to four-feet thick. There must have been literally tons of sandbags used, and there was comm wire leading from it in all directions. It had a corrugated tin roof. We on the front lines had not thought of having to keep these things dry during an occasional monsoon. The bunkers would fill up like septic tanks.

The island was crescent shaped from east to west, the eastern end being more open and free of brush. The tiny trench lines with their high sandbag walls resembled the great wall of China at a long distance; a ribbonlike mass arching over each knoll, then broken and hidden in the valley, to appear and disappear again.

I waded through the normal CP activity: men standing around drinking water from a lister bag that stood in the middle of the area, swinging freely on three poles fashioned in teepee style. The canvas bag of water was always saturated, which created evaporation and dropped the temperature of the water a little. I decided to try some.

The eighty-one mortar team was going through mock drills. Other than that, it was a siesta lull. I heard little bits of chatter and laughter coming from the bridge and decided to investigate. A little coke on ice, and maybe a glance at a pretty girl.

I started down the trail past the CP. It was already a well-used path down into a gully and up the other side to the road. The gully was full of brush, cool and hidden from the sun, and on the opposite bank hidden back in the shadows was another bunker.

There were two marines sitting on the roof, relaxing in the shade, one reading and the other wiping down his rifle. I recognized the one with the rifle as Cable, and realized that this was the third platoon area. Cable and I had gone surfing together at San Onofre Beach—or at least he had tried to teach me. I was a hopeless case. I could not keep from slipping off the board, even with tons of wax. Then I got a brainstorm. I put on some tennis shoes and paddled out. I caught a couple of good ones coming in and actually looked like I knew what I was doing. I wasn't hanging five, but it felt good after all the frustration. I got a lot of laughs for lack of class and being square, but it had worked.

"Hey, Oggie, what are you doing?" He chuckled to his bookworm friend, "I love that name."

"Just out roaming the neighborhood. It's changed a lot since I moved in. I think the value of the property has gone down considerably."

"I bet you are. I bet you heard about the fine little chickies, and you're sniffing around. There's been some fine-looking stuff coming across that bridge. Asshole here," he nudged the bookworm with his foot, "could have had one a couple of days ago, if he had been cool. Some of these gook broads are looking so fine."

"Can't hurt to look," I said. "See you later."

I started up the bank, got up on the road, and headed toward the bridge. The bridge itself had become a regular carnival. Giggling, screaming, naked kids were jumping off the bridge into the slough. Every now and then a Marine would grab a skinny brown little swimmer and hurl him out into space. He'd scream, fold up, and do a cannonball on his friends below. The little one would surface again, yell, and shake his fist in mock protest.

There were dozens of vendors just off the east end of the bridge. I enjoyed the mayhem on the bridge for a while and then decided to do some shopping. Everyone mobbed the potential buyer. The ages of the competitive hard-selling group seemed like eight to eighty. The ladies were clad in their pajamalike satin traditionals, baggy pants, and a long-sleeved, no-frill blouse. Their blouses and shirts were of neutral colors. It was plain, hard-working, practical attire, loose-fitting and cool, and served no other purpose than to cover the body. There was nothing garish about these people.

Betel-nut blackened teeth glistened like slate from under conical grass hats. It was said that black teeth was a sign of beauty. I'll leave that up to personal taste. The grossly deformed lips, and mud-and-cow-dung hairdos of Africa are also considered beautiful.

Age was very difficult to determine. Some were wrinkled and some were not. There seemed to be no in-between. The young girls stood about and smiled. They had not yet been blessed with the black-beauty syndrome, much to my satisfaction and approval of pearly whites and unstained lips. I determined their ages to be from fourteen to sixteen, or even more, because of the nicely shaped breasts. Their long, lovely, perfectly straight hair would have fallen somewhere to the midpoint of their backs had it not been tied up in a bun. Their eyes were big, brown, and bright, like soft velour. On their faces were tiny beads of perspiration that left a subtle sheen, soft and golden as the purest honey.

One girl, slightly smaller and more beautiful than the others, turned away, embarrassed at my prolonged staring, obviously more sensitive than the others. She aroused my curiosity and maleness so strongly that I was embarrassed myself, and hoped that my suntan hid my blushing. She was so small and beautiful. Tiny, silklike hairs waved with the breeze from the nape of her neck and all along her hairline in the back. They were yet too fine and immature to be restricted within the confines of the mature hair that made up her bun. Curves—youthful and not completely mature—did not give way; or were they restricted by the baggy shabbiness of her clothing? Even her small, dirty bare feet that protruded out from pant legs that were too long and dragged in the dirt, could be forgiven. I knew she could be no more than fourteen.

I was brought abruptly out of my enjoyable trance by a little boy about five years old tugging on my utility coat. "You number one, you number one, okay?"

He was dressed only in shorts and was very brown. He pointed to an unlit cigarette he had stuck in a cavity where two front baby teeth were missing. He kept pointing to the cigarette as though he wanted me to light it. I reached into the deep baggy pockets of my utility pants, pulled out a candy bar, and took off the wrapper. I took the cigarette from its neat little toothless holder and replaced it with the candy bar before he had time to protest. He immediately bit down on it, nodded with approval at the transaction and beamed in delight. I threw the cigarette down on the ground and stepped on it. I shook my head. "Bad, bad, number ten, number ten."

One of the mamas handed me a nice, cold Coca Cola and I gave her more than enough piasters to cover the transaction. I didn't feel like bartering. I tipped it back and opened my throat, letting it fall unrestricted into a deprived and deserving cavity until the nerves, activated by the cold, collided with each other somehwere in the back of my head and throat, causing a painful signal that my lungs and pipes were about to collapse from the carbonation. It was absolutely exhilarating! Thank God Coke can be purchased anywhere in the world. I bought some more Cokes, some of Fred's favorite green stuff, and a couple of loaves of French bread for later. It would be nice to empty their little bamboo carryalls, but I was short on piasters. I had a few greenbacks, but it was illegal for Americans to have them in their possession, let alone spend them. They were of great black market value to the communists, and I didn't want to finance someone's AK-47 and end up on the wrong end of it. I waved to the mamasans and kids, winked at the beauties. We exchanged smiles, and I started back across the bridge.

By now, the slough was even more alive with action. Troops were now jumping off the bridge and having as much fun as the kids. My short excursion was a pleasant and much-needed diversion. Under different circumstances, this could indeed be a paradise.

115

I headed back to my position. It was the hottest part of the day. Ed was sitting in the shade of the lean-to that extended down from the top of the bunker. He seemed to be in deep thought, gazing out across the rice fields. I sat myself down in the shade.

"What's happening, Oggie?" he asked, with a smile that quickly faded away. "How did you like those foxy chicks at the bridge?"

"I tell you what, I was sure surprised. The women here are better looking than in Okinawa, Japan, or the Philippines."

"Look, I'm gonna find me the right one, marry her, and take her home."

I couldn't believe what I had heard, and laughed. I guess it was the depressed, melancholy way he said it. I almost thought he meant it.

"You attempt a numbskull act like that and they'll have you in the brig or in a straight jacket for sure. We're not here to marry the country and take it home with us, we're here to save it and leave it here. What's the matter with you, anyway? You're acting kind of wierd. You're not thinking of bailing out, are you?"

"No," he said as he abruptly threw away the twig he had been sucking on. He looked back over the sandbags and pushed his cap back on his forehead. "You remember the tall redhead I introduced you to at Mission Beach?"

"Yeah, I think her name was Sharon, wasn't it? She had great legs and good chocolate cake."

"Yeah, that's the one, the bitch. I got a letter from her. She's going with somebody else."

116

"I didn't realize you were so hung up on her."

"I'm not hung up."

"Then what's your problem?"

"They can't write me off like this."

"They?" I asked. "You mean you have letters from others?"

"Yeah."

"Well, buddy, what do you expect them to do? Stand in platoon formation down at the docks in San Diego when the ship comes in? I can see them all now. Sitting around at a Tupperware party biting their nails and waiting for The Horn to come home. The Horn's gonna show up in San Diego with a little nasan bride and a couple of little babysans! That oughta fix them!"

He smiled. "Shut up!" He swung at me playfully. I ducked.

"Here, Casanova." I handed him a not-so-cold soda pop and a loaf of French bread. "This ought to take care of a broken heart for a while."

He popped the top off with his belt buckle and proceeded to examine the contents of the bottle, especially the sediment on the bottom. He cracked open the loaf of French bread to examine any impurities, and picked it apart like a hungry raccoon. Occasionally there would be grass, twigs, or a tiny stone, but nothing we couldn't get around. After all, the bread was baked in the village; and, in fact, sometimes it looked as though they had rolled the dough on the ground. Other than a few pickings here and there, the bread was great, and it smelled too good not to eat. It was made out in the open in a not-too-sanitary bakery, but as long as half a bug didn't show up. I was not going to worry."

I was always entertained and totally amazed by Ed's sterile, antiseptic fetish. It was not quite to the point of mental imbalance, but very comical. He checked all the food and drink of native origin like a mad pathologist. After all the films and lectures we had in training about V.D., Ed took it much more seriously than most of us. Although we were aware of the problem and took it seriously, Ed was totally consumed with the idea. On his first liberty in Okinawa, after a cute but commercial date, he raced back to the barracks and scrubbed himself vigorously for hours. The whole platoon had become aware of his feverish sterilizing process and gathered around to watch. Two days later, it was confirmed, he had contracted something. He was the first, and one of the very few, who contracted anything. The platoon screamed and howled for days. I felt a little sorry for him, but it was indeed classical. He was the butt of every V.D. joke for months.

"Oh, I almost forgot." He pulled a letter out of his breast pocket. "They had mail call while you were gone. This is for you."

The thickness of the letter was unusual. Mom didn't usually write long letters. My heart stopped when I recognized the flawless, beautiful handwriting on the envelope. No one will ever write my name so beautifully in longhand.

The postmark was a month ago. I hesitated, almost too afraid to open the letter. I let the faint perfume do its provocative work inside my head. Why now, after all these months? I took out my pocketknife and slid it under the flap so as not to destroy the envelope. The small pages of stationery were robin-egg blue, with a tiny forget-me-not monogrammed on the upper left-hand corner. It's a strange sensation to hold something clean and fragrant, with words beautifully written and passed secretly and silently from one mind to another, like the private communion of two people who have only eye contact across a crowded room.

My mother hated the nickname "Dick," but I liked it. Only my grandfather and one other person used it. The letter was from her:

Dear Dick:

I'm sorry for not continuing to write to you after I became a mother, but things became terribly hectic. I'm sure you can understand, though, being from a large family yourself. You were like a brother to me, always kind and understanding, and quite mature for your age. Although you were younger and shy, you were unique, and you were my friend.

I remember when you came and told me you had joined the Marine Corps. I laughed at you and you got angry. I'm sorry for that. It was only a reflex. I thought we were both too young to accept something so worldly, within our idealistic and immature world. Silly girls grow up too, and I was proud of you. I was especially proud when you came home on leave and stopped by Dad's in your uniform and met Bob.

I don't want to burden you with my problems. I'm sure you have all you can handle right now in the war, but we were close, and I know you'll understand. We had been married almost two years, and he's gone now. He was killed a month ago, when his truck overturned on the way to work. I can't believe it has happened to me. I still cry at night. Sometimes, when I'm in the kitchen in the late afternoon, I hear him coming through the front door and I run to the front room, and there's no one there.

He left something behind, so precious and dear, that enables me to carry on. A part of himself, a part of us, a part of what life is all about. Bethany is ten months old now, and just as beautifuil as her daddy. The same hair and nose, and when I look into her eyes I feel a mixture of great joy and heartache.

I've been wondering how you were and where you were. Writing a letter to you has always been special to me and has always lifted my spirits. I hope you'll take care of yourself and come home soon. We've both come a long way from the strawberry fields.

I don't know if you've heard or not, but I got so excited when I read about it in the *Herald*. It seems that you and your family are becoming celebrities in town. There was a half-page article about your little brothers John and Mike, and the Cedarcrest School. You are the only one in town who is in the Vietnam War, and the kids at school wanted to do something for the cause. It was in the Sunday supplement. There they were in living color, Mike and John and the other kids, holding a large care package with cake and cookies. I thought it was marvelous . . .

She continued on about her plans and the security that Bob had left her. She said that no one need worry about her, as she was in good financial shape. She also included a little typical small-town gossip. Diana had invited her to a dinner party, but she said she couldn't handle the seaweed hors d'ourvres. I was already aware of Japanese customs, food, and beauty.

Our families had known each other for many years, and Diana and I practically grew up together. I remember once when I was home on leave, and Diana called to ask me if I wanted to go horseback riding. I told her I would be delighted. She was fifteen at the time, and I was seventeen. I was somewhat puzzled when she showed up with only one horse, since they had a full stable. But Diana was no longer a skinny-kneed silly little girl, and I learned that a horse was very comfortable carrying two people.

The letter was signed, "Love, Elizabeth. P.S. Do you still have the St. Christopher medal I gave you?"

I got up and stepped out from under the lean-to. I noticed Fred peering at the last ounce of green stuff in the bottle and eyeballing it clinically, looking for impurities. The bread looked as though an unhungry but inquisitive raccoon had gone through it.

"You don't look so good. Did you get a Dear John letter too?"

I didn't want to go into it with him just then.

"See, I told you them broads have no heart." He went back to picking at the bread and putting little pieces in his mouth.

A gust of hot, moist wind blew directly into my face as I walked along the barbed wire barrier and squinted out across the rice fields. The smooth bronze embossed figure felt comfortable between my thumb and index finger. I remembered meeting Bob before they were married, the only time we ever met. He was tall and good looking, with dark hair and eyes and fair skin. Elizabeth seemed electrified, with a sparkle in her eye I'd never seen before. I sensed a slight uneasiness in her when she introduced us, and thought that perhaps Bob didn't understand our relationship. Somehow her uneasiness made me feel more important to her and seemed to add substance to our unique relationship. I did not want her to feel uncomfortable in any way, though.

Our love, as I interpreted it, was a mere fantasy—and I flagrantly indulged myself. Much like a sister, she would introduce me to some of her dates and then ask me what I thought of them.

I gave earnest congratulations to Elizabeth and Bob and did not prolong my stay with them. I left with a feeling of consolation: I had known her and loved her first. In a fantasy, you can get bruised a little; but in reality, you can get hurt.

Looking back on it now, I thought I needed love

then. But when all in my life seemed lost, she was my first real friend. She took a genuine interest in me as a person, and she made me feel unique. She added an entirely different dimension to a dull, insecure life. She was the most beautiful girl I had ever seen, but I never looked at her as if she were a girl. I always looked at her as a woman. I was totally captivated and mesmerized by her at age fifteen.

From the day I met her, the changes that came over me were humorous and immediate. One day she asked me if I would like to read a book she had enjoyed, *The Jungle,* by Upton Sinclair. I was a poor student, and hated books and reading, but I wasn't about to let her know that she had a dumbbell friend. I took the book and read it frantically. I read through each class in school, and at night in the bunkhouse by candlelight, until it was completed. I was amazed at what I had done, since she had only casually asked me if I wanted to. It was the first time I had ever read a complete novel. I was so proud when we got together and discussed our enjoyment of certain facets of the book. It was strange and exciting to listen to myself discussing an important literary work. (I later learned that my objectionable attitude toward reading was due to headaches related to a minor eye disorder.) I did a book report on *The Jungle* and got the first *B* in English I ever received. She also introduced me to Steinbeck's *Of Mice and Men.* It was fascinating.

My entire outlook on education changed, and all of my grades improved. My whole attitude toward myself changed, as well.

What a strange relationship we had. I felt bad because I thought I was not repaying her for what she was doing for me. I did not have a car, and did not even have any money for dates. Sometimes we just went for walks and I would buy her an ice cream at the general store. For the first time in my life, I was in love. I was proud and happy, and it made the rest of my life bearable. I didn't care if it was half fantasy and half reality.

She would call on the phone and invite me over to her house, where she lived with her father and younger brother. Her mother had died. We spent endless hours talking about everything and nothing, laughing and having fun like two friends will. I adored her, and at that time in my life, I needed her.

Now was my chance to repay her for saving me. But I was so far away. I let the medal slip through my fingers and fall back on my chest. The sun was going down. I turned and walked back toward the bunker. I took the first watch of the evening and let Ed sleep until early morning.

I knew that my head would be full of the letter for some time. I tried to picture Elizabeth's little Sherry as she had described her, but I couldn't. My mind didn't register dark hair and eyes, but rather large pools of deep liquid blue, rich auburn hair, a full round face with high cheekbones and dimples, a short, perky nose, and a small upturned mouth showing extraordinary pearly teeth.

CHAPTER ELEVEN

The days at Iron Bridge Ridge had become long, hot, and uneventful. Our bunker was no longer a cool quiet refuge from the heat of the day. At no time could we risk using a light during hours of darkness. Toads, salamanders, and other nuisances were inadvertently crushed underfoot in the darkness. Even after a daily policing of casualties, the air in the basement was still somewhat less than fresh.

The evenings were becoming increasingly more active. 81mm mortars were called on to illuminate the area. We hoped to catch the enemy with their pants down out in the open, but the pop out of the tube and the crack in the air before the flair hit left ample time for them to hit the ground and hide among the rice stalks, if, in fact, they were there.

Weapons platoon, on our right, seemed to be more active (or skittish) than anyone else. Periodically, someone would hear something, or think they heard something, and lay on the trigger, sending tracer rounds skimming out over the tops of the rice for hundreds of yards into the darkness. It became so frequent that other platoons started joining in. Some fool along the line would open up arbitrarily to create some excitement in order to break up the boredom. It was fine for those who were on watch, but it was hell when you were trying to sleep. Weapons platoon said they had heard voices out in the fields, and other strange sounds. But we never took seriously anything those idiots said. I figured it was just the sound of the sand shifting between their ears.

The fire watch games at night had also gotten out of hand. It looked as though Iron Bridge Ridge was under siege all the time. I enjoyed popping a few rounds of H.E. (high explosive) myself, to see them flare.

During one of the fun-and-game periods, Fred and I decided to throw our first hand grenades at the enemy to see who could outthrow the other. Ed claimed that he won by default because I threw a dud. It bothered both of us. The first time I had thrown a grenade in Vietnam, and it malfunctioned. It wasn't very good odds. It left me with the burden of wondering whether I had received all of mine from the same crate. Maybe they were all defective. Without blowing, they are heavy enough to crush a man's skull. Of course, the Vietcong may grin and kill you for trying to take him out with a rock. Grenade throwing was finally wisely curtailed by the command post, or they would have had to call San Diego and request another freighter of ammo.

The next morning, third platoon reported that someone had tampered with the booby traps on the claymore mine. A Ho Chi Minh sandal print was discovered. These sandals are popular native footwear. The soles are punched out of old automobile tires, and when you walk around they leave tracks like an old Chevy.

It took a lot of guts to crawl in there with all of the trigger-happy thrill seekers. To get close enough to fool with a booby trap in total darkness either takes someone brainless or someone with a frightening amount of talent. In any event, the fun was over and the heat was on. Everyone felt a degree of believability in the rumors, which made us very alert.

The short-scan method was the most effective way to get optimum vision at night. It did not allow one to see in total darkness, but it was an effective method that allowed one to see things otherwise obscured or overlooked by tension in the eyes. Straining, by trying too hard and moving the eyes from side to side, created undue stress; but locking the eyes within the sockets and moving the head only from side to side in short scanning movements was more effective. For terrain directly in front, we started in close and used the same method, moving the eyes and head in short increments outward to infinity. It was like looking at squares on a checkerboard one at a time, but never allowing the eye to become fixed on one square for too long. Focusing too hard and allowing the eyes to become fixed on one object or area for more than a moment aroused the imagination. We began to see things that did not exist.

Obscure, inanimate objects began to move almost invariably during periods of mental or physical fatigue, or excitement. The secret was to relax the eyes and keep them moving.

Listening had the same peculiarity, even in total darkness. I would cover my eyes and my ears seemed to be more effective. A blind man can hear more than a sighted man could ever think possible because the energy is channeled in one direction instead of two. The eyes, although they may be looking into total darkness, are still drawing energy from the brain.

I squirted some thick, greasy bug repellent and rubbed it on my face and neck. It burned the skin a little and was too strong for the sinuses. But it was a minor nuisance compared to feasting mosquitos. Somehow, Supply had screwed up and had filled all the little containers they issued with repellent designed to saturate tents and to spray in billetting areas. No one had yet discovered whether it was toxic or lethal. You could hear the hungry hum all night, but no way would they try to penetrate the invisible iron curtain.

An eighty-one mortar popped out of its tube with a hollow, airless sound. Several seconds later, at about six hundred feet, it cracked and illuminated, swaying back and forth gently in its tiny silk parachute, giving all the scanning eyes on the ground a well-needed break. The shadows around me created by the flare also swayed in gentle unison. I eyeballed as much territory as many times as I possibly could before the flare went out. I hoped to have the first crack at some sorry soul with no place to hide.

The flare began to sputter and go dim. To the left, I spotted something out of the corner of my eye that didn't feel right. About twenty yards out between the wire and the slough was a bush about three-feet tall. I concentrated and tried to visualize the area during the day, but I couldn't remember if it was there or not. My imagination must be working overtime; still, I wondered why I wasn't drawn to it the night before. Perhaps it was the height and angle of the flare that illuminated it differently and made it more predominant. My God, what was I worrying about a damn tree for? I knew what kind of an answer I would get if I had to bring it to anyone's attention. Maybe bushes grew fast around here.

Ed and I were enjoying a quiet breakfast. By the luck of the draw, we had drawn too decent meals for breakfast instead of his ham and lima beans and my beans and franks like the morning before. We decided to pool our groceries. We took his canned ham and mixed it with my chopped ham and eggs in a canteen cup. We heated it over a couple of heat tabs. It smelled and resembled a Denver omelet that was grossly overloaded with ham. I added a little sugar to cut the salt. Fred sliced little pieces of French bread and toasted them on a twig, then spread them with peanut butter and marmalade. I brewed a canteen cup of hot chocolate. Everything was going fine at the breakfast table until tasteful Fred pulled out a warm bottle of his favorite green elixir, followed by a chocolate-covered coconut candy bar.

"How in the hell can you drink that warm nasty crap so early in the morning and ruin a good breakfast?"

"No problem. I just pretend it's orange juice."

"I'll bet from green oranges. That crap is so dark green, it's probably artificially colored."

"What's wrong with that? There's nothing wrong with artificial colors." He paused. "What's wrong with artificial colors?"

"Well, in the village they probably use algae to color things green."

"What's algae?"

"They're tiny microscopic green bugs that live in water," I lied.

His eyes bugged; he choked a little and blew out the remainder of the soda pop. He poured some of the contents of the bottle into his palm, eyeballed it closely, and sniffed it like an inquisitive chimpanzee.

I looked at him with a stern, sober face. "Fred, you're sick." I cracked up and fell over backward in a screaming howl. I was rolling around in the dirt, totally out of control.

The seriousness of his expression began to fade. "Why, you little bastard!"

He lunged for me and I rolled out of the way and stumbled out of the canopy into the sunshine. Still hysterical, I nearly ran headlong into Trudeau. Fred was close behind me.

"What are you guys up to? Cut out the grab ass."

"The Horn here gets a little frisky after breakfast."

Trudeau, as usual, was not interested in our fooling

around. "Well, he can get frisky on a work party at the CP this morning. First, I've got to talk to the squad."

Fred raised his eyebrows and smiled. I couldn't figure his angle. Nobody's happy to go on a work party. Then I remembered the girls on the bridge.

Trudeau yelled for squad leaders up, and in a few minutes we had a small huddle eager to hear the day's news.

"We've got trouble. The Vietcong are moving in and probing at night. The corpsmen carried away Chavez, from weapons platoon, practically in a bag. The Lieutenant says he'll probably get discharged with a Section Eight."

"I guess he really took a jolt last night. He went out to bring in his claymore and found that somebody had deactivated both of the mousetrap devices and disconnected the lead wire. They turned the whole damn thing around and re-imbedded it in the ground facing the squad area. For some reason, they didn't re-booby trap it, but reconnected the lead wire. They could have gotten him for sure, and took a hell of a lot of other people, too. The strange part is that he was awake all night listening."

"Get this: rearming it was not an oversight. They left a piece of paper attached to the claymore with his name on it. He was considered the best booby-trap man that weapons platoon had. Now he is a basket case."

This information was more than a little unnerving. In the raw sense of the word, it was frightening. Behind young faces, minds labored quicker than high-speed computers, racing through years of index input, searching for answers, ideas, and rationalizations. For the moment, the imagination applied small amounts of pressure on the circuits and resisters of the mind.

The enemy was no longer warm flesh and blood; they were now an intangible, evil, macabre force. They were a commando raid of microscopic saboteurs entering the mind undetected to sever and splice intricate circuits of communication, causing havoc within the integral part of the computer, altering circuits, changing impulses, then escaping to safety to watch the huge, magnificent war machine self-destruct.

Neither tanks, machine guns, mines, barbed wire, nor indestructable bunkers—no amount of physical arsenal or defense—can deter such a haunting and effective invasion. Only an informed and alert mind is invulnerable.

I stared out into the darkness, sometimes forgetting my night-vision techniques. A dull, unhelpful moon was obscured by a thin cloud layer which broke up the monotony of the invisible black ceiling. It glistened like a sullen ghost squirming on the surface of the slough. I sat erect, legs folded Indian style. I had the forty-five in my lap, a round in the chamber on half-cock. Fred's oily M-14 lay at my left knee; and on my right, within finger's reach, lay my six hand grenades, all in a row.

I turned my head to the right sharply as someone came scurrying along the trail. I picked up the forty-five, pulled back the hammer, and challenged.

"It's Sheldon." His voice was low, almost a whisper, and out of breath.

I recognized the voice and didn't bother to ask for

the password. I released the hammer back to half-cock and laid the gun back on my lap. I told him to come in. He dropped down beside me, out of breath, and I could see the dull moonlight reflect off the sheen of his sweaty cheekbones and forehead. The whites of fearful eyes scanned the darkness too erratically and too intensely. His voice was shaky and unnatural. It scared the hell out of me.

"Oggie, they know my name, man. They know I'm here."

"How do you know they do?"

"I heard them, man, in plain English. Morales heard them, too." There was more stress in his voice. "How in the hell do they know me?"

Sheldon was a natural leader who probably dominated all of the basketball courts in the east side of Detroit. He was built like a thoroughbred racehorse, and was intelligent.

The Marine Corps could care less who you are or what race you are. Early in training, if they sense any leadership capabilities, they will give you every opportunity to develop them. I had blown it miserably. I was just too young and insecure. I could have probably succeeded in a limited degree if I'd let myself become an unconscionable tyrant, pushing around guys who were more intelligent, and older and bigger than I in order to compensate for my inadequacies—but that was not my style.

Sheldon didn't appear to have any insecurities. He kept up his courage even under the pressure of Jason and Trudeau. He never had any of the problems I did.

His bag was security. He was a better leader than either Jason or Trudeau, who were older and supposedly more experienced.

"Listen." He grabbed my arm. "Listen."

He was on his knees. He sat back on his heels, facing me, swaying back and forth gently, trying to ease the tension. We both held our breaths and concentrated with everything we could muster.

Then I heard it. My whole body shuddered with disbelief. It was impossible to locate the range. The low-key perfect English floated in from the darkness, riding on the warm breeze.

"Corporal Sheldon, we want you."

If they had used my name, I probably would have cracked. It was frightening enough to listen to them use someone else's. How could we be so inept, unprepared, and vulnerable? We didn't even know what they looked like or anything about them. They seemed to have us all figured out, and they were applying effective pressure. The microscopic commando teams were here.

Ed woke up, rolled over on his sleeping bag, and sat up. "What's going on?"

"Shut up and listen."

The voice spoke again. He heard it, but didn't believe it.

"Sheldon, somebody's bullshitting around with you out there. It must be a joke."

"Just listen and shut up, Ed, goddamn it."

Ed realized what direction it was coming from. He scrambled after his M-14, took the safety off, and let the bolt go home. Sheldon did the same.

"Come on, you guys, cool it. Sheldon, you're playing right into their hands. You can't see a thing out there. If we start to pop off, they're going to know they've already got to us."

Before we could take another breath, an M-14 opened up in weapons platoon area. Sheldon sat down. Whoever they were shooting at was right on top of their position. The tracer rounds bounced off the ground at such a sharp angle, it was as though someone had crawled into their position. Tracer rounds bounced off the ground and streaked out into the darkness like tiny comets. We asked each other what in hell could be going on over there. Maybe someone got through the wire and into a foxhole.

Sheldon stood up. "I think I had better go on down the line and make sure no one panics, before these motha fuckas start name-dropping again."

"Just think, Sheldon, you're a celebrity to them creeps out there. They must think you're awfully bad."

"Them sneaking, little motha fuckas are gonna know I'm bad, and I ain't gonna do no talking about it. You all take it easy, now."

He disappeared into the darkness. He was immediately challenged by the next position. He seemed to be less nervous and a little more confident after realizing that he was being used by the Vietcong as a football in a game designed to bend us all.

Ed challenged someone else scurrying down the trail, and we both concurred that it certainly wasn't a boring night. The new arrival was Jason. He was more out of breath and more excited than Sheldon had been. I wondered if he, too, was receiving little love calls through the night, or whether they even cared enough about him to bother.

Jason squatted native style and leaned in our direction. He whispered, "You know that kid, Smith, the quiet one in weapons platoon? He just blew up Osborne, his team leader, with twenty rounds. Osborne was sound asleep outside their bunker. He just blew half his head right off at point-blank. That's what all the tracers in the sky were."

"Yeah, we know, we saw them."

"The captain's calling it murder. They want me to take him back to the division tomorrow because of my M.P. experience. The company is on one hundred percent alert for the rest of the night. That means every swinging dick stays awake all night."

He disappeared into the darkness.

Both Ed and I agreed that Smith was kind of weird and that Osborne was a complete asshole, but that he didn't deserve to die for it. We wondered how he'd made team leader. There was definitely something wrong with that pack of hyenas. It was probably the reason they suffered more casualties than the other platoons.

Another mortar left the tube and cracked over our heads and blossomed out. I grabbed my pop gun and stood up. My peek-a-boo tree had moved a good ten feet. I pulled down on my gun and blew it into a fine mulch.

"What in the hell did you do that for?"

"I'm getting tired of it creeping around on me all

the time."

He looked at me strangely. "What?"

"I'll explain to you in the morning."

We sat down.

"Since we're going to be up for the night, do you have anything to eat?"

"There's some crackers and peanut butter around here somewhere."

"That sounds good to me."

We started looking, taking advantage of the light.

"Oh, I could probably be persuaded to try some of that green slime you call orange juice, too."

The only other event of the night was a med-evac chopper sent to haul out the murder victim. It could have waited until morning. That would have been less risky.

How do you explain to a mother that her son was murdered in combat by a foxhole buddy? The incident seemed to jolt the company back to a rational consciousness. We agreed that the enemy was here and they were actively attempting to destroy us. We discovered that their effectiveness was not due to genius or superhuman powers, but to their audacity, guts, and ability to play effectively on our naivete and carelessness. We discovered that the docile farmers planting rice around the Iron Bridge Ridge were Vietcong! All eyes, all ears!

CHAPTER TWELVE

I scrubbed my greasy, salt-encrusted utilities, underwear and socks with a ball of crude, scented Vietnamese hand soap, and spread everything out on the bank to dry. I scrubbed off the dead hide accumulated by weeks of neglect. After the much-overdue chores were completed, and the childlike frolicking (disguised as swimming) in the dark, still, unstagnant slough was over, I rolled over on my back. The air and water were very near body temperature. I lay motionless, senses almost in a state of meditation, trying with reasonable success to purge my mind of thoughts. I closed my eyes and felt no physical sensation at all. I experienced a combination of euphoria, vertigo, and ecstasy. The nerves slowly and reluctantly gave up their desperate hold on muscles, allowing them to give up the strain on tendons. The body floated listlessly, as though it were a wooden puppet with members and joints fastened together with a single thread. To relax any more would give the heart an unexpected, premature rest. The controllable revolving carousel of a free-wheeling mind slows down to a near standstill and strains to keep from becoming motionless, allowing the various steeds of emotion to catch their wind and continue to endure. To stop this endless revolution is to withdraw and deteriorate. A nebulous group of complex entities drifting through time and space, the mind is suspended like the universe, confined only by the word "infinity."

The bump of tiny, fingerlike minnows subtly disturbed the total experience. A frog in the cool green shadows stirred and watched the forlorn, dubious monster climb up the bank and out of sight, carrying an odd-looking bundle.

Our first monsoon pounded us throughout the night. It kept us busy trying to sleep and keep dry. The bunker provided some protection from the relentless downpour for the lucky men off duty. It was like sleeping in a leaky cavern with six inches of water on the floor and the constant siege of dripping from above. We fashioned a cot of sandbags to keep out the muck and hoped the water wouldn't rise much further. We wrapped the neoprene poncho around the sleeping bags, but little snakes of water still somehow found their way inside.

The canopy outside had become a nuisance. It caught the rain like a funnel and poured it directly into the bunker. We pulled it in and wrapped it around the body, as it was first intended.

The rain was heavy enough to tear up the ground and carry it away. There was virtually no watching or effective listening while on watch. The only pastime of the evening was to stare at a perfectly good luminous wristwatch that you knew beyond a doubt was malfunctioning when it took the second hand a full hour to make a sweep; the hour hand seemed to be rusted in place forever. Even when counting off the seconds in the mind, a minute still took an hour. *(We humbly repented our transgressions of cursing the inferno that besieged us by day. May we not curse the flood of night, for fear of releasing the wrath of holocaust which would surely destroy the earth.)*

The rising sun revealed that the world had been washed away and a new one had taken its place. The loose earth and our positions had been washed into the bunkers and trench lines like a sewer system.

The spirit of the morning was like that of spring, purged and cleansed. The breeze carried the sweet fragrance of rice flowers. Shy and simple flowers seemed to be coaxed from their hiding places, and indistinguishable birds sang enthusiastically of the welcome change. The overall landscape seemed to be more green and lush than the day before. Even the sky seemed to be a deeper, richer blue, with a handful of tiny white fluffs racing toward the east to catch up with the storm that had left them behind. To my amazement, the dark slough had vanished. It had climbed its banks and flooded the surrounding rice paddies, creating a sizeable lake no longer segmented by a variety of dikes.

Steam rolled off everything and everyone as we prepared for a long-range patrol, a search-and-destroy mission across the valley and up into the foothills. First squad moved out led by Lieutenant O'Connor. There was a bunch-up at the small opening in the barbed wire in front of my position. It was just large enough for a man to squeeze through if he was lucky enough not to get hung up on it. With my size, I had no difficulty; but I had to hold the PRC 6, usually called by its more fashionable acronym "Prick," over my head and inch sideways through the opening in the wire.

The radio was not too heavy, but was bulky and cumbersome. Having the responsibility of the radio meant that I didn't have to participate in the flank security or point. They could have stuck me with the big brother PRC 10, which required a packboard.

The squad had finally spread itself out to normal intervals, and our first heading was south toward a small crude footbridge across the slough. We sloshed along in knee-deep water, giving the hidden slough a wide berth in fear of the deep. The sun began to burn and the perspiration began to pour. At least there were no flies or mosquitoes to clutter up the air. The water was drawn in with each step and squirted out again through the portholes in our canvas boots. It was warm, and massaged our feet.

Nellis was well out in front of point man, and by the time he had reached the end of the small bridge, he was up to his waist in water. He was six feet tall. I began to

141

worry. Unlike going off the end of a landing craft and going over my five-foot-five limit, there wasn't anyone near enough now to grab me by the nape of my neck and drag me to the surface. I began to walk more carefully and in a direct line with Lieutenant O'Connor in front. I wished I had a walking stick. The amount of water that had accumulated overnight in these fields was unbelievable.

Lieutenant O'Connor put a hand up to his mouth. "Nellis, take it nice and easy, and watch your step. We are in no big hurry today."

Nellis stepped up onto the footbridge. There was a single log running down the middle for walking on. On each side, at about shoulder height, there were railings. He slung his weapon and hung onto the railings. He was now in knee-deep water. He felt along the submerged log one foot at a time. The submerged log was suspended in a cradle of bamboo strips laced to the two rails on the surface.

Nellis turned around and grinned. "Don't worry, sir, frogman school was my second choice."

Before he could turn his head back, his foot had slipped and he had crashed into the water up to his neck. He hung onto the right rail with one hand. The bamboo strips had helped break his fall, and one leg was still hanging over the submerged log. He slowly pulled himself back until he was on his feet again.

I continued to worry. In boot camp, I had drunk, breathed, and puked a lot of chlorine water. They had physically thrown me into the deep end time after time, poking me with long rods as I wildly thrashed the water to get to the side of the pool. Undisturbed, I could float on my back. But to this day, I have never experienced swimming strokes without terror.

With the radio and grenade launcher hanging around my neck, jaw locked, and knuckles white from holding on, I started across the bridge with the caution of a blind man exploring the Grand Canyon.

After Nellis got off the bridge, some yards further on, he took a second unexpected plunge. I froze on the bridge. Morales waded frantically in his direction, feeling the bottom so he wouldn't take the same plunge. The long seconds and the stillness of the water where Nellis had gone down were terrifying. It was as if a great shark had grabbed him from below and pulled him to the deep. Finally, a convulsing hand broke the surface. Morales laid a rifle stock right into the clutching fingers. You could see the power generated in the quivering fingers almost as though they were strong enough to squeeze the linseed oil from the hardwood of the stock. Morales closed his eyes, gritted his teeth, and strained. Nellis's helmet broke the surface like a hard-hat driver. He blinked a half-dozen times and sputtered.

Morales grinned and spoke to Nellis, almost falling in himself. "How did you like it down there, frogman? See any Victor Charlies?"

Nellis clawed his way back up to the shallow water. Despite the gravity of the moment, I could not help but wonder whether Nellis was carrying his volumes of *Hamlet* and *The Taming of the Shrew* in his pack, and whether they had gotten wet. He was a tall, skinny Jeff

Chandler type with a flat top. He was from Chicago, and Charlie called him "Richard III." Nellis seemed to have an innate passion for Shakespeare. On several occasions I would find him reading feverishly, then breaking up in heavy laughter. He would ask me to read a paragraph. I would oblige. He would ask me what I thought. I would lie and give him a bemused smile. I didn't want to appear totally illiterate and foolish, which I was. I didn't understand a word of it. There were words I had never seen before, and I couldn't quite get hysterical about them.

I did feel that I was missing out on something. I had served two terms in the fourth grade and had walked away from school in the ninth grade, still reading on a fifth-grade level. Any more than plain English and I was out of business. I guess that was the reason I enjoyed Steinbeck; I had something in common with his characters.

I hadn't really wanted to leave the classroom. The mysteries of education still fascinate me, and I plan to do some heavy digging at my first opportunity. Friends who attempt to placate my embarrassment often remind me of numerous millionaires who never made it through grade school. I appreciate their kindness, but doubt that there will be very many dropouts in the seventies and eighties. I'll start somewhere, but it won't be with *The Taming of the Shrew*.

I hoped that the fruits of Bill Shakespeare's labor hadn't gone to ruin at the hands of a frogman. Nellis's rifle was lost forever somewhere off the Great Barrier Reef. I knew how he felt. Get yourself a fork and spoon, boy!

The patrol moved on, fighting a slow, tedious, unsuspecting battle, sloshing and sliding and being sucked in and out of the toothless jaws of the greasy, plasterlike mud. It could easily suck off a boot and leave it several feet under the surface. An entrenching tool would be needed to rescue an important part of oneself, like a foot.

Nellis finally pulled the patrol up out of the quagmire to high ground toward some high elephant grass growing along the base of the foothills. We had already burned up too much energy in this morning's water and mud fest, and we vowed to find an alternate route back. The tiny bleeding cuts from the savage, towering elephant grass added to the discomfort from the ten o'clock ball of sulphurous hell. With each movement the dry mud dropped away, leaving dust on the surface or mixed with perspiration and saturated along with the salt that crusted on the fabric.

My dog tags were heating up and burning my chest, so I slipped them around to the back. I was glad I had risked the opportunity to take an unwarranted, unofficial, against orders, court-martial offense, firing-squad level, refreshing dip in the slough yesterday.

I noticed while on long patrols that if the inside of my thighs were unclean, they became easily chafed when rubbed with the utility trousers. The buildup of salt and filth contributed to a raw, bone-crushing agony. I seemed to sweat more and expend valuable energy. It takes a little of the fun and glamor away from a combat patrol. Something so minor and simple could be crippling. I hope some brasshead dies of terminal jungle rot.

I lay face down in a clear, fresh creek and drank as much as I could hold, then popped in a couple of salt tablets and washed them down. I filled up both canteens and faked putting the brackish, iodine-tasting halazone tablets into each canteen as we were ordered to do. If we had to resort to drinking out of rice paddies or out of village wells, I could see it; but a mountain stream is the purest of water.

It was nice to know there would be an abundance of water to drink at will instead of sipping and conserving as much as possible, as we did when we were out on the flat ground in the direct heat. But drinking all we wanted, with the heat and exhaustion, would be dangerous if the priceless, life-giving salt tablets weren't used.

The cliffside was green, lush, and dangerous. We were poking around in Victor Charlie's backyard, and the odds were in his favor. He had more control of the situation and more mobility, knowing the gorge we were entering, the high ground, and our lack of experience at jungle fighting. They wouldn't be able to wipe us out unless there were a lot of them, but they could pick at us and make it rough if we weren't careful.

Nellis was relieved at point and Ed took his place. The point man is in the most dangerous, vulnerable position on a patrol in dense jungle. The enemy lies in ambush waiting for the point man to come into very close range, then they hit him and run like hell. I knew Ed was nervous enough to stay alert all the time; and with those big, lemur-like eyes, nothing would escape him.

The creek had a good swiftness after the running off, but it was the only way we were going to penetrate the mountains. The years of erosion had left steep banks on both sides thick with brush and vines. We tried putting out flankers, but it was impossible for them to move effectively.

We penetrated deeper into the mountains. The walls began to jut up on each side like skyscrapers, and gigantic boulders that had been carved loose lay in midstream. We waded through the deep, dark, but still-moving water with equipment and weapons held high over our heads. We crossed the sand bars and entered the current again.

Every so often Ed would raise his hands. We would freeze and listen. We waited for him to check out possible ambush sites such as blind bends in the creek. His job was to stick his neck out to keep us safe. This whole gorge was filled with ambush sites.

They could probably see us frolicking across the muddy valley floor, coming haphazardly in their direction, from the trees that towered high on the hillsides. It would give them plenty of time to set up for us. Or maybe they thought they were really dealing with kids who cried in the night and had their boots and equipment stolen.

We moved deeper into the bowels of the massive green sauna. The surrounding mountains blocked out any hope of a light breeze. When not fighting the current, we were still drowning in our own sweat. The surrounding jungle steamed as though it was reaching its kindling point and would burst into flames at any moment.

Lieutenant O'Connor halted the column for a ten-minute break. When we had relaxed and gotten our wind back, the complainers complained and the smokers smoked. I sat down on a rock. I was starving. I popped open a can of sticky fruitcake. It was sweet and nourishing, and it only took a half-quart of water to get it down.

I stared down into the crystal-clear pool at my feet. Minnows darted in and out of the shadows. I was homesick for fishing, picnicking, crawdadding, bull-frogging, dam building, the old swimming hole, the beatings I got for catching a cold, the nearly drowning and dragging in mud.

The sound of anxious, predestined water flowing licked at my ears. I was far away. "Goddamn it! Goddamn it!" Morales began to yell and jump forward.

We thought at first that he had been hit. He flung his butt down on a sand bar and hastily began to untie his boot. He quickly pulled it off and tipped it up. A mixture of blood and water poured out. We knew he was hit. He pulled off his socks and pulled his pant legs up. He was covered with leeches!

I shuddered, afraid to examine myself. My next thought was of Ed. If he found anything like that, he would die of a coronary.

Everyone began pawing and examining themselves. The smokers began puffing on several cigarettes and handing them to the nonsmokers. A touch on the back from a hot cigarette, and the ferocious little vampires would unleash their jaws and could be easily flicked away. A series of good and bad blood jokes broke the tension of working loose from these tiny sucking invertebrates.

I was amazed at my luck; I fit under the "bad blood" category. I found one under my jacket sleeve that was rolled above the elbow. Like pigs, they had aggressive, voracious little appetites, and wasted a lot of what they craved. There was blood running from almost everyone afflicted. Just as I should have imagined, Ed found one clinging to his testicles. For a moment I thought he was going to be in desperate need of a sedative—but we all managed to survive, and we saddled up and continued on.

The terrain became rougher and steeper, and the current swifter. We slipped, slid, and crawled over wet slimy boulders. We clung to roots and vines hanging from the canyon wall, trying to stay out of the white, cascading water. We helped each other with a hand or an occasional extended rifle butt while keeping an alert, wary eye over our shoulders and the high horizon.

The front of the patrol seemed to have reached a summit, and some disappeared over the top. Past the boulders at the summit there was a wide, still pool. It was nearly motionless until it spilled over the rim of the rocks and down the canyon. The left side of the gorge gave way to a small canyon that ran perpendicular to the gorge. Thick colonies of green moss clung to the bare face of the rock that towered above. Outcroppings of short, indestructible brush grew between the cracks and crevices. Below, there was a thicket of bamboo surrounding a small clearing.

Trudeau dispatched a man to keep a watch down the canyon, and another to watch the area ahead of us while the rest of the patrol went in to poke around the clearing. Somehow we had caught them by surprise—but not quickly enough to overtake them at their rice and fish-sauce lunch, which was thrown around on the ground. The campfire was steaming. There was a large lean-to at the far end of the clearing and about four or five smaller ones scattered throughout the area. There was a lot of debris strewn around, old tennis shoes and trash. We were surprised to find out that they were eating as well as we were. There were C-rations and garbage strewn everywhere. A slovenly lot, these Victor Charlies.

Trudeau, along with Morales's fire team, was probing through the trash behind the large lean-to with their rifle barrels when they called for the lieutenant. We hurried over, hoping they had found something important. Trudeau handed the lieutenant the remnants of a small, white, heavy cardboard box. In his other hand he held some gauze and used syringes.

"Look, sir. It's some kind of a medical kit. Look where it's from, sir."

He looked at the other side of the sopping-wet cardboard. In big, black, bold letters it read: "The University of California, Berkeley."

"Where in hell are they getting this stuff, Lieutenant,

sir?" Red asked.

"Probably the same place they're getting the C-rations. Captured from the ARVN."

Charlie spoke as he took off his helmet and scratched the back of his head. "Berkeley is too liberal to openly oppose a nice Marxist like Uncle Ho Chi. Something smells."

The lieutenant gave him a funny look that I did not understand. No one else paid any attention to either of them.

The lieutenant scanned the periphery of the rocks high above us with squinted eyes. The rest of us followed suit. We all agreed without a word that they were probably watching us right now.

"Trudeau, round up your men and let's get out of here fast. We've found out what we want to know. This place is suicidal. Make sure your front and rear guard keep their little eyeballs open. We're like fish in a barrel all the way down until we reach the valley floor."

We kept a good interval and moved out quickly through the waist-deep water.

CHAPTER THIRTEEN

Like a thousand leather whips cracking in the air, M-2 carbines blasted down on us like a shower of hail. We were all out in the open, and there was a moment of confusion over which way to duck for cover. The squad split right down the middle, and the front half thrashed and clawed to the other side of the pool at the base of the wall. The fire was coming from over their heads, and they made it safely. The rest of us had to backtrack. Four of us, still in the line of fire, slammed into the water and slithered in between some rocks on the opposite side.

Charlie emptied a magazine into the brush along the top of the canyon wall so at least they wouldn't be able to breathe, squeeze, and pick us off.

Red, still scrambling from the pool, let out a yell and went down. He was fighting to keep his head above water. "I'm hit bad!"

Nellis jumped out from behind a rock with my forty-five still barking in his hand. He dove out into the water and grabbed Red by his jacket collar and dragged him back to safety. Red screamed in agony but never let loose of his rifle. I helped Nellis drag him to cover.

By the size of the hole, it looked like a thirty caliber round had smashed through the thigh bone.

The troops on the other side of the pool were safe from enemy fire for the moment. They searched in vain for a firing position to get a shot at the enemy, far away up the embankment. When a lull in the firing came, I yelled across to them and shook my M-79 over my head. They quickly got the message and moved downstream away from the impact area. Looking over their heads, they clung tightly to the side of the gorge.

We still couldn't pinpoint precisely where the firing was coming from. There was no flash and no smoke. I aimed the pop gun high into the trees that hung over the gorge. With an air burst, maybe I could rain shrapnel down on the angry lunch crowd. I pulled the trigger, and the explosion severed a four-inch-diameter bamboo trunk. It came crashing straight down into the water.

The three of us were on our knees in water up to our waists behind a huge boulder. Nellis and Charlie had a rhythm going; one flared while the other one loaded a full magazine, which kept the automatic weapons fire constant on the ridge line. I fired as fast as I could open the breech and pop in another shell. The others helplessly cheered us on.

Red was still conscious but in agony behind us. He had taken off his helmet, filled it with his own magazines, and with his upper leg blown all to hell, he managed to crawl over next to Nellis and sit up with his back against the boulder. He cradled the helmet full of magazines in his lap while he lay his head back until he was facing the sky. His eyes were closed and his teeth were clenched. Tears of pain rolled down his face and dripped off his chin into the helmet.

Nellis looked down on him, and smiled and patted him on his wet bristly head like a mother would a little boy. "It's okay, champ. You're still cooking. We'll get you home."

Red opened his eyes, registered a faint smile, and handed Nellis a magazine. It was the first time I had experienced something they call "guts," and it was moving.

I saw Ed waving frantically from the other side and hesitated on the trigger. I guess someone from the other side was bound to try something out of sheer helplessness and desperation, but I didn't think it would be Ed. But why not Ed? He always managed to be amusing, if not crazy.

He quickly stumbled out into the water, armed with only a hand grenade. As soon as he was beyond the overhang of the embankment and waist deep in the water, he let the spoon fly on the grenade. It popped and fizzled. He threw it up over his head and waded frantically back to safety. The grenade hit the top of the cliff, fell back into the pool, and blew harmlessly in the same spot he had thrown it from. Another foot and he would have made it. Another display of guts.

We continued to chip the jungle with a barrage of fire

until we heard a hideous scream only a human could make. A body crashed through the brush on the cliff. I could see the grotesque, twisted face as the body seemed to fly through the air in slow motion. It hit the water face and belly first with a stinging, hollow slap. It spasmed and flopped in the water like a downed goose for a time, then it was still. When it stopped bubbling, a slick of blood began to appear on the surface around the body. Again it was silent. In this forbidden land, the only sound was water on the rocks echoing down the canyon.

When we were certain the enemy had disengaged, at least for the moment, the rest of the squad moved over to what Charlie jokingly called the business side of the canyon and set up a perimeter. Red was fading in and out of consciousness as we carefully carried him back to the clearing to prepare him for the long, hard journey home. There was no chance of a med-evac until we got further down the gorge.

We hoped there would be a break in the jungle canopy. No one could remember when he had last seen blue sky or sunlight on the way up. The radio still hung around my neck, useless in these mountains. I chopped some small but sturdy bamboo stalks and lashed them to Red's leg as tightly as I could with several rifle slings. Morales and Trudeau were fashioning a litter with a couple of poles and a poncho.

We headed down the canyon as quickly as we could go. Going down was more difficult than going up, not only because of the litter but also the ominous threat of another, and perhaps more successful, ambush. All eyes and ears were turned to the ridge as we listened and tried to keep our hand- and foot-holds at the same time. Knuckles and knees were barked, swollen, and numb.

We switched carrying the litter often. Nellis was reluctant to give up his turn and rest. He barked orders to whoever was carrying the other end to be more careful.

Because of our hasty withdrawal, I did not seem to recognize any of the terrain. We hadn't given too much thought to the terrain on the way in, but the canopy was now beginning to thin and sunshine illuminated the gorge below. Without luck, I kept trying to raise the company on the radio.

After checking the overhead thoroughly, Lieutenant O'Connor held up the squad. Red was unconscious, with a quick heartbeat but normal breathing. I unslung the radio, turned down the squelch, and turned up the gain. Nothing. Trudeau, the lieutenant, and I were sitting on our heels around Red.

"Anything at all?" the lieutenant asked.

"No, sir, not even a break on the other end."

"Okay, Ogden," he pointed over his shoulder. "See that knoll up there over the ridge? I think if you get your butt up there, you can probably get some reception."

"Yes sir."

I gave Nellis my M-79 and took the forty-five back. I took off through the water and up the bank. I leaped, scratching and clawing at the bank, and managed to get hold of a securely anchored bush and pull myself up.

The bank was going to be the hardest point of the climb. The rest of it was steep but not impossible. I had toed, kneed, and knuckled it as fast as I could go all the way up the side of the slope. The urgency of the situation warranted no less.

The breezeless heat, the fatigue of the patrol, and the under-four-minute scaling of the "Matterhorn" left me strangling for air and almost nauseous as I crawled over the summit and lay on my back. I waited for a moment to see if I was going to come back to life and stop breathing like a carp out of water. I stood up, faced Iron Bridge Ridge, and pushed the button.

"Hotel One, this is Hotel One Bravo, over."

I took my finger off the button and listened intently to the relentless hissing sound of the open channel, waiting for it to break. Waiting for a voice.

I did everything I could think of for the next ten minutes, playing with the switches and jockeying the antenna around. Everything but throw it away, like the sole surviving legionnaire who never believed or appreciated such frivolous technology and knew the only hope of survival would be to march five hundred miles across the scorching sand dunes to be saved.

Then I thought of the extra battery. I started back down the slope. I followed the trail I had unknowingly gouged out like a heavy land turtle. I jumped in awkward leaps and bounds. I lost my footing and slid for what seemed like ten or twenty yards at a time. At one time I curled up in a ball and got off the trail and crashed through the brush like a lifeless rock. In the last roll, the radio slammed into my jaw and left me senseless. I lay on my back, with lungs and mouth full of dust and anything else I had stirred up. I was like a maniac running aimlessly and dangerously out of control. I laid on my back looking up at the sky from under a small shrub. I began to laugh out loud. I finally got a hold of myself and continued the rest of the way down in a more sure and constructive fashion.

When I reached the bottom, I filled my helmet with water and poured it over me. I told eager ears that I had had no luck. I quickly changed the battery.

Nellis kept wetting a handkerchief and applying it to Red's forehead. He lay motionless, and it was pointless to ask how he was.

I immediately took to the slope again, trying to muster as much strength and exuberance as the first time. But the legs began quickly to give out, and then the arms. The healthful flood of perspiration began to dry up, the solar plexus began to ache, and the whole stomach cavity began to send out its own subtle warnings that the body had very little left to give. Someone else could have just as easily made the second trip, but the lieutenant had entrusted me with the responsibility of getting a chopper in here and getting a man out. I took it on as a personal test, and I was going to see it through to the end with gratifying results.

By the time I flopped down on the summit again, I had a mild case of the shakes. I was out of salt tablets and nearly gagged myself on half a canteen of water. I stood up a little unsteadily and faced toward Iron Bridge Ridge.

"Hotel One Alpha, this is Hotel One Bravo, over.

Hotel One Alpha, this is Hotel Two Bravo, over."

The radio ignored me and continued on its dead, unconcerned hissing sound. Then it broke, and my heart stopped!

"Hotel One Bravo, this is Hotel One Alpha, go ahead."

I squeezed the button and opened my mouth; then it dawned on me that I didn't know what to say. I knew what I had to say, but I was not competent with radio procedures, I was like a child learning to talk on the telephone.

A carbine cracked, sounding like the snap of a large branch. They were above me in the tree line. I flattened my body like a large halibut at the bottom of a bay, pretending to be invisible. I was right out in the open without even a blade of grass to hide behind. I drew the forty-five and pulled the trigger fast, not even knowing which direction the Vietcong were firing from. When I had run out of rounds the hammer was still hitting an empty chamber as I flung a rubbery, scared body down the slope again. I slid a couple of yards to cover, hoping I could once again make radio contact. I waited till I had caught my breath.

I stuttered a little at first, but then began. "Hotel One Alpha, we have been ambushed and have one severe casualty."

"Hold on, Hotel One Bravo."

I waited for an endless three or four minutes. Finally, crazy with impatience, I began to shout into the mouthpiece.

"Hotel One Alpha, what's going on?"

I waited for about another minute, then the silence broke. "Hotel One Bravo, this is Hotel One Actual, do you read me?"

I recognized Captain Martin's voice.

"Captain, sir, this is Ogden. We ran into an ambush at an enemy encampment. We have one man severely wounded in the leg, and he is being carried in a litter. We have one confirmed enemy KIA."

I was surprised to hear myself speak in a calm, confident manner, remembering the important details and explaining them clearly. I fumbled in my breast pocket for a piece of paper that Lieutenant O'Connor had given me with our coordinate numbers.

"There was no paper or weapons confiscated. We made it back down the gorge to where we think is the most accessible med-evac area. We will use yellow smoke. Over."

"Hotel One Bravo, hold your position. Repeat, hold your position and wait for further transmissions. Hotel One Actual, out."

I headed back down my favorite ski slope with rubbery legs. I hoped that I had thought of everything, because I wouldn't be making another trip back up. I relayed the final instructions to the lieutenant. He thanked me for a good job and asked if I was all right.

"I'm okay," I lied.

I felt weak and shaky, as though I had contracted some kind of exotic bug. But an "I don't feel well" comment didn't seem appropriate with a man in shock who had a leg nearly blown off.

Part of the patrol was assigned to fan out around and

make a perimeter while the rest of us began tearing out the jungle with our entrenching tools and the only machete we had to clear out a reasonable landing zone. I began to move about as though I was programmed, a mindless machine with the batteries nearly gone. I kept looking up, wondering if the hole in the canopy would be large enough. We only had a few minutes to chop out the brush so the heavy bird could settle down. If it punctured the underside, damaged the oil lines, or started whacking at the jungle with its rotors, it would self-destruct. With enemy in the area, the pilot had only a few seconds to drop into the hole, pick up our man and be out of here.

"I can hear it!" We stopped for a moment of silence as we listened to the welcome, unmistakable sound of heavy metal wings chopping through the hot, dense tropical air.

With no breeze, the bright yellow smoke feathered itself and lay for a time on our hastily prepared LZ. Then it slowly began to ascend from the depths of the jungle, guided by a thick, heavy green chimney big enough to land a dinosaur.

The heavy piece of machinery hovered over us, blacking out the sun like a magnificent prehistoric insect. Its invisible wings created a hurricane as it descended upon us. Flying debris made it almost impossible to see or maneuver. The front landing gear that projected heavy rubber tires telescoped back into itself as the tires slowly accepted the weight of the heavy bird, allowing it to settle gently on the ground.

I held up one of the corners of the litter as we

crowded the hatch. We lifted Red safely inside. The last surge of energy was too much. My legs gave out as though they weren't there any more. For a moment, I hung onto the bottom of the hatch with one hand and tried desperately to keep from dropping my corner of the litter, until someone from behind rescued me from the weight. I fell to the ground and my mind spun out of control with dizziness and delirium, like a little kid jumping off a playground merry-go-round.

I hadn't completely passed out, but I felt as though I were on the opposite end of a long tunnel. I could see a light and hear voices.

"Ogden passed out cold, sir. He's white as a sheet!"

"Load him up. Keep the M-79 and the ammo. Climbing that hill in the heat would have killed anyone. He deserves the ride home."

With all due respect and very little reverence, they lifted me to the hatch. The corpsman grabbed me by the limp arms, dragged me in, and laid me down on the deck face down. Still semiconscious, I seemed to know what was going on. I began to crawl away from the hatch with great effort, dragging a dead body.

"It looks like heat exhaustion. Take her away," the lieutenant yelled.

The chopper began to shake as it developed power to take off. As we lifted off, the corpsman quickly rolled me over, unbuttoned my jacket, belt, and fly, and sloshed me down with water from a five-gallon can. Then he immediately went to work on Red. The water was warm, but quickly evaporated with the cool air whipping through the hatch. I felt a chill, and it quickly

162

brought me around. A little dizzy but coming back to reality, with a body still like putty, I managed to sit up in the corner against the bulkhead.

The corpsman was on his knees working feverishly over Red. He clawed through a medical kit, and brought out a syringe and gave him an injection. With the engines screaming, there could be no conversation. He looked over in my direction and gave me a thumbs up. I returned the gesture. He pointed to Red and gave another one to indicate that he was going to be all right.

After making sure that his patients were stable, he quickly went back to his secondary job. He sat back in the gunner's chair by the hatch to search and traverse with the M-60 machine gun, anticipating enemy ground fire.

Red began to stir back to life. I envied him. He might end up with a bad leg, or it could heal perfectly, but one thing was certain: he was going home. He would be in Fenway Park rooting for the Sox in no time.

My head was clear, but I had mixed emotions. I was very glad to be sitting here in a nice cool breeze, heading back to the rear, but guilt kept creeping in over leaving the others behind. I felt like I had somehow managed to get out of something. Too bad they all couldn't have piled in and flown back. It was such a long, arduous, and dangerous journey back for them.

The doc quickly glanced at his patient, then went back to the business of the machine gun. There wasn't much to tell about him except that he was tall, lean, and blond. I wondered if while going through Navy boot camp he'd ever dreamed of ending up as a crew chief and corpsman aboard a marine Med-evac. Most of the corpsmen I knew had no idea that after training they were destined for a marine grunt outfit. Most of them didn't care, but they were excellent at the job. When we'd sat in the classrooms in boot camp, no one dreamed for a moment that any of us would be out running through the rice paddies in combat.

The chopper sat down in its torrent of wind, dust, and debris. Four men came running from the cluster of squad-size tents that made up the division medical unit. I tried to assist with the litter, but realized I'd be doing well if I could get off the chopper under my own steam.

After jumping down and grabbing my pack, helmet, and cartridge belt off the deck, I smiled and waved to the flying doc and mimed a thanks. They rose and banked into the breezeless late-afternoon sun.

I turned in the dust and followed the entourage of medical people fussing over their new patient. Once inside the tent, one of the corpsmen noticed that I looked a little ragged around the edges. I told him that with a few salt tablets and six months sleep, I would be fine.

I sat outside the tent on a bench under a sign that said "Sick Call" to wait for the word of Red's true condition. I scanned the surrounding terrain and wondered where I was in relation to the battalion area. I wondered how the patrol was doing and how Nellis was handling my M-79, radio, and his old buddy Shakespeare. I sat on the bench, fighting to stay conscious. I felt a faint sadness, as though I were the only survivor of a tragedy.

I was brought back to my senses by the unsympathetic slam of a spring-loaded screen door, which hung on the wood-frame tent and kept the flies in. A young corpsman stepped around the corner.

"Ogden, your friend's going to be okay. He's going to need surgery to get the bullet. It's going to take pins and a lot of mending, but he's going to be all right."

"Thanks, Doc. Can I see him?"

"I'm afraid not. He's completely under anesthetic already."

"How can I get to Second Battalion CP?"

"Wait and I'll check for you."

CHAPTER FOURTEEN

I jumped out of the jeep, thanked the driver, and went into the CP tent. I was assigned a cot, but I didn't need one. I could have dropped and died anywhere.

The last squad tent in the row was sagging miserably as though it were an afterthought and no one cared if it stayed up or not. It was crowded with empty cots that seemed to cling desperately to the ghastly, uneven ground that ran steeply downhill and to the right. I found the only level cot in a dark corner. I dropped my gear and kicked it underneath, and died while falling onto the cot.

I must have gone into a deep coma. When I opened my eyes, I was startled by the strange surroundings. Then it all came back: the patrol, the ambush, and the evacuation. The computer, clogged with fuzz, was slowly starting to warm up.

I sat up to test the mechanical parts. Everything seemed functional. Up on my feet I was still a little weak, and I noticed an enormous cavity where my stomach used to be. The sun had gone down and it was cool and peaceful. I felt like an invalid who had been locked away for a considerable length of time and suddenly turned loose to go out and check the new world. Everything looked strangely different and non-routine. There was not a soul in sight.

I decided I had better start begging and scrounging around for something to eat, for I knew that chow call was over. I decided to begin at the CP tent.

The company sergeant major sat behind a green desk with green utilities and shuffled through a green folder. The only things amiss were the green goat eyes of Lucifer himself. He had a heavy, hairless, glowing head like the Wizard of Oz, and a grotesque, carniverous beak.

The sergeant major and I had less-than-warm affection for each other. He had unsuccessfully run me up for battalion office hours, a lesser facsimile of a court-martial. The incident stemmed from the seasickness and missing sea bag and the subsequent disrespect to Jason. He had had to settle for company office hours. I spent five days at hard labor in the bilge of the ship—an obviously sensitive antidote to a helpless, chronic seasick victim.

The sergeant major had not seen me standing in the doorway. I wasn't hungry enough to dicker with him about why I had missed the chow call. I went immediately to the radio shack to see what the disposition was on the patrol.

Kruger, the weight lifter, was on radio watch. He sat

at a small table with two PRC 10 radios propped up on an ammo can. They were connected to a high aerial outside and made up a crude, makeshift field radio communication system.

Back in the States, Kruger had convinced me to explore the rewards and benefits of weight lifting. I was curious and had tried it for a few weeks, but quickly came to the conclusion that I would remain a ninety-pound weakling. It was just too much work.

Some of the typical nuisances snickered behind his back—way, way behind his back—because of his size and bulk. They thought he was a little slow and dull upstairs, and maybe on the gay side; but I knew different. He wasn't the brightest guy I knew, but he was pleasant. On the weekends, we hung around the cantinas in Tijuana, daring each other with the fattest and ugliest señoritas.

"Oggie, what are you doing here? The patrol isn't supposed to be back yet, and I heard you talking to Captain Martin this afternoon."

"I decided to ride back in style with the med-evac. I hailed a taxi and rode her home."

I could tell he wasn't in the least amused by my attitude.

"Two more are coming home, but they're not coming home in style."

I knew something was wrong before he completed the sentence. There was no sparkle in the voice, no comedy.

"What happened?"

"They were hit again. There're two dead."

He hesitated and turned away. Kruger had been part of the first platoon and had gotten to know everyone before he had become the company radio operator.

"Who, goddamn it, who?"

"Charlie and Nellis."

"No!" I yelled as I threw a tightly clenched fist through space, trying to crush the invisible source of my anguish. I began to rant and rave like an actor, giving wild gyrations in all directions of the stage. Kruger sat quietly as I kept yelling, as though there was something he could have done to prevent it or something he could do now to change it.

"They should have been pulled out of there with Red and me! The whole damn gorge was a death trap and the whole patrol was ill-fated from the start! Nellis damn near drowned before we got to the foothills, then he risked his ass to save Red's. All for what? Just to take a fatal bullet later on in the afternoon!"

I began to laugh. It was a frivolous attempt to try and cover it up, to black it out.

"We all laughed at the idea of stuffing each other in plastic bags when we first got here, didn't we?"

The scene was over. The actor was exhausted and in tears.

I stepped outside and was brushed by a young second lieutenant I had never seen before. He didn't even have a tan. I felt numb and mindless, like a cloud of lethargy had just descended and was choking off the air. I heard music and voices coming from a tent down in the wash. It was a makeshift bar, better known as a "slopshoot."

I handed a dime to a corporal I had seen before but didn't know. He fished out a can of Schlitz from a washtub of ice. There were about twelve men sitting at picnic tables, some talking about going home and some idiot talking about being extended for about a year to grab the combat pay. I tuned them out and guzzled my beer, which I had already begun to feel. The mood was bad and the decor of the bar was rotten, but the price was right.

I was sitting close enough to the washtub bartender that I didn't have to get up. I am sure he had his orders not to serve anyone he considered drunk. I had four, then put number five in my pocket. For a nondrinker, that would be enough.

I stood up, and only then did I realize I was totally paralyzed from the eyebrows down. I managed to make it to the doorway. Only drunks have a talent for finding hidden things to trip on. I ended up sprawled out in the road face down. The deep powdered dust was like falling into a vat of dry flour. I rolled over and sat up slowly. The open can of beer I had shoved into one of my lower utility pockets trickled down my leg. I retrieved it and took a long drink to wash the dirt out of my mouth. I was disoriented and felt no pain—like a forlorn clown who had gotten into the wrong-colored makeup. I sat in the roadway with thick dust clinging to my skin, eyebrows, and eyelashes. Only the wetness of unclear eyes gave the lifeless face of the sad mannequin away. When I had tipped the can of beer too far, a huge muddy frown appeared, extending from my lips to the corners of my mouth and down to the base of my jaw. I sat with the world whirring around me and wondered if I should get up or just sit there and finish the beer.

Four men came walking down the road and stopped where I was sitting. I couldn't see too well for the dirt and the booze.

One spoke in a mock Irish brogue. "Well, lookee here. A wee little drunken leprechaun."

They surrounded me and began to taunt and sneer. One took the remainder of the beer and poured it over my head. I didn't care. I was a clown, and they were the laughing audience. I got to my feet unsteadily, and they realized I was totally helpless. They started shoving me around playfully, curious about the drunk. One would shove me and the other would catch me.

"What's the matter, drunk, can't you handle your booze? Or maybe you can't handle the war? Maybe you're drowning your sorrows and you want to go back home to momma? Maybe you're just a scared little chickenshit, afraid they're going to send you to the front lines."

Even through the fog and the catch-push game, I knew the dialogue couldn't be coming from anyone who had been here for any length of time. No one ever talked to anyone like that—not even his enemy. They had to be replacements; very young, green, and stupid.

As far as I was concerned, the fun was over. But they got caught up in the fervor of their own game and began to get rough. The ground under my feet was listing and rolling like the deck of a ship. The four hyenas weren't big—they were just bigger than me.

I took a hard shot from the back and went careening

toward another grinning punk ready to catch me. I came in way off balance and fast; and to his surprise and mine, I managed to smash him in the face with as much of an off-balance fist as I could muster. In a cloud of dust, he went down on his back. I fell on top, knocking all the wind and pride out of him.

I rolled off him slowly, got halfway up on my feet, took a direct shot right in the face, and went back down again. Someone got a firm hold on me from behind and dragged me to my feet. I couldn't shake loose. Another one threw a fist into my midsection. It was hard enough for me to give up a little Schlitz, gag, and nearly pass out. I still felt I was good for one more shot—one of theirs or one of mine. The drunken leprechaun coiled, still being held by the goon from behind. With proper timing and the spring of a grasshopper, I scored a direct hit with both feet to the chest, sending a no-longer-grinning idiot about ten or fifteen feet into the tent. He nearly tore it down, bounded off, and finally landed on the ground.

The force of the kick brought us all down. Somehow I had managed to bring down three of the four pimply faced juvenile delinquents to the leprechaun's level.

The next thing I remember was being smacked lightly on my crusty, muddy cheeks. I came to. It was the young second lieutenant with no suntan.

"Are you all right? What happened?"

Still in a drunken stupor, I grinned. "Playing volleyball, sir."

"Volleyball? You look like you went through a shredder before you went through the brewery. On your feet. Let's go to the CP."

Next morning, I stood before the battalion commander like a ruffian grade-school kid standing before the principal. My head and body ached so bad inside and out that being reduced in rank from pfc to private didn't faze me in the least. At least not for the moment.

I was marched over to the company CP, where the great wizard informed me I was being transferred into a new green outfit, Third Battalion, Third Marines. He assured me that my office hours had no bearing on this. Many men from this battalion would be transferred into that battalion to give them combat-experienced men. I grinned. Sure, Wiz, I believe you.

I found an unattended jeep parked alongside a tent. I lucked out; the keys were still in the ignition. I only had an hour before I would have to board a C-130 heading for Chu Lai, wherever that was.

The sides of the tents were rolled up and secured, allowing plenty of sunlight and fresh air in. Red was lying on his back staring up at the ceiling. He heard me clomping across the wooden floor.

He smiled. "Well, look here, if it isn't the fucking midget." He got up on an elbow.

I could tell by the tone of his voice that he was feeling pretty good. I sat down on a locker box.

"How are you doing, champ? I hear they're going to put you aboard one of these big, fancy, sterile hospital ships today."

He clenched my fist and shook it and beamed with a big smile. "I'm going home, too. Hey, where are the rest of them assholes? How come they aren't here to see me off? What in the hell happened to your face?"

"Playing volleyball," I answered.

"You must have had a pretty rough game by the looks of that eye. Where's the rest of them, huh?"

I swallowed, emotion beginning to build. Even though he was being transferred away I knew I had to tell him, as he was a letter writer and would find out anyway.

I finally forced it out. "Charlie and Nellis didn't make it!"

Without a word, he quickly flopped down on his back and stared up at the ceiling. There was a long silence.

"I'm getting out of this neck of the woods myself. I'm being transferred to 3-3."

He continued to stare at the ceiling. His eyes began to glisten and a small tear developed out of the corner of his eye. It quivered but didn't break off. He turned to me without a word and stretched out his hand. We squeezed hard together.

"Good-bye, champ. It was good to know you."

He smiled but didn't say a word. I replaced the steel pot on my head, clomped across the wooden floor, and got back into my grand-theft auto.

CHAPTER FIFTEEN

My mind wandered back and forth, in and out, like a C-130 dodging turbulence, drifting, correcting course and heading for a new outfit, new terrain, and new circumstances. It couldn't possibly be as much fun as the one I had just left. I had to reach hard for a tiny shred of optimism. I felt like a child bride after the wedding: misused, abuse, annulled, broken in spirit, abruptly packaged up and sent parcel post, stamped "last priority," and given no consideration. I was a goodwill package consisting of old, discarded necessities with some use left in them on route to another needy, unappreciative group of morons. Yes, the honeymoon was over—and so was the marriage.

The fog of frivolousness had dissipated and the path forward seemed sharp and clear. There is a strange feeling of uniqueness that comes with being on the very bottom of the social order; like an ex con, feared, misunderstood but romanticized, a threat and an enigma within a dubious social order, and no longer a slave in the realm of mediocrity. I believe in rules, laws, and order much like Hammurabi. My rules, my laws, and my order, all of which will be implemented toward my survival. There is nothing further they can do to me. If necessary, I will fight on two fronts: against them and the enemy.

I walked down the ramp and out of the belly of the huge cargo plane. I could have been stepping onto an eight thousand-foot prefabricated aluminum runway somewhere in the west section of the Gobi Desert. A green nylon, overweight, weather-faced crew chief checked our manifest cards like a good little stewardess. I slung my seabag and followed a line of men toward a group of tents a couple of hundred yards from the aircraft. The temperature was well over one hundred degrees.

The view in any direction was obscured by hot, forceful gusts of wind laced heavily with sand, dirt, and dust as though there were far less gravity here on this newly charted, uninhabitable planet. It was nearly impossible to look beyond the air base to see what kind of terrain lay out there. The heat waves reflected off the griddle-hot runway, reflecting like a glossy, mirrored lake. The heat rays played havoc with the light rays, everything partially visible waving and dancing.

For a moment, the gust of wind subsided, releasing its grip on the sand. And without warning, the thunder of an aircraft vibrated the aluminum sections of runway underfoot. An A4D Skyhawk rocketed into view, heavily laden with bombs. It screamed down the runway. The pilot flipped the switch, igniting the jato rockets strapped to the belly. They exploded like a truckload of TNT, catapulting man, machine, and tons of death into the sky.

After a lot of names were called, we boarded trucks headed for our designated companies. There are approximately sixty miles of sandy coastline between Danang and Chu Lai. The rapidly growing air facility takes up only a tiny portion of the many square miles of the white, sandy, almost totally arid territory stretching from the sea inland ten or fifteen miles to the low-lying mountains that run all the way into Elephant Valley.

At the end of the not-completed four-thousand-foot runway is jungle. It hides a network of small villages.

A comfortable grove of pine trees between the runway and the beach protects hundreds of the Marine Air Group, Third Battalion, and Third Marine headquarters from the sometimes one-hundred-thirty-degree heat.

I waited for hours outside the company CP tent with the others. We were interrogated and given a pep talk by a tall, skinny, bald, middle-aged captain who looked more like a retired major general. I felt more uneasy than I had expected, coming into a new outfit with the left side of my face still purple and puffed. I looked and felt like I'd been KOed by Jake Lamotta.

With all the questions he fired at me about my conduct and recent office hours, plus the addition of his own personal L Company discipline dissertation, I felt like either a prisoner of war or a slave that has just been traded from one tribe to another. At any moment, one of the NCOs standing there would step up and rip off my shirt, open my mouth, and check my teeth. With my five-foot-five frame and unruly, spirited disposition, the bidding would have to start low.

After a few more minutes of waiting, a young corporal came out of the CP tent with several service-record books under his arm. He called out three names, and we climbed aboard a jeep. He introduced himself as Corporal Daniels. He was average sized, with sandy hair, brown eyes, and cheeks that had been ravaged by years of acne that had since healed, leaving a relief map of the moon on either side of his face. The jeep sped off through the pine trees and down a back road. The Third Platoon was down at the north end of the runway, he said.

He turned around. "Which one of you is Ogden?"

I tipped the helmet back off my face.

"Oh, I didn't recognize you from your picture here in your record book with your helmet on and your new face."

"I feel a little different too, Corporal. Like a new man," I said sincerely.

"What happened, anyways?"

"Playing volleyball," I answered.

"It looks as though they were using you for the ball."

I didn't need to invite any further humiliation by letting him know how right he was.

The driver of the jeep, who looked only twelve years old, almost had control. He was driving much too fast and was trying to hit every chuckhole and loose rock on the newly graded roadway. The road ran straight and narrow down the backside of the airstrip.

Between the road and the open air hangers that housed individual Skyhawks by the dozens, a number of gigantic rubber bladders filled with jet fuel lay exposed on the surface of the sand. Each of them stretched over an area the size of an Olympic-sized swimming pool, and when completely filled they were about four feet thick. In such heat, I wondered how they kept the gas from evaporating, expanding, and exploding the tanks.

The airfield was now obscured by sand dunes as we came to a Y in the road and the driver kept to the left. The road divided a large sand dune, and we drove out toward the end of the runway and cut back along the edge. The Third Platoon CP tent sat on top of the dune that ran parallel to the runway and was about twenty yards away.

The jeep whined and slipped in the sand as it labored up the incline. The twelve-year-old stepped on the brakes, nearly throwing us all over the windshield or through it. I grabbed my gear, readjusted my helmet and jumped down.

"This guy's terrific, Corporal," I said. "You ought to get him full time. I think he thinks he's A. J. Foyt."

The twelve-year-old going on eighteen gave me a dirty look; and when everyone had bailed out he ground the gears, floored it, tried to twist the wheels right off the axles, and headed out of the pit area.

I followed the others to the platoon CP tent. Starting

from this end of the platoon area, there were sandbag positions protected from the sun by shelter halfs, and ponchos stretching south along the runway as far as I could see. They appeared to be facing the runway. To the rear lay the fuel bladders, and one hundred yards south to the rear was an extension of the maintenance and refueling area. It was like a long dock or peninsula extending out into the sand to the fuel bladders where the planes would taxi to refuel.

It looked like the Third Platoon Lima Company was right in the middle of things. But why in the middle and not on the perimeter? It could only be the very last defense. There must be perimeter after perimeter out there, and this is just the last hope. If they get this far with all this fuel and equipment lying around, somebody's going to play hell.

It took a while for the eyes to adjust from the white sand and sun to the gloom of the inside of the tent. The tent smelled of coal oil and musty close-quarter living. The platoon sergeant stood behind a cluttered table in the middle of the tent. There were several lanterns, half-burned candles, C-rations, map boxes, binoculars, and a chess set with captured pieces lying helter skelter as though it were the last game that would ever be played and they would never be needed again.

The sergeant was about five-foot-ten inches, small-to-average build with too much gut, an olive-brown complexion stretched over fine features. His eyes were like cigar burns in a terry-cloth hand towel. His head was literally shaved from the tops of his ears down all the way around the back. A small dark island of stubble remained on top of the head.

This polished dome syndrome, radical beyond the regulations haircut, seemed to exemplify an acute fanaticism among lifers. FOR OURS IS NOT TO REASON WHY, BUT OURS IS TO DO OR DIE. The unbending, unyielding android that prayed to no God but to its true creator and savior, the Marine Corps, had a name that had too many *l*'s and too many *p*'s, and not enough vowels, and stretched endlessly across his left breast pocket.

Sergeant Nickopoppollopales (I couldn't spell it or pronounce it) began to speak louder and more authoritatively than was necessary.

"Lance Corporal Rudy, you go with Corporal Anderson of second squad. PFC Sims, you go with Corporal Burnett here of third squad. Now get out of here. Ogden, you stay put."

To one side of the tent was a sergeant sitting on a cot. He looked like a very young Glen Ford with a close, light-brown flattop. He fondled and rubbed with an oilcloth what appeared to be a British Sten as though it were a delicate animal. He probably bought it from someone but would brag of its capture.

The cigar-hole eyes began to assess the purple and puff.

"So we have ourselves a real live shitbird here, just busted this morning. You've got two choices. You can do things my way and do your job, or you can go to the brig. I'm not about to put up with some scum from another outfit."

He turned to Corporal Daniels and started to yell as

though Daniels was responsible for my past.

"If this shitbird fucks up just once, I want to know about it. And if you don't straighten him out, your ass is in a sling."

He pointed back at me with his finger, still ranting. "Go ahead and screw up, and I'll clobber the other side of your face."

I began to boil. You'd better bring your volleyball team, sergeant. That's what it took and that's what it's gonna take from now on, I thought.

The diatribe continued. Yelling at an NCO in the presence of junior rank is irresponsible and shows weakness and insecurity. It's like Dad yelling at Mom, or vice versa, in the presence of the children. It promotes confusion and erodes the virtues of respect and discipline. Whether it was Nickopoppollopales . . . or Napoleon, I was in deep trouble again. I hoped I was not dealing with another personality with a hairline fracture lying dormant, just waiting for the right pressure in the right place at the right time.

I hoped it would not be me again. How could I be so lucky? I felt like I had a clandestine role in an intelligence-type high command investigation seeking out character aberrations in staff NCOs. Okay, General Walt, you keep transferring me from unit to unit and I'll come up with a psychotic every time. I will apply the thumbscrews and the electrodes to the head and flush them out into the open so special troops can bag them, take them to a lab, dismantle them, discard the old, defective parts, replace them with new ones, and send them to the Marine Corps Recruit Depot to train "boots."

Daniels and I were dismissed. The sergeant on the cot continued to fondle his over-the-counter war trophy. He must be the platoon guide. I wondered where the platoon commander was.

Once outside, we headed to the nearest position next to the CP tent. I stopped for a moment.

"Tell me, Corporal Daniels, is our leader always that nervous?"

He didn't stop or speak. The reluctance to discuss it was either out of loyalty, out of respect for the rank, or a belief that you do not talk to shitbirds about such matters.

I caught up with him outside the sandbag hootch. "What's the platoon commander like?"

"Sergeant Nick is the platoon commander."

So that's what it was all about. That explained the nervousness and the tantrumlike attack. A staff sergeant playing first lieutenant and platoon commander and not quite sure he could handle the job.

"Johnson, get your black ass out here." He began to grin as Black Johnson stuck his head out of the hatch.

"Yessuh, Boss, is that you, Mr. Benny?"

Black Johnson was grinning also. He was on his knees with just his head sticking out of the hootch.

"I brought a new foxhole buddy for you. This is Private Ogden. This is Lance Corporal Johnson."

"If he's a bigot, I'll frag and eat him for sure." He scanned me up and down. "On second thought, he's too damn little and skinny. Now, Corporal Daniels, why can't you get me somebody big and mean and ugly I can fight with?"

"I think he'll work out all right. Ogden here likes to play contact volleyball. He looks almost like a brother with half his face black and blue."

Daniels unslung his M-14 and reslung it on the opposite shoulder. "You remember what Sergeant Nick told you, Ogden, and maybe both of us will stay out of trouble. Just maybe!"

Rochester disappeared back inside his sandbag hootch. I was not sure, but I felt as though the welcome mat had not been dusted in quite a while.

With an armload of gear, I ducked into the shade of the hootch. I dumped my gear in the corner of a patio arrangement attached to the pup tent like a front porch. I sat on a sandbag in the corner. The roll of sandbags that encircled the patio were about shoulder high, and I could see in all directions.

Johnson was sitting inside the two-man tent on one of two cots that were dug down into the sand so they would fit but still remain about three inches off the sand. A great idea; I knew some people who would dig and pick their hearts out for a cot in a foxhole.

Fighting holes were obviously impossible in this sandy country. Each position was just a ring of sandbags around a two-man tent.

My new residence sat on the end of a large fingerlike sand dune. It was cut through abruptly by the access road that led to the runway, and the dune continued on

184

toward the jungle. There was a position on the other side and I assumed there were positions all the way to the edge of the jungle, some two hundred to two hundred and fifty yards distant. At the very end of the runway stood air traffic guide-markers, lights on stanchions of various elevations. They were visible signs for pilots that said, That's all there is. And if you don't make it over us you'll tear out a chunk of jungle big enough to build a supermarket, parking lot and all. On the opposite side of the runway lay a massive junkyard, piles of empty oil barrels, heaps and miles of broken aluminum runway.

As a kid I was always fascinated by junkyards, dumps, or vacant houses. At home there was no such thing as trash. Sometimes, in desperate need of something to do, I would paddle my bike some four miles further into the country to an illegal dump site. I rummaged through it as though it were a staging area for Santa Claus. I would claw feverishly through fragmented treasure. On one rewarding day, to my astonishment, I found a J. C. Higgins bold-action twelve-gauge shotgun in perfect condition with only a minimum amount of rust.

My mother sharply curtailed my bountiful treasure hunting when I arrived home on another day after several healthy spills off my bike on the mountain road coming from the dump with a shirt pocket full of dynamite blasting caps. I had positively no idea what they were. I had found them all nicely packed in a small cardboard box, bright and brassy. There was enough explosive to slip me into a plastic bag, size small. "One man's trash is another man's treasure" was still the most eloquent phrase I had ever heard. In the case of this junkyard, one man's trash could be another man's warning. I thought I saw a blackened wing tip from a Skyhawk, the eyesore maybe just enough to take the edge off an overzealous pilot.

CHAPTER SIXTEEN

My reluctant host continued to ignore me as I went on with the visual orientation of the hot, lifeless, disgusting terrain. What irony! How could I already miss the slop and stink of rick paddies, the humidity and leeches of the mountainous jungle?

I decided to break all the rules I had hastily formulated for my new environment about keeping my mouth shut and staying on the defensive. An excellent way to keep from drowning is to stay out of the water— but what happens one day when you inadvertently fall off a bridge?

My interpretation of the Monroe Doctrine would not work. Sometimes standing off and keeping to one's self is misconstrued as arrogance and conceit. The world is too small, the hootch too cramped. The smell of defensiveness hung in the air like a gas to warn me that I was in the wrong league. Notwithstanding, I took the initiative to break the ice.

"Johnson, what happened to your partner?"

He continued cleaning his M-14, running a small patch through the grooves of the fire suppressor.

At this point, I did not want to be proven right about my frivolous, philosophical rhetoric. As the seconds ticked by, and as the cleaning patch passed through another groove, insecurity began to grab me. Insecurity, paranoia, and needless defensiveness; garbage packed into the mind like bundles of old useless newspapers packed tightly in the attic. There is no room left for fresh air.

I wanted to jump up and tell him to get fucked in big red letters. Talk to me, anything! But then with the timing of a brilliant comic who waits until every tear has been wrung dry and the fatigue of laughter has subsided, he let me off the hook. He began to speak. And to my astonishment, he spoke in flawless, elegant diction unhindered by colloquial dialect. It was as though he were miming a Sidney Portier soundtrack. There was an air of "Let's make everything perfectly clear."

"He contacted an acute case of dysentery from field mess. Sergeant Nick accused him of malingering." His eyes never seemed to blink, and they never once left me. "He was a very sick man. I knew for a fact that he was bleeding. He was my friend, and yes, he was black."

He went back to rubbing his M-14. If the ice was melting, I did not want to inhibit it. Now at least we had conversation, even though it was tainted a bit with a wisp of anger and discord.

"I'm sorry for your friend." I decided to jump in with

188

both feet, foolish and naive but in earnest. "Is there a racial problem in this platoon?"

"There is racial tension throughout this entire planet. Have you ever been to L.A.?"

"Once, coming through on the way to boot camp."

"There's a section of Los Angeles called Watts, and right this very moment black people are burning, rioting, and looting that part of the city."

I sat and listened like man's best friend, alert, cocking head and ear to the master's voice, ready to spring to any decipherable command. But nothing came—just words I did not understand. Flashes of Seattle burning, people running through the streets in horror, came to my mind. Seattle, Los Angeles, and San Diego were the only large American cities I had ever seen.

"You've got to be kidding. Burning and rioting doesn't happen in the United States. Here, maybe, but not at home."

"It's true! It's my neighborhood! My momma has been keeping me posted. It's been coming for a long time."

"But why?"

"Do you know what the word bigotry means?"

"No."

"Do you know what ghetto means?"

"No."

"Mr. Ogden, where pray tell have you existed your whole life? Another plant, perhaps? Maybe a white, upper class, sterile capsule?"

Neither one of us knew what kind of an animal we

were up against, but the common denominator obviously became curiosity. When the heat of animosity becomes dampened, healthy little specks of perspiration begin to appear on the ice that forms on and cripples the vital communication systems. Curiosity has done more than just kill the cat—it has evolved society from frolicking in the trees to landing on the moon.

"I'm from Washington, the state of. I was raised in the woods on a tiny ranch."

I no longer found myself reluctant to tell what I always considered a rather grim story. Instead, a feeling of exuberance and pride seemed to have taken over. He listened intently as I babbled on and on. From time to time, I would patch into the system and listen to myself. I was good.

As I listened to myself I realized that I may have traveled eighteen years of rough and crazy terrain—but now, in a strange and subtle way, I began to be less sensitive. For the first time in my life, I was appreciative of my background; but I did not understand why.

"When my mom and dad separated, we would go live with my grandmother. She owned and operated a restaurant on the Yakima Indian Reservation. I was six or seven years old. I still remember so many different kinds and colors of kids that lived around the neighborhood on the reservation. There weren't too many white kids, but there were Indian kids, Mexican kids and Negro kids. We had a lot of fun.

"Grandma treated us all the same. In the mornings

and evenings the family would eat together, but at lunchtime every kid in the neighborhood would end up out back of the restaurant. We would all eat sandwiches made from the leftover bread. Grandma was a hard woman and sometimes difficult to understand, but she loved kids. She treated us all alike, even though I was the grandchild."

I was so caught up in my own storytelling I didn't realize Johnson had put down his rifle and leaned back on his cot to listen.

"Grandma had a very good friend whom I remember well. He used to drive by after working in the woods logging to help with the few heavy chores around the restaurant. After the work was done he would bounce me on his knee and sing crazy songs like 'La Cucaracha' and 'Open the Door, Richard.' He was always singing and smiling. He had a gold front tooth that was fascinating to me. He would let me fondle through his pockets like a raccoon, and I always found the one full of candy corn.

"Sometimes on the weekends he would drive us out to his little ranch not far away in an old, rickety pickup truck. His little, old dilapidated farmhouse looked worse than ours on the coast, but for some reason it seemed a lot nicer. It smelled like disinfectant and chili peppers. Sometimes we would stay for lunch, and he would put too many peppers in the peas. I would cry and my nose would run into my mouth, but I wouldn't give up. He really got a charge out of it because I would come back for more. He had a pack of hounds that I liked to play with. We had hounds of our own at home, and when I got bigger the old man would take me out coon hunting on the weekends."

"What kind of coons?" There was a faint curl of his lip that could have been misconstrued as a wisp of a smile.

"I don't know what you mean."

"Forget it. Continue on."

"Yeah, old Tom Jackson was just like one of the family. He was like one of my uncles. They all worked in the logging camps. In fact, he became one of the family. My grandmother married him. I guess you could say he was kind of a grandfather."

I didn't purposely intend my story to come off as a setup or to have a punch line, but that was exactly where it was heading. I was almost reluctant to finish. I did not know how he was going to take it. He allowed me to talk at great length, and that in itself was encouraging. I knew I was into things I had been exposed to from time to time, but I was still naive about racial problems. If I knew or felt anything from childhood, it was very minimal. The only thing now was to be honest and take the consequences as they came.

"You see, Tom Jackson had skin darker than yours. He was a negro, and I liked him a hell of a lot. If there was any hatred in the family or the community, and I'm sure there was, they kept it from me. I thank them for that. It may have left me confused all these years, but they didn't pass on their own hatred to a dumb little kid to carry around for the rest of his life."

There was a painfully long silence. Then Johnson

sprang up from the cot. He slapped both knees, looked me right in the eye with a straight face bearing a serious, inquisitive expression. I knew I had pulled the trigger on everything.

"Mr. Ogden, that's the most contrived crock of honky bullshit I have ever heard in my entire life."

There was another long, painful pause. Then the corner of his mouth went slightly taut, a tooth was revealed, and then another, until there was an actual full-blown smile.

In a calm breath, he said, "I believe you! Like the Irish say, I don't think you've been blessed with the virtue of blarney; you're too naive. Your grandfather Tom sounds like an 'Uncle Tom' to me."

"What do you mean by that?"

"Far be it from me to puncture your low class, poverty stricken, country-bumpkin capsule."

He began to chuckle. I smiled out of relief. Most of what he had said had gone over my head, but I knew from the tone of his voice it was not malicious.

"What became of this Unc—I mean, Grandfather Tom Jackson of yours?"

"I was told somebody murdered him. He was shot over some kind of gambling thing, and my grandmother closed the restaurant."

"That doesn't surprise me at all. Just another hustling nigger!"

That statement really shocked and confused me.

A gust of hot wind rattled the hootch. The hot sand that traveled with it stung momentarily like ground glass. Johnson rummaged around in a haversack, a large pouch that hangs independently from the bottom of the pack. It is designed to make a twelve-pound pack twelve pounds heavier if necessary. He dug out a couple of cans of rations and threw one in my direction.

In this climate and these circumstances, canned fruit was valued far more than gold. Peaches were the most coveted of all and it was unthinkable to give them away, even to your best friend. In an amazed state, I thanked him and we both ate. Even at ninety degrees plus, the fruit slid down the throat with the tantalizing excitement of melting ice cream.

Between bits, slurps, and licks, I listened while Johnson showed his hand at storytelling. I interrupted him from time to time to get a clarification on what a ghetto or a bigot was. A dormant, frozen mind was beginning to thaw. I thought poverty and degradation were only indigenous to rural areas. I thought all city dwellers had nice houses and fancy apartments, ice cream parlors, movie shows, bicycles and paved roads, no fields to hoe, no wood to chop, and no water to carry. What I was hearing about ghetto life was scaring the hell out of me.

I sensed a subtle mood change, a sense of pride and enthusiasm, perhaps much like I felt when I told my own cluttered epic. He had an extraordinarily large family who clawed and scraped together. He told me of his success in high school, a basketball scholarship to college, the dream of becoming a teacher, and the idealism of perhaps going back to teach at the same junior high school or high school.

"With all that going for you, why did you join the

'crotch' like the rest of us meatheads?"

"I'm a meathead, as you call it, just like everyone else. I wanted to get away for a while, affirm my convictions, and make sure beyond a reasonable doubt that that's what I wanted to do. I wanted to get my head straight. And besides, my friends were getting drafted. I wanted to have some choice in the matter. On the other hand, just like all the other meatheads, I wanted to find out if I could hack it."

"Well, I knew I could hack it. I've been going through pre-boot camp all my life. What's liberty like here?"

"Liberty? You've got to be out of your mind, boy. There aren't even any towns around here."

"Shit! I knew it didn't look so good from the air, but I didn't think it was this bad. What's the scoop on Daniels and Nick? I want to know what kind of a circus I've been sold to."

"Daniels is cool. We get along fine. Nick leans on him hard and runs the jesus out of him. He has to pass Nick's bullshit along. He gets frustrated, but he's fair. Anderson's leadership is silly and simple, but okay. He's trying to do a good job, but he has too much fun at it. The tall skinny redhead is Burnett. He thinks he's gunnery sergeant already. As far as Nick is concerned, my first preliminary prognosis was paranoia. I've come to the conclusion, however, that it's an acute case of schizophrenia brought on by the insecurity and inability to accept the responsibility of leadership. Some days he's amiable as your best friend, and some days something will set him off and he's into a tirade and everyone catches hell."

"I'll let you explain the scientific jazz later, but it sure doesn't sound good."

"We're just one big happy family."

All the time that Johnson was talking, something was buzzing around in the back of my mind. It finally landed on the wall, like a listless fly. I had never before in my life sat down and had a lengthy discussion about myself and then listened to someone else. The storytelling had been a lot of common ground, and I took for granted that the feeling was mutual.

Several uneventful days passed. We rotated the watch, staring out into the empty white hot desert by day and the emptier blackness by night. We entertained each other with more storytelling. Can you top this one? As we grew short of material, another fly buzzed the darkness of the inner cavern that housed a small but imaginative mind.

"Know something, professor? Seeing as how we're stuck in this big happy family of yours, I've got one brilliant idea to help pass the time. We can make it worthwhile. You want to be a teacher, right? I don't know anything, right? I'm as dumb as a post about a lot of things. I never went to high school. You could teach me. I could be your first student."

He laughed and shook his head. "No way. That would be kind of counterproductive, wouldn't it? Me teaching a dumb honky everything I know."

"I think I read somewhere that the key to the peace and goodwill among all mankind is education."

He raised an eyebrow and began to smirk. "Don't

patronize me." He paused, looking at me for a long time. "Well, you may not be as dumb as you look. But if you're as dumb as you are small, we may have to ship over for four more years to get you educated."

We chuckled. It felt good. I was long overdue for a good laugh.

CHAPTER SEVENTEEN

After sundown, I got a chance to meet some of the "family" hanging around the platoon CP next door. The professor's quick summary was very close to the mark.

Roy Anderson was not very tall, but had thick arms and legs and massive shoulders. His size twenty-two neck and twelve-inch grin made him look like he had swallowed all of an accordian but the keys.

Burnett was tall and gangly with bushy red hair. He could have passed for Red's older brother. I sensed him watching me without emotion. His features reminded me of a petulant, dry redbone hound puppy. They are forever grinning and slobbering.

A blond lance corporal came out of the CP tent and announced there would be a squad leader's meeting in ten minutes. I recognized him as a replacement from the old outfit. He had a medium build, blond hair, gigantic ears, and no lips. He had just a slit where a ticket came out when you pushed a button, and you had to read what he said if you were not from Alabama. He was in Burnett's squad, and apparently Sergeant Mick had taken a liking to him and made him a house mouse, or the gofer. Go for this, go for that.

Sergeant Mick noticed me outside and called me in. I entered the dragon's smoky den. He was sitting behind his makeshift desk with a dead cigar butt in his mouth. He had his shirt off and his dog tags dripped with perspiration. In his surroundings, as he shuffled the papers on his desk, he looked like a porno theater manager skimming off the profits of skin money.

"Ogden, I'm screening a few people. What was your job in your old outfit?"

"Grenadier."

He looked surprised. "You were? How come it's not in your service record book? How come it doesn't show you qualified with either the forty-five or M-79?"

"It was a last-minute change before we left the ship."

"Are you good with the M-79? I'm looking for someone who's really good."

"I'm the best there is in combat."

"What makes you so sure?"

"Sure has nothing to do with it. I just know."

He stopped chewing his cigar and looked at me. No one was more surprised at my candor than I was. He waved me out.

"Get out of here. You've got the job. Have Corporal Daniels take you down to supply after the squad leader's meeting. We are going on an operation tomorrow."

I had surfaced back into the fresh air with a smile. I had just bluffed my way back into my favorite job. I gave myself a mental pat on the back. You've got your shit together, boy!

I went back to the hootch. The professor was still wiping down his rifle. I sat down in my favorite spot in the corner.

"You know, you're gonna rub the blueing right off that thing. Then you'll really be in trouble with rust."

"Cleanliness is next to godliness. May my blueing never come off, praise the Lord." Before I could say another word, he began firing questions. "What do you know about the United States government?"

I stuttered. "I don't know very much."

"What are the three branches of government?"

I was delighted, but my mind began to whirl. "The executive, the ah . . . I've got it, I've got it, the legislative. Oh, damn it, I used to know it. I can't think of it."

"Two out of three isn't bad. It's the judicial system. Do you know what each of them are?"

"Yes. The executive branch is the presidency, the legislative branch is the Senate and the House of Representatives, and the judicial branch is the Supreme Court."

"That's good, Mr. Ogden. Now you may sit back down and contain yourself, please. I appreciate optimum enthusiasm from my students, but please keep your seat."

I sat down. I was exhilarated that I had remembered a few things.

"Do you know what the first amendment to the Constitution is?"

"No."

"The first amendment is the freedom of speech, which is essentially one of the cornerstones and the key to a democratic society. Do you know anything in particular about the Constitution?"

"Ah, let me see. 'We hold these truths to be self evident, that all men are created equal and they are endowed by their creator with certain inalienable rights. Among these rights are life, liberty and the pursuit of happiness. To secure these rights, governments are instituted among men, deriving their powers from the consent of the governed. When any form of government becomes destructive of these ends, it becomes the right of the people to alter or abolish it.'"

"Not bad, Mr. Ogden. That's from the Declaration of Independence, not the Constitution, but your memorizing of it shows that your learning ability is notably unimpaired. At least with a retentive mind, we have something to start with."

"Professor, could you do me a favor? I feel kind of funny when you always call me Mr. Ogden."

"We must maintain a student-teacher rapport to keep discipline and respect in their right perspective."

He was having fun.

"Look, all I want is a tutor—not Sidney Poitier."

"Ah, that's very good." He drew an imaginary score on the air with his finger. "There's one for good old what's-his-name."

"By the way, what is your first name?" I asked.

He stood up at attention and put his hand over his heart. "Elgin Walter Johnson the second."

"Wow, I'm sorry I asked."

"What's yours?"

"Richard Edwin Ogden the first. I never heard the name Elgin before."

"You mean you've never heard of Elgin Baylor?"

"Oh sure, I remember. It's just that Elgin sounds different all by itself. I'll just call you Professor, okay?"

"Let's see . . . what shall I all you? Richard seems a bit Victorian. Aha, I've got it! Has anyone called you Oggie Doggie before? You know that cartoon that used to come on on Saturday morning?"

I said no a little too abruptly.

"Ah, just as I thought. They did, and you loved it."

"I can't stand it."

"I christen you Oggie Doggie, in the name of the Father, the Son, and Victor Hugo. May you never grow a hump on your back. Amen!"

"What the hell are you talking about?"

"Never mine." We both laughed. "Back to school, Master Oggie."

"Yes sir, Sidney."

"What kind of exposure have you had, if any, to the fine arts?"

"Drawing was my favorite subject."

"That's not what I mean. I'm talking about the family of arts."

"Oh, I got straight *A*'s in art and music, and an occasional *A* in writing, but only if I got to write about what I wanted to write about."

202

"Who was Matisse?"

"I remember him really good. He drew funny, naked, fat women."

"That's not all, but that's good. You remember who I'm talking about. I think we will have you in UCLA or Harvard in no time. But seriously, I think we can get you ready for the GED test to get your high school diploma."

School was out, and I promised an apple a day—or at least half a peach.

An unexpected but welcome thunderstorm blew in off the South China Sea. I brushed heavy gun oil on my new forty-five and twenty millimeter. There seems to be something personal and intimately comforting about having a forty-five on your hip or tucked in your belt. This issue to certain special weapons carriers was a last-chance resort. It is only reasonably accurate at twenty-five yards, depending on the talent of the trigger finger. A forty-five caliber round traveling at nine hundred feet per second is like a shot put compared to the high velocity 7.62 rifle round, but it is still capable of stopping anything made of flesh and bones with one hell of a wallop. I put the toys to bed within reach inside the hootch. I did not bother to cover up.

I tilted my head back to the falling sky, stuck out my tongue, and let the warm refreshing rain rinse the salt away along with a great many of my cares. Every now and then I would probe the upper extremities of my mouth with my tongue and feel the tenderness of the hemorrhaged, nearly broken cheekbone. It was a harsh reminder of bad times. I am getting a fresh, clean start, I recited to myself. I am going to make the very best of it. I am stuck in another psycho circus; but I think I have a friend, and that will make a difference.

The chopper flew us westward over the short mountain range bordering the desert around Chu Lai. From the hatch door, I could see two other choppers flying to our right flank in formation. Their windshield wipers flapped in sync. We flew through a clear but wet corridor of air hemmed in on all four sides by the dark mountainous jungle below. The ominous, dark ceiling of storm clouds was above, and to the sides was an infinity of invisible mist.

Once again the exhilaration of the hunt; with the cold dampness of the morning altitude, the body jittered and chattered along with the vibration of machinery.

I remember back to other mornings, when I was ten or eleven years old, when I'd lay in the hay in the back of my stepdad's 1946 Chevrolet pickup with a couple of hounds on each side. They kept me warm on our way to a hunt in bear country. We would rendezvous with a dozen other people who had their own packs of hounds. These hunters were friends of my stepdad. He called them Tarheels because they lived far deeper into the wilderness than we did. They also lived more off the land. We were urbanites compared to these modern-day mountain people.

Early in the morning, with that many people and hounds, there was always mass confusion. An exuberant hound would get a whiff of a trail and the whole menagerie would be set into fierce motion, like a British foxhunt without the horses. My stepdad would make sure I survived the ordeal and did not get lost by literally tethering one of the hound's leashes onto my arm and putting a large piece of rat cheese in one of my pockets and a pint of loganberry wine in another to keep me warm. The dog lashed to me, in its excitement with the scent of the trail, would literally drag me up the most rugged, mountainous terrain in the state. All I had to do was hang on.

Black bear meat is good eating. I felt sorry for the bear only when the meat was discovered to be unpalatable because the bear had been fishing for salmon in the rivers and creeks rather than foraging in the orchards. a fishing bear will take on the smell and taste of fish.

I was taught to hunt anything to keep from going hungry; but now, in retrospect, I realized it was basically sport disguised as survival.

We second-checked equipment, buckled chin straps, and braced for a landing. Daniels crouched by the hatch. He kept us at even intervals as we bailed out into the cold, wet, turbulent elephant grass. The snake eyes of the gunner crew chief scanned the LZ over the top of the M-60 machine gun as it traversed back and forth, hoping to see or hear something in time to strike (or, hopefully, not see anything to strike at). As the empty choppers lifted off, the rotors seemed to slap the wet air more than chop it.

The ceiling finally cracked open all the way and the downpour restricted visibility to near zero. In a half-crouch position, we ran around in the confusion of the LZ until we got our bearings in conjunction with the rest of the platoon. When we finally got on line in proper interval with everyone facing the same direction, the sweep began.

This was the best weather the Vietcong could hope for. We wouldn't be able to hear snipers over the downpour. We prayed for relief, and when it came it was so abrupt that it startled us. It was as if a big hand had reached over and turned off the spigot, bringing back the squeak of wet gear and the clinking of canteens.

Lakes and channels of waist-high elephant grass lay before us, broken up by peninsulas of dense jungle. At times, the vast body of grass doglegged out of sight, about a par five. It was like a massive Pebble Beach that had been unkempt for centuries.

We began to draw sniper fire from the right flank, and we hit the deck. The right flank of the company broke off and started an assault in the direction of the firing. The word came down for each platoon to take cover in the jungle a squad at a time while the rest laid back to cover them. First squad held ground until it was our turn. At any other time, running thirty or so yards fully laden with gear in waist-high jungle would have been nearly impossible; but under the circumstances, it was almost effortless.

Someone to my right rear yelled that he was hit. I looked back. It was the assistant machine gunner who was, surprisingly, still burning up real estate with the rest of us. He finally went down. The professor and I were closest, and we went back to get him. I put his machine-gun tripods around my neck, and we both grabbed an arm and began to run like hell. We were able to drag him over the slick, wet elephant grass with ease, but we were seriously lagging behind. I was taking three steps to the professor's one. I tripped and brought us all down. We gathered up our patient and took off again. The troops already in cover cheered as we stretched to make the final yards. Everyone was smiling and happy, and congratulated us as though we had just won a sack race at a picnic. Even the patient was grinning.

"What in hell are you grinning about?" I asked. "Where are you hit?"

"In the leg."

He pulled up his trouser leg. There was a small hole in the calf, clotted with blood but not bleeding to any degree, and another clean exit hole where the round had penetrated the entire calf without striking bone. He had gone as hard and as far as he could until the muscle had seized up.

"Someone call for the doc," I yelled. "You know, this looks like a million-dollar wound to me. You'll be home by Christmas."

The adrenalin began to subside and the pain started to catch up. He winced but continued to grin, like a defensive lineman who had intercepted on the fifty-yard line and gotten racked up in the end zone scoring his first and last career touchdown.

CHAPTER EIGHTEEN

The assault on the snipers was fruitless. It only drew them out of the area to come back and hit from another direction, at another time. Their spooklike hit-and-run tactics left gaping holes in our morale. The frustration of not being able to react in time creates a condition of tired, angry blood. It is a common withdrawal symptom like the aching of a junkie in need of a main vein surge of adrenalin that sends the whole body system into a high and renders thought effortless and almost euphoric. Sometimes it is a good feeling, and sometimes bad. Perhaps it is the very last sensation before death, when the pilot light flickers and goes out.

The Vietcong knew exactly what they were doing, and they were effective. Their continual harassment and evasion kept our anger, frustration, and jagged nerves at an optimum peak. Sniping inflicts minimum casualties; but its ominous danger can keep a well-trained alert mind from thinking of the ambush that may lie ahead.

A single casualty can preoccupy an entire crew of men—a crew designed to handle many men, but that must go into action for just one. It brings into play the med-evac chopper, a slow, easy, lush target. It is a slow but constant attrition of manpower, logistics, and morale. The enemy risks everything in the process as they have no immediate resupply, no adequate medical treatment, or hospitalization. He is restricted to lightweight, small-arms weapons, mortars, and rockets, for mobility. And if there is any hint of concentration in numbers, an air strike is called for—something he cannot outrun.

The smell of yellow smoke subsided as the med-evac chopper flew steadily out of earshot carrying our grinning wounded. The company continued its sweep through a sector of very dense, difficult jungle laced with footpaths that had to be meticulously searched for booby traps. We had to push, pull back, and fake out the plant life that seemed to be alive in order to get through.

The man-versus-plant contest stopped immediately as the sound of heavy volumes of automatic weapons fire bounced off the wet jungle. The volumes seemed to increase to enormous proportion. The left flank of first and second squads had stumbled into an ambush for sure. The volume of firing increased as though the outcome of the entire war would be determined here and now. The rest of us lay on the jungle floor, maybe fifteen or twenty yards to the right of the invisible ambush, waiting for orders.

The word came down for the grenadier up. I nearly passed the word myself, then remembered it was for me. I took off, following the line of prone bodies laying in the jungle. I tripped over Daniels and nearly landed on the professor.

"Keep your head down, Oggie. It sounds kind of interesting down there."

"Don't worry, Professor. I won't be missing any class."

Everyone continued to call for the grenadier. I pressed forward as fast as I could. I fell at the base of a hedgerow, out of breath. This time I wanted to take a look before I took a leap.

We had been ambushed at the edge of a river. It was slow moving and more than a hundred yards wide. There was fire coming from the opposite bank. It crashed through the trees just above my head. On our side of the river was a tiny ornate temple with a tile roof, oriental carvings, and paintings on the exterior walls. It faced the river squarely and the machine gun teams had set up on each corner. It looked like the entire platoon had taken cover behind the structure.

Both gunners were firing at a tremendous rate, neither releasing their trigger until the entire belt of ammo was gone. Some fools were leaving cover and firing from the hip, then stumbling back behind the structure.

Ten yards to the right of the temple there was a man down. He was lying on his back. He was a big man with a huge chest and gut. For some reason, he had managed to get his shirt off. I could tell he was alive; his arms moved and he tried to sit up, then lay back down. Why in the hell hadn't they gotten him out of there? He was drawing fire. Incoming rounds were leaving tiny divots in the packed barren soil around him. He took off his helmet. The fool must have been delirious and in shock.

I crawled over the hedgerow, hooked the canteen on a vine, and fell hard on the other side. I slid across the ground on my belly as fast as I could go; but like a baby alligator, I was not quite confident with my technique. When I got to him, I realized that with his size it would be a good idea to keep him between me and the river.

I looked up at a sweaty face. He was grinning. I swore if I ever saw another wounded Marine grinning, I would kill myself! What was wrong with these people?

He tried to sit up. "I'm going home. I'm going home."

I shoved him back down and put his helmet back on. "Sure you are, partner. In your own plastic sleeping bag if you don't stay down."

Lead bumblebees were passing by my ears at over a thousand feet per second. There was a huge earthen jar that must have held thirty gallons within reach. I rolled it over in front of him to give us a little protection. He continued to babble about going home.

Just below his navel there was a hole about the size of a quarter. A very big gut with a very big hole in it. I wondered how he was still alive. His mind was probably on a first-class champagne flight back to the States instead of the burning deep in his guts. For some reason, it was not bleeding like other stomach wounds I had seen. A geyser of blood should spurt out with every inhalation, but it was not occurring in this case.

The machine guns still chugged away. Reeves, the corpsman, flopped down beside me.

"Hello, Doc. Nice to see a friendly face. We've got a very sick boy here."

The friendly face was full of terror. "What am I gonna do? I've got Thompson back there with half his groin shot away."

"Pull yourself together, man. There's not a hell of a lot of you can for either one of them. Give me your B-1 unit."

I reached in the doctor's little black bag and pulled out the biggest bandage I could find. I tore open the wrapper with my teeth and unraveled the ties. I held it against the wound until I figured out how I was going to tie the ties around this huge gut. I began to realize just how green this outfit was; the corpsman had never seen a gunshot wound before, and he had panicked.

I shoved his B-1 back to him. "Go back and take care of the other patient, Doc. And don't tell anybody I'm practicing without a license."

A round hit the large earthen jar and rung it like a bell. I noticed on my patient's lower forearm what looked like a self-inflicted tattoo. It was a large heart that said "Jim and Sue."

"Okay, Jimbo, see if you can help me. I'm gonna

have to get this strap around you so I can tie it down and you won't bleed to death."

"I'm starting to go numb all over."

"Relax, then."

I finally worked my arm underneath him. I grabbed the tie on the other side and dragged it through. There was a slight lull in the machine gun fire, and I heard Sergeant Nick yell.

"Ogden, put some rounds out there!"

I yelled back to get some help out here and get this man back to cover.

Another round hit the bell. Big Jim was no longer grinning or mumbling about going home. He was beginning to bleed badly. I wondered where the other grenadier was. I hadn't heard one all day. The ties on the bandage were too short to tie in a knot, so I held it in one hand and reached for my cannon that lay across big Jim's huge thigh. I felt like a buffalo hunter hiding behind his downed quarry while being attacked by angry red men.

I was in a very curious firing position, in refuge behind the hulk of a body. My right hand pulled the ties under his body, applying pressure to the bandage, while with the other hand I put the cannon to my shoulder and let a round fly. It fell miserably short and blew in the water. Loading with one hand was slow and tiring. I was only guessing where the target was. The tracer rounds from the machine guns were only a partial clue. They were traversing the whole wide front of the jungle, so I concentrated on the center of the field of fire.

As I was loading, the cavalry came. Before I could pick myself up out of the mud, they carried Jim back to safety behind the temple. I crawled behind the Liberty Bell, hoping it would not crack with another direct hit. I launched a couple more rounds, but they did not seem to be effective.

I alligatored my way through the mud to the back of the temple, which was overcrowded with heroes and casualties. Sergeant Nick was screaming at his machine gun crews like a madman. He turned to me.

"Goddamn it, Ogden, when I call for the grenadier up, you'd better hustle, damn it. We've got corpsmen to take care of casualties."

I knew at that moment that I disliked the man intensely; but this was no time to let him know it.

The temple was good cover, but it rendered us ineffective as a complete team offensively. There was only room for a machine gun team on each corner. The rest of us were huddled behind. Anderson's grenadier was the other casualty. Anderson had taken over the weapon himself, but there was no firing position from behind the temple for either of us. We were totally useless back there.

Then an idea came to mind. From where the Liberty Bell was, I noticed there was a front door on the temple facing the river. There was also a side entrance. I explained to Sergeant Nick my idea to turn the temple into a bunker to be more effective. All Nick said was "go."

I beckoned for Anderson, who fell right in behind me. I got next to the machine gunner and tapped him on the helmet, and told him what I was going to do. He nodded and kept firing. I held my breath and thought ahead to exactly what I was going to do in the next thirty seconds.

I slung my cannon and lunged forward. I put my head down and slithered along to the side entrance. It seemed further than it was. I flung myself in and rolled. Two idiots were already inside playing John Wayne. They were taking turns firing from the hip in full profile of the door.

"Get your goddamn asses down!" I didn't need any more grinning idiots today.

They looked at me funny but did not argue. Anderson flew through the doorway in midair like a running back on fourth down at the goal line, and landed in a heap in the corner. We lay flat on the floor. Rounds were coming through the doorway and bouncing off the hard adobe walls. The John Wayne brothers began to realize how foolish they had been.

I began to have reservations about my brilliant plan. Outside the hive, we had only had to worry about bees going in one direction. Now that we had so intelligently crawled inside the hive, we were vulnerable from every direction.

I yelled to Anderson. "Do you know how to use that thing?"

He held up his finger, indicating he had fired it once.

"Corporal, that's all you need. That's all the training

I had when I started out."

We took prone firing positions on each side of the door. Chinks of plaster kept popping off the walls in our little bunker, creating a dust we could taste and smell. To expose one eye to get a fix on the target was unnerving.

I told Anderson I would fire a couple of rounds to get the distance and true elevation. Most of my rounds were falling short. I gave the barrel a lot of elevation and pulled the trigger. The round blew just outside the temple. I was so conscious of getting dinged in the head that I had failed to look up. I had blown off a large tree branch, and it had come crashingdown. Anderson just grinned. Now we had a clear field of fire.

I reloaded and took aim again. The enemy did not seem to be rousting very easily. They must be dug in. The bamboo grove on the other side was about thirty feet tall. If I could land a shell midway up I would get a good air burst showering down on them. I pulled the trigger and watched the round travel in a high arc against the backdrop of gray sky. As it plunged toward the jungle I lost track of it. Like magic, it seemed to land just where I wanted it to. A patch of large, sturdy bamboo splintered and tumbled to the ground.

"Got it! Just keep your barrel at the same angle and let it fly!"

We fired together, both right on target. Both rounds detonated about ten feet apart, bringing down a curtain of jungle. We fired as fast as we could load. I thought I heard cheering out back above the machine-gun roar. Each time I reloaded, I had to flip over on my back. I noticed the dust was settling. There were no more bees buzzing around inside.

Someone right outside began to yell. "They're running! They're running! They're on the run!"

Machine guns began to slacken up, and only sporadic fire was mixed with the cheers from outside. Neither one of us had even seen the enemy. No one cared. We had rousted them and put them on the run. Morale was back! Everyone got their badly needed dose of adrenalin. Two unlucky ones got a dose of morphine.

The depression of a long dreary day was forgotten. Everyone seemed to be in a jubilant mood, like tarheels after a wild bear hunt. I watched a pack of less experienced kids pat each other on the back for a job well done. They were high from their very first taste of combat.

Thunder clapped around us. The hand reached once again and turned on a warm, steady downpour. It was a refreshing shower which washed the tainted battle area clean.

It was not known what casualties lay on the other bank. The river was too risky to ford. Whatever there were, we had paid for them. The company formed up and headed to the LZ with casualties in tow.

Jim and Sue were very lucky people. A thirty-caliber round had tipped his belt buckle, spun out, and dug out a chunk of flesh, instead of going through and blowing out his spine. It had penetrated into his massive gut but did not pierce the stomach cavity. I learned that Jim's last name was Tweedy. With a name like that, it was no wonder he survived. He had to be damn tough.

The grenadier was not so lucky. And after I saw him, I kept visualizing myself lying on a stretcher, delirious with morphine, with only half or nothing left of what I was born with.

CHAPTER NINETEEN

We sat for days and watched the rain come down from inside the comfort of our hootches. The lack of visibility kept the aircraft grounded, and the total activity around the airstrip was minimal. The ever-drifting, white powdered sand was now a dingy gray. In contrast, all objects throughout the landscape were dark with wetness. It was like a vast countryside winterland, where the rains had come and washed away the crispness and cleanliness of the snow.

To break the monotony, there were occasional work parties. No one seemed to mind because the effort expended in storing water was in direct relation to our comfort. In the vast junkyard on the other side of the runway, we salvaged fifty-five-gallon drums. We chiseled out the ends and cleaned them out the best we could, then sunk them into the ground to catch water for bathing and other utilities. We saved the drinking water that had to be transported in. It was a good idea because we remembered how scarce water could be when the sun was high. The weather of late seemed like a freak of nature, as there is rarely any water in the desert. But I had to keep telling myself that this was not a desert; it was only extended beach.

One morning as I was chiseling out the top of a drum, Simms walked up. I had worked up a sweat and had already cracked a portion of my thumb, a good one, between two pieces of cold steel. I had never spoken to the man, and I was surprised at the contempt in his voice. It went beyond contempt; it was the most vile form of hatred.

"I heard you and the nigger have become good old buddies. Why, I heard he gave you that stupid nickname. If a nigger ever did that to me, I would skin him alive."

My ears started to singe, but I kept chipping the steel. Others in the work party had heard the dialogue and began gathering around.

"Why don't you leave him alone, Simms? He's not doing anything to you."

Now that Simms had an audience, I knew he was really going to let me have it.

"This here is a nigger lover, boys. You know what we do with people who fraternize with niggers? We hang them, that's what we do. We don't mess around back home." He turned back to me. "I heered you think you're a bad ass. I heered you took on three boys in your old outfit and really gave them a roust. I think you're a little sweet-ass cunt."

Sweat began to roll off the end of my nose almost in a

steady drip. My muscles became taut from holding in the reins of emotion. I had promised myself I would stay out of trouble. I was hoping to keep that promise. But this degenerate throwback from fourteenth century Alabama had become tight with the platoon sergeant in just the short period of time he had been here.

"Leave him alone, Simms."

I did not look up to see who was making sense. Instead, I tried to continue working; but my hands were sweating and shaking too badly. The hammer and chisel began to slip through my sweaty palms. I was still down on one knee, and Simms began to crowd me from the rear.

"You know what I think, boys? I think Miss Oggie here is sucking the nigger's cock. That's got to be the reason you're so tight."

I took in a deep breath, dropped the tools, and shifted my weight. I shoved one leg nearly three inches into the sand for support and spring, then twisted my body and let out a massive grunt. I caught him with my left shoulder below the rib cage and sent him sprawling.

He was so unprepared that his helmet came off and slammed into mine. The impact knocked him a couple of yards. Still on my knees, I dug and clawed at the ground to get momentum to rush him. He had tumbled over several times and had ended up facing me. He got to his hands and knees. I clipped him under the chin with a twenty-yard onside kick. His jaw slamming shut sounded like the tailgate of a dump truck as he went up over backward. A fifty-yard field goal attempt would have killed him. Why I held back, I will never know.

I jumped on him, coming down as fast and heavy as one hundred-forty pounds could fall. I grabbed a handful of yellow thatch and scalp, and cracked his face on my knee several times to make sure he was out of commission. An interesting, if not funny, thought occurred to me: He has no lips; but when I get done with him, he will.

His mouth was agape and gasping like a freshly caught red snapper on the deck of a boat. I grabbed up a handful of wet sand and packed it into his mouth tightly. His eyes bulged nearly out of their sockets. I pulled my K-Bar out and placed the blade under his jaw. I put the flat part of the tip against the underside of his jawbone—not to draw blood, but to apply pressure on the mouthful. In a whisper of controlled rage, I spoke.

"You little, filthy mouthed, bigot motherfucker. If you ever open that slime trap around me, or even come near me again, I'm going to give you lesson number two. Do you hear me?"

I applied more pressure to the jawbone. He went completely white. He nodded furiously as he choked and gagged. I got up and grabbed him by the lapels, pulled him partway up with me, and threw him back down. I got to my feet and looked around. Everything had happened so fast that the group gathered around us also looked like they had just been popped out of deep water. I turned and walked away. I could hear Simms cough and puke as I walked the entire distance to my hootch. It was music to my ears.

I decided to bypass the hootch and instead walked out to the end of the sand dune, where I could sit and relax alone to take the edge off the moment. I knew that all hell would break loose soon. These moments of peace were earned. I set my mind on low frequency and sent it home.

It had been so long that I got a foggy picture in return. Things about home that were particularly unsavory at the time now seemed to have lost their significance. Let's face it: I missed everything about home—even the smell of the barnyard. Homesickness had reached its highest ebb. I thought of what I would do when I got home and out of the Corps. Maybe I would work construction or get work in the woods logging for a while, at least until I could get enough money to go to school. Maybe there was still a chance for Elizabeth and me. Maybe I would become a family man, work days and go to school at night. I wanted to accomplish something, be somebody.

I must have sat in the sand, totally consumed in my problems and my future, for nearly an hour. Then I sensed someone standing behind me. It was the professor.

"I heard you had quite a row with Simms."

My arms remained folded around my legs and my chin rested on my knees. "He's got an ugly way about him and a filthy mouth."

"I know. That's what I want to talk to you about. I know what it was about. I don't need you or anybody to fight my battles."

I looked up at him. "What are you talking about?"

"You bashed Simms because of me, didn't you?" The voice began to change, and he pointed down at me. "I don't need you or anybody else to fight my battles! I'm an intelligent, rational human being, and I can take care of myself! Mind your own business!"

The stress in his voice was real, but the confidence in what he said was not convincing. This tiny shred of weakness and insecurity left me confused. My easiest and most predictable attitude was to get angry. I jumped to my feet.

"Let's get something straight, brother. That sick son of a bitch was headhunting for me. I busted him for what he said about me, and nobody else. I mind my own business! I fight my own battles and look out for number one! I don't fight for anybody except me! I don't know about the rest of the world, but I'm gonna survive assholes like that! I'm here to stay. The world's full of sick degenerates running loose. They come down on people like me to show their manhood, and they come down on people like you to show how ignorant they are. I don't want to hear any shit about fighting your battle. I fight for me!"

There was a long silence. He looked down at the ground before he spoke. "Sergeant Nick wants to see you." He turned and walked away.

Once again, the tattered green knight in rusted tomato-can armor was summoned to the high court. What else could happen today?

"Ogden, you're a walking contradiction far beyond

anything I've ever experienced before in the Marine Corp. You transfer into this outfit busted and beaten. Your service record book is, in part, one of the best I've ever seen. But the last twelve months of it reads like a toilet novel. Now this."

Nick was referring to a piece of paper in his hand.

"According to this, First Lieutenant O'Connor has recommended you for a Bronze Star. How does one go about getting office hours, getting into a brawl, being transferred to another outfit, and getting a medal on top of it? It's insane!"

"I agree, Sergeant. It's insane!"

"Don't get smug with me. What's Lieutenant O'Connor recommending you for?"

"I don't know, Sergeant. He didn't say anything to me. We were pretty busy up there."

"You must have done something to have your platoon commander bestow such a high honor on you."

At the blink of an eye, his mood changed. He paced back and forth behind his desk, arms behind his back with fingers laced. He walked around behind me and placed his hand on my shoulder.

"Look, you don't have to be modest. You can tell me. I'm your platoon commander, remember? Listen, how would you like to be the platoon runner? You could have that cot right over there. Simms has been screwing up lately, and he has a big mouth."

That's not all he's got, Sergeant, I thought.

"I don't think I would be very good at that sort of

226

thing." I was confused again, but I decided not to get mad. Instead, I would go along with what was happening for a while.

He walked around behind his table. "Now, tell me all about your getting a Bronze Star."

I began to get impatient. "Sergeant, I don't have a Bronze Star. It's only a recommendation."

"It's as good as in the bag. I know about these things. Before I head stateside, I'm gonna have me one. Maybe even two."

He was no longer looking at me. His stare went right on by. His grin was disturbing. He was no longer in the tent or in the present; he was out winning handfuls of medals on the battlefield.

"Sergeant Nick, may I be excused?"

His trance broke. "What? Oh, not until you tell me how you got your medal."

"Like I told you, I don't know. I don't even care about the medal if it's gonna create a fuss."

His mood changed again. "What do you mean? You don't care! You . . . don't care? The country is bestowing an honor on you for a job well done, and you don't care? Boy, there's something wrong with you!"

He started to lose control and shook his finger at me. "You know what I think? I think you're a smartass! I think you're smug and arrogant! You shitbird, you disgust me! Get out of my sight!"

By the time I got outside again, I was really confused. I didn't know whether to get mad at a psycho sergeant or rejoice at the fact that Lieutenant O'Connor had remembered me. It was the only time I had the opportunity to display an individual effort. Pride, and the idea of a medal, did enlighten my spirits. It is gratifying to know that someone has confidence in you; it fortifies your own. I think I know how it feels to be nominated for an Academy Award. "For best supporting actor in a foreign campaign, the nominees are . . ."

The professor was wearing off some more blueing with an oily rag. I flopped down on my cot.

"What did Sergeant Nick want?"

"Oh, he just wanted me to become his new house mouse or runner. I figured he'd run me up for shaking up his number-one boy. I guess he wants me to tell him how he can be a hero."

"What?"

"I think he's more schizophredic than you thought he was."

"It's schizophrenic."

"Well, whatever! He's giving me the creeps. A letter came from my old outfit recommending me for a medal, and Nick started to act kind of funny about it."

"Well, what did you get it for?"

"Come on, not you, too."

"I'm sorry about coming down on you today."

"Forget it."

"How about a peace offering?" He uncovered two cans of Budweiser and I sat up.

"Sounds good to me, but you don't have to." I nearly dropped it because of the shock of the unexpected pleasure. "It's cold! Really cold!"

We'd been getting a warm beer ration every day since

I had been here, and a can of cold Budweiser made peaches look like a can of ham and lima beans. The professor did the honors of opening.

"Give a toast, Professor!"

"Why not. Here's to all the bigots and schizophrenics in this fucking war!"

We clicked cans and tipped them up.

CHAPTER TWENTY

The resonance of my name came slashing through the night, like electricity through a conduit to a brain partially deadened by sleep and an accumulated ration of Bud, Schlitz, or Ole. The professor's hideous scream penetrated the inner cosmos of my mind, reaching beyond my soul. It would never be penetrated again—not even by a host of psychiatrists.

I sat up on the cot. Dreaming!? Having a nightmare!? The area outside the hootch was lit up and the shadows were doing the dance of fire. I tried to assess what was real and what was not. I remembered the professor taking the first watch after our little party. I had gotten tired and crashed . . . or was I drunk?

An explosion outside set off another charge of electricity, this time to the heart. We're being attacked! We're being overrun! I rushed outside. The platoon CP tent was in flames. An exploding Skyhawk sent a huge bolt of fire into the sky like a nuclear bomb. There were people running and yelling. But I saw no enemy. I thought I would wake up in a cold sweat and it would be over. How could they have penetrated so many perimeters of defense? The sight was so awesome and unbelievable that my mind had not begun to function properly.

My total attention was diverted to the left where the action was, but out of the corner of my right eye I saw something that froze my warm blood to a sludge and jammed my nervous system with an overload of confusing signals. My entire system nearly shut down, causing near-total paralysis.

Not more than ten feet to my direct front, halfway down the side of the sand dune, it stood, partially lit by the dancing flames of the burning tent. It was barefooted, with black shorts that seemed too large. The sleeves of its black shirt were rolled up past the elbow and protected the skin from bandoliers of hand grenades that hung across the chest. A bandanna across the forehead hung down the side, like an Apache warrior. Highlights frozen motionless on highly polished steel eyes reminded me of a humanoid built to pass as the real thing. Its engineer had been unable to duplicate the spirit of life, as can our true Creator. It smiled, showing black polished teeth.

A physical tremor began to develop in my gut. I started to shake all over. Bud, Schlitz, and Ole soaked my trousers and ran down the inside of my knees. I had never had a weak bladder before.

He held a hand grenade, while I had no weapon. One thing was for sure; whether it was human or not, it was the enemy. I was caught cold, suspended in my own terror, entrapped by a lifeless creature from some science fiction novel. He broke off his hypnotic stare that flowed like electrons and began to work the pin loose on a hand grenade. I wanted to cry. I wanted to get on my hands and knees, to ask forgiveness and make amends.

My body hurled through the air. Whether it is true, imagination, or just a contrived cliché, odd lengths of footage of my entire life did race across my mental screen. I landed on him hard, like a terrorized house cat, grabbing and clawing and holding onto anything that would fit my paws. We hit the sand and rolled around endlessly out into the darkness.

He was more powerful than I could have imagined for his size. He must be on drugs; that would account for the dazed, lifeless expression. His muscles were hard, lean, and taut like knots, from years of toiling in the fields. My own strength seemed nonexistent . . . just enough to hang on. The greasy, rotten clothing and the putrid stench of body odor, mixed with my fear of not finding the necessary energy reserves, made my stomach begin to retch. I also had a fear of one of his comrades coming up and blowing the back of my head out.

Each time we rolled over and over, locked in a death embrace, more sand got into my eyes, nose, and mouth. We each had an arm around the other's neck. I held his wrist that clawed at my face, keeping it from extracting my eyes. I managed to turn my face away, and his clawing was ineffective. He was arching his back; and just by brute strength alone, I was losing my hold on him. He tried to roll one more time to take advantage, but I flattened my body and stiffened. I began to ride higher on his body. He bucked and kicked in all directions.

It was perhaps a lifesaving thought that entered my mind: One of us was going to die at the hand of the other. Another thought dripped from the roof of the dark, icy cavern of my mind: If one of these grenades blows we will both go, and they will find a pile of bloody arms and legs they will not be able to explain.

I took a chance, freed one of my hands from its hold, and slammed a clenched fist into his groin. He began to yell and spit. I knew I had just taken the advantage. The more he yelled, the more I hammered. Then I went for the kill. I reached up under the baggy leg of his shorts and grabbed a handful of testicles. He began to scream. I took one massive yank, using all the muscles in my body clear down to my thighs. The flesh gave and tore in a silent, fluid, surprisingly easy motion. Once it gave way it was like stripping the excess fat from a chicken before broiling.

At that moment, I knew I was going to live. I was running on the last of the adrenalin. The barrel was dry. His relentless, high-pitched scream pierced both sides of my head like a sharp probe. I let go of what he did not have left and shifted my body. I slammed my fist into his vibrating throat, crushing the tiny frail bones of the larynx and the trachea. His screams were diminished to the sound of a toy doll whose whine is generated by a tiny bellows inside. His body convulsed and twitched. Blood bubbled from his nose and mouth as the air continued to escape slowly, vibrating tiny broken bones in his throat like the reed in a clarinet.

I staggered back up the hill, fell down, and crawled the rest of the way to the hootch. The CP tent was still burning. The ammo stored inside was going off. I found my pop gun and forty-five belt, slung a bandolier of twenty millimeters around my neck, and crawled out the back. Flares from eighty-ones began to pop overhead, lighting up the area. I scrambled down the other side of the sand dune and took up a firing position facing the edge in the direction from which I had come. My mind was still teetering on the edge. I knew the Vietcong would storm over the top by the thousands to get revenge for their comrade.

The professor was attending to someone on the ground. Sergeant Nick was walking around in a daze. He walked over in my direction. He was dressed only in a pair of trousers rolled up the knees, with no shirt, boots, or weapon. He was disoriented and nearly in tears.

"I lost my equipment, weapons, and everything. What am I going to do?"

I tossed him my forty-five, but could not resist a smart remark. "I want it back after this is over."

The fear of the unknown lurked everywhere. We did not know how many there were or what they were doing. The most frightening thought that came to mind was that they had probably already wiped out the entire squad closest to the jungle.

We started to yell for them. I was afraid that the

Vietcong might have found somebody asleep and cut throats along the line to get to the CP tent. But the return yells of a live and kicking squad gave us new confidence, and we organized a counteroffensive. Rounds continued to pop intermittently in the smoking rubble of the CP tent, and we crawled to the crest of the sand dune as more eighty-one flares ignited over the area and illuminated the junkyard.

The Vietcong left the temporary cover of the junkyard and ran for their lives out across the open sand. They ran one behind the other, entrants from the same country, one running for the gold medal and one for the silver in the one hundred meters. They were coming into the last stretch and heading for the tape, two men running for their lives. They could have made a new world's record. A strange remorsefulness came over me as I watched their final seconds. Even with all that effort, there was no way in hell they were going to make it. M-60s cut loose a thousand yards away, and the first burst was miraculously on target. The tracer rounds burned through them and streaked off into the darkness. The impact of the bodies in full stride seemed like slow motion. The bodies flew end over end, seven or eight feet in the air. They plunged to the ground and plowed through the sand like wiped-out downhill racers through the snow, and then came to rest.

The ten- or eleven-man suicide squad had been reasonably successful. They had completely totalled one Skyhawk, and a chain reaction had set off some highly volatile liquid oxygen that damaged two more planes. Sergeant James (the Sten-carrying platoon guide whom I had not met because of his time-consuming duties as platoon supply sergeant and scrounger) had taken shrapnel in the leg.

The professor had initially spotted four or five Vietcong running across the runway toward the CP tent in the dark, but he was unable to get the tape off his magazine or his hand grenades. Because of a bureaucratic safety precaution after some fool had shot his foot off in the rear and another had accidentally blown up a truckload of troops playing with a grenade, an insane safety program had been initiated. So the professor hadn't been able to stop them.

The Vietcong had thrown incendiary grenades into the CP tent. The professor returned the fire with a barrage of hand grenades with the spoons still taped. He actually hit one and knocked him down. He would have been just as effective with a bucket of rocks, like a caveman. He had screamed my name as he ran toward the flaming tent, and his scream saved my life. They would have blown me away in my sleep and I would have never known a thing.

The occupants of the CP tent were nearly overcome by the heat and the smoke. They were confused and disoriented. The professor rushed in and dragged each one of them out, then threw them into the sand to safety.

There was a one-hundred-percent alert for the rest of the night. We watched and waited for another attack, but it never came. I tried in vain to keep my mind occupied with something other than the dead body that lay somewhere out there in the darkness. There were reoccurring memories of terror laced with the sadness of destroying another human being, especially hand to hand.

Dawn came like a repealed death sentence, and a warm comfort of joy began to grow inside as the light in the sky widened and brightened. The dismal, bleak, but absolutely beautiful countryside that I would have missed began to unfold. I told myself that never again would I feel remorse or sadness for killing, because I was alive and it felt wonderful.

I searched the sand; the body was gone. I was glad. It was probably dragged off by a comrade and buried in the sand nearby without a trace. It relieved me of explaining the details of the savagery and the method I had used to initiate the kill. I knew, though, that if necessary I would do it again and again.

It was still dark inside the hootch when I felt around for a canteen. Everything was in disarray because of the attack. There were full C-ration cans strewn around the sand. I picked them up and threw them into a pile underneath the foot of the cot. The last one I picked up I thought was probably a can of ham and lima beans, but it seemed heavier. I shook it. It rattled. I turned around on my knees to find the light coming from the hatchway.

I froze and stopped breathing. The can of ham and lima beans had a bamboo cork and a braided trigger release that had already been pulled, and it sounded like it was full of black powder. I inched out cautiously on my knees through the hatchway. I yelled loudly but in fear that the vibration of my voice alone would set it off.

"I've got a live Vietcong grenade!"

The activity around the rubble of the CP tent stopped. Everyone froze. They grabbed their helmets. Still on my knees in a praying position, I cradled the bomb with both hands in front of me.

"Take it easy, Ogden. What are you going to do?" Sergeant Mick asked.

"I'm going to throw it. The pin's pulled. I can't tell right now, but if it's the type without a primer it's live as hell, and it might blow at any time. I don't know how far I can throw it underhand and in this position. Would somebody put my helmet on?"

The professor scrambled over and placed the helmet gingerly on my head as though it were a crown in a holy ceremony.

He smiled at me. "Take it easy, Plato. The republic will miss you."

I smiled back. "Don't worry, teach."

I was sweating and beginning to chill in the cool of the morning.

"I'll count to three and throw it. One . . . two . . . three . . . *fire in the hole!*"

I threw my whole back into it to get as high an arc and distance as possible. We flattened our bodies into the sand. It blew on impact. I lay in the sand, exhausted. I did not ever want to get up again. They rallied around me, cheering, banging me on the helmet and patting me on the back as though I had something to do with their salvation.

The grenade must have come with the first volley through the hatch, landing under my cot just three inches from my body. All of a sudden the war seemed more personal, as though they were after me and me alone. They had missed twice. What were the odds?

The professor went with the patrol that was sent out to find bodies and weapons. To their astonishment and discontent, they found no bodies. The professor did find a Thompson submachine gun that was overlooked in the dark. Third platoon had two enemy kills and the bodies to prove it. One of their "kills" was found at dawn wandering around close to the perimeter. He was shot in the gut, and he held what he could inside with his hands while he dragged the escaped intestines behind him in the sand. As the Vietcong soldier shuffled his feet forward through the sand, the second platoon commander stepped behind him and drew his forty-five. He placed it at the back of the head and pulled the trigger. It was a mistake he was never likely to forget. He did the man a kindness, but in the process he blew flecks of flesh, blood, and brain all over himself.

The body count and kill ratio were considered by the experts in the Pentagon the most important factors in determining the progress of the war, at least in combat. Each unit leader's efficiency was unofficially judged by the number of enemy KIAs to his credit. Each kill was treated as though it were a trophy. The Vietcong picked up their dead and weapons at any cost in order to refute any compiled statistics against them. It was demoralizing to find just specks of blood and rarely ever find a body. It made them seem elusive and impossible to kill.

Evening came. The professor offered to take the first watch, and I did not argue. I lay down, exhausted. I had nearly dozed off when the familiar scream rocked me wide awake again. I sat straight up in the cot, just as I had done before. The professor was sitting out in the patio on an ammo can, wiping down his new-found trophy. I realized that I was getting a videotape rerun of the night before. I got up and went outside.

"Why don't you hit the sack if you want to? I can't sleep at all."

"I can sleep any time. Are you all right?"

"My mind's still going around and around about last night and this morning. I just thought of something: did anybody thank you for bailing them out last night?"

"I don't know. I can't remember. I think you had a lot on your mind."

"You can say that again. But goddamn it, I'm thanking you right now. I owe you a lot."

"It's okay. I hope I don't have to collect."

He got up and handed me the Thompson, and I sat down.

"Go back to bed. You need your beauty sleep."

"Who, me? The pride of Watts? Beauty sleep?"

"Good night, pretty boy."

As the quietness of the dark, warm evening lingered on, I became uneasy and unable to relax. Instant replays kept cropping up. I tried to think of more pleasant things, but the override was too much. As a diversion, I began rubbing down the Thompson. In the moonlight, I noticed there was dried blood on the cloth; and when I looked closer, I found small flecks of dried flesh and skin in the crevices of the weapon. I was repulsed, and leaned the weapon against the sandbags.

Something flicked out of the corner of my eye. I gasped and froze, then relaxed. It was just a mouse scampering along in the sand outside the patio. I was not intimidated by mice; but for some reason, every tiny movement caught my attention and my heart stopped. Hair has the uncanny ability to stand up by itself, and mine seemed forever on the ready. My goose bumps also seemed to be out in force on this warm evening. Why was I so uptight?

The warm wind changed direction and blew in from across the sand. It brought the stench of blood and remains that had baked all day in the sun. It was the smell of death, strong and revolting.

The Thompson kept drawing my attention like a magnet. How could an intelligent, educated, sensitive person like the professor relish this thing so much when it was covered with blood and guts from its previous owner? I could smell it. He must be sick. That's it, sick like the others, and I didn't even sense it. I was the only one left who was sane and rational. The only one.

I heard the professor scream again. Then the Vietcong hand grenade exploded the hootch with me in it. I smelled the rancid, greasy body odor, and a hand yanked unmercifully at my testicles. I began to shake, sweat, and my mind whirled. I picked up the Thompson and slammed a round into the chamber. They were coming back! They would do anything to get their Thompson back and avenge their comrades!

I stood up. I could hear them yelling and screaming. There must have been a thousand of them! I could hear equipment banging and metal scraping. I could see flashes of swords and machetes in the moonlight.

I sensed someone directly behind me. Without turning, I saw a piece of shadow cast on the sand. I dropped the Thompson, whirled, and grabbed the figure by its clothing. I pulled him around and threw him down on the sandbag parapet. I got ahold of his throat. I cut off most of his wind. Then he managed to say my name, and I snapped out of it.

"Doc? What are you doing here?"

I let him up and pulled him to his feet. He spoke as he assessed his neck.

"I didn't sleep, so I got up. But I didn't expect to be mugged by one of my own troops. What are you so jumpy about? You're shaking apart."

"Doc, I was having a nightmare, but I was awake! I was hearing things and seeing things. Stay here and talk to me for awhile, will you? Are you all right? I'm sorry about grabbing you. I think I completely flipped out until you came along. I mean, damn near totally crazy!"

"The stress just finally caught up to you, Oggie. You had a pretty hairy twenty-four hours. I'll send you back to the rear for some rest."

"Come on, Doc, I haven't completely jumped out of

my tree. Stay here and talk to me. Now that I know what's happening, I'll be all right. You don't know how glad I am that you're sitting there and you don't hear or see anything. From what I've heard about nut houses, I think I'd rather go home in a rubber bag than in a straight jacket."

CHAPTER TWENTY-ONE

The war had the earmark of going on for another hundred years. There were rumors of massive escalation, rumors of being extended as much as a year after we had served the first year, rumors of only spot bombing in the north instead of total destruction, rumors of Russian supply ships still entering Haiphong Harbor in the north, rumors of corruption and military coups within the Vietnamese government (the government we supported and were fighting for), and rumors of drug experimentation among troops in other outfits. That was impossible. Marines didn't take drugs—just more than a crippling share of booze when it was available. Captive and isolated in the jungles and paddies, there was no way to refute any of the rumors. They were depressing, demoralizing, and probably true.

The unexpected rumor of "R & R," rest and relaxation—or "rape and ruin" in Bangkok or Tokyo, as it was more accurately referred to by some—lightened my spirits until I was told I would be on the bottom of the roster with the rest of the troops that came from Second Battalion. We were expected to rotate home before all the troops in this outfit. This was a marvelous rationalization. We had been in the bush fighting three months longer than Third Battalion, but we were going to be the last to enjoy any relief. We were still the bastards of the regiment.

One rumor—that we were moving out to become part of a large operation somewhere to the south—lasted for only a few days. No one was impressed. We had all been there before, or to a place just like it. No one seemed to care.

We were transported from Chu Lai beach through choppy seas in an LCU, the big brother of the landing craft family designed to carry a medium-sized tank to the beaches and back. We climbed up the debarkation nets of the LST and got a surprisingly warm welcome from the navy. They pulled us aboard, showered us with kindness, and overwhelmed us with questions about the fighting. It was like a big, noisy press conference held for the dead who had just returned from hell, and curiosity was killing the living.

Most of them expressed a willingness to take our places just to get away from the boredom of the ship and find out what combat was all about. But we knew that a couple of days in the jungle and they would be crying for clean sheets, real mattresses, the ship's store, showers, air-conditioning, fresh vegetables, red meat, bread, milk, apple pie, ice cream, nightly movies, and all of the other "boredom." We would be staying with this glorified floating day-care center for only a day and a night, then make our beach assault at dawn.

We took full advantage of the entire ship, everything but the bridge and the engine room. The galley was the most celebrated area. We nearly bathed in gallons of reconstituted milk, and ate until we were sick. The months of C-rations and bad field chow were forgotten for awhile. Sailors catered to our every whim, and the mess hall became a madhouse. We indulged like looting conquerors or death-defying prisoners from a concentration camp. We were trying to press a whole week of liberty or R & R into a few hours.

After the Roman feast, I took an endless, scalding shower. I wasted enough water to make the Indian farmers in Arizona weep. I put on clean underwear and crawled into a cot. It was difficult to remember when I had last had a full night's sleep. I grinned inside from ear to ear, jubilant over a few hours of peace and rest. I did not care to think about tomorrow. Today was wonderful! I closed my eyes and saw Elizabeth waving at me from the strawberry fields . . .

School was out, and for the four of us it was going to be a long, hot, wonderful summer. We were going to fish, camp, play baseball, and take long bicycle hikes. Somehow, I would have to work at a part-time job so I would have new clothes for school next fall.

We were fourteen and fifteen. We ran around together in a small pack, forever thwarting the pangs of boredom. I was considered the runt. We were not really mischievous, but the sisters who were a few years older thought we were obnoxious and unruly. Each of them had a sister. I liked the sisters and got along with them, but I was still condemned for associating with an entourage of brat brothers.

This summer we found ourselves hard-pressed for cash for important necessities like a new baseball, a Coke, candy bars, and other life-support items. We decided that for a couple of weeks we would lower ourselves and join the annual migration to the berry fields with all the boring and practical kids in the neighborhood.

Getting up at five o'clock in the morning was not as tough for me as it was for the others because of the crack-of-dawn chores I had. We were a pretty loyal group; if one could make it, even the slowest and most reluctant seemed to close up ranks. The bus picked us up at the general store, and it was a forty-minute ride into the Snohomish Valley to the fields. We quickly captured the rear of the bus and took it over, far from the authority of a reasonable but still adult lady bus driver.

Picking strawberries was hard work and boring. We all vowed we would not come back the next day. But at the end of the day, we added up the money we had made collectively. We were amazed at how well we had done, in spite of eating and throwing away so many strawberries. We had thought we would be thrown out by the straw bosses.

By the next afternoon we had become more restless

and bored than usual. We were loud and obnoxious, much to the dismay of some boring, practical girls who sat in front of us on the way home. The more they turned around, raised their eyebrows, and stuck up their noses, the more we showed off.

During these free-for-alls, the runt always seemed to be the brunt of the practical jokes or the teases. This time it was "keep away the baseball cap." I was proud of the cap. My uncle had given me his gold wings from World War Two to wear on it. I hated to admit it to myself, but I didn't mind being teased some of the time. It was a small price to pay for acceptance.

During the free-for-all, my hat went sailing up to the front of the bus. I went up to see where it had landed. A voice from behind me asked, "Is this yours?" I turned and reached for it, but she seemed reluctant to hand it over. When she spoke again, I detected a light wisp of delightful perfume. She asked me why I let them pick on me.

Her presence and attitude left me overwhelmed, speechless, and confused. She looked up at me with beautiful sky-blue eyes and a lovely smile. Her hair was gone in a French roll and held with an attractive pin, which added to an air of sedateness about her. She wore a red, short-sleeved print blouse and blue jeans cut off at mid-thigh but neatly rolled up and creased. Her beautiful, short, tanned legs and bare feet with red-painted nails rested on dirty, strawberry-stained sneakers.

Still partially tongue-tied, I explained to her that they were my friends and I didn't mind them. She moved an eyebrow as though she didn't quite understand. I asked her if I might have my hat back. I thanked her and walked back to the rear of the bus.

I sat by myself, no longer interested in the gang and their stupid games. Something had happened! Even my prized hat no longer seemed significant. I did not eat or sleep that night. I tossed and turned and thought about her. Why did I feel so strange, as though she had some sort of power over me? I was totally consumed with the thought of her.

I popped out of bed the next day, more enthused about the berry fields than ever. I rummaged through the dresser and found a white shirt that my mother had just bought for a dime at our most frequented department store, the Salvation Army. I left the baseball cap with the gold wings hanging on a nail. I applied Wildroot Cream Oil and attempted to find a long-lost part in my hair. I rolled my shirt sleeves up to my elbows and did my chores. The white shirt was not the most intelligent choice for picking strawberries, but I didn't care. I wanted to look nice. It would detract from my dirty Levis and sneakers.

After breakfast and a nice, cold sponge bath from the livestock spigot, I headed down the narrow gravel road to the general store. The sun was coming up. Hundreds of frogs croaked along the way, and a robin sang. It seemed as though I had never heard such delightful sounds before. What was happening to me? I had to run most of the way to make sure I did not miss the bus, because my bicycle had a broken chain.

The others noticed that something had come over

me. I did not ignore them completely, but sat quietly alone. My heart stopped when the bus pulled up to her stop and she got on and sat with her girlfriend. I noticed how nicely the top of her brown paper lunch bag was folded, just like her jeans. Mine was always crunched and wadded at the top. I tried to straighten it out a bit. I had made my own lunch. Since I was tired of peanut butter and rhubarb jam, I had decided on cheese and mayonnaise. I was tired of that, too, but the other options were even less appealing.

The gang was carrying on as usual, but I rode the whole forty miles without an incident, except for an occasional hair rearrangement from one of them. My hair was hard to keep combed because it was very curly, and when it dried out the Wildroot made it wilder.

I wondered how it had come to her attention that my friends were always picking on me, when she sat so far forward on the bus. I did not mind them, but I wondered why she cared. I sensed in her tone of voice the day before that she did not approve. No one would pick on me again if I could help it.

The bus reached the fields and the straw bosses waited outside, like Georgia prison guards, to assign each person to what seemed to be a ten-mile-long row. One person on each end picked toward the middle, and they might meet each other around noon. Everyone was assigned as soon as they got off the bus.

An idea came to me. When I got up to file off the bus, I stepped in behind her girlfriend. They stepped off the bus together and both were assigned to the same row, to their dismay. I was assigned to the row adjacent. My scheme had worked.

We got our flats off the stack and began picking; to my astonishment, she picked so fast that my whole gimmick to be close to her was crumbling before my eyes. I panicked and began ravishing the plants, making sure I left no berries behind, because the straw bosses would come and spot-check the row. I managed to keep slightly behind her, but I could not believe the amount of strawberries I was picking. This girl had come here to make money.

I looked around. We were pulling well ahead of the others around us. The wild bunch were about fifteen rows over and well behind us, so I decided to relax. I began whistling along in good spirits when she stopped to stretch.

"What are you whistling? It sounds nice."

I smiled and told her I really did not know, and kept on picking. She asked me what my name was. I tripped over my tongue, but managed to answer. I concentrated on picking to cover my shyness. She told me I should take a breather, so I stood up and stretched, too. We talked for awhile, and I could hardly believe it when she told me her father was the barber at the general store. They were planning to move into the neighborhood across from the store. Her father cut my hair every other week, a daring attempt to rectify a hopeless ball of fuzz.

My shyness began to dissipate as we went back to work. I was glowing inside. We had something in common. I learned she was a year older and was going to be a junior in high school. I did not have the guts to tell her my age or where I would be in the fall. Her name was Elizabeth. It fit my image of her; it sounded sophisticated. She asked me if anyone called me Dick instead of Richard, and I told her only my grandfather. She told me she liked the name Dick very much.

Something whizzed by my head. I stopped to look around. I thought I was seeing or hearing things, and went back to work until a soft strawberry hit me on the back of the head. The wild bunch had jumped their rows and had the two of us surrounded. I was steaming. I did not need these clowns fooling around in the presence of a lady.

They moved in and introduced themselves in a silly, pretentious manner for my benefit, keeping one eye on me to see my reaction. Each handed her a full box of strawberries. She gave me a brief, inquisitive look, shrugged her shoulders, and gave them a nice thank you. They continued to pick for her. I was furious, and went back to ravaging the plants. They were older and bigger, and all was lost. My jealousy was running wild.

The noon whistle blew, and to my absolute shock she asked me if we could have lunch together. She placed two boxes of strawberries into my flat to give us both half a flat so we could have our tickets punched together and go to lunch. What an incredible triumph! The berries they had picked for her she gave to me. I picked up both flats, and we headed for lunch. Cheese and mayonnaise never tasted so great.

On the way home I sat with her and her girlfriend, and never heard a whisper from the rear of the bus.

Something was brewing. As soon as we got off the bus they grabbed me, wrestled me to the ground, and pulled off my jeans. It was the current fad. The bus drove on, and I hoped she did not see me in my most undignified hour.

From that moment on, none of us was ever the same. They congratulated me for having such a fantastic girlfriend. I was never again the subject of their jokes or pranks. We had all grown up a little, and I was in love. The whole world took on a slight rosy tint. Nothing else mattered.

CHAPTER TWENTY-TWO

A massive charge detonated, splitting the air like an axe. It knocked us to the sand, blowing others in the platoon back into the amtrack. L and M Companies found themselves right in the middle of a fortified beach assault. A barrage of rockets, mortars, and machine-gun fire pinned us to the sand. Ironically, it was beautiful sand, and over the jungle towered lush coconut palms. The only ingredient missing was Sergeant Striker, the "Duke."

The clash and roar of all-out combat to get inland off the naked dangerous beach was so deafening that it numbed the senses, leaving the strange silence of animation only. Slightly bulging eyes reacted and overreacted to take in such an awesome, incredible scene. A cross wind carrying the black smoke of burning diesel fuel temporarily blinded us, and the stench of detonated sulphur was sickening.

Over the roar I heard men screaming. A barrage of

B-40 rockets hissed out of the jungle, and one slammed into an amtrack partially loaded with troops. A tank rolled off an LCU and took a direct hit, blowing off one of its tracks and rendering it immobile but not ineffective. Its big gun traversed the tree line spitting out shells as fast as the loader could load, exploding large chunks of jungle to dust and vapor. A constant rain of machine-gun fire kept the sand around us boiling. Our mission was to put a cork on a bottle that surrounded a regiment of over two thousand crack North Vietnamese troops.

We had landed on the southernmost coast of the Van Tounge Peninsula. The peninsula itself was discovered by reconnaissance to be a staging area, or jumping-off point, for attacks on the air base just a few miles away. It had only taken a handful of suicidal junkies a few weeks ago to give us something to think about. The airfield was not impregnable.

The campaign was officially called Operation Starlight. Companies from the Fourth and Seventh Marine Regiment were heli-lifted deep into the jungle to set up a blocking force, using six-inch naval guns, Skyhawks, and Phantoms. They were pounding the center of the arena with cannon fire, bombs, and napalm. The idea of getting off the beach and buying some real estate with cover was our only thought the first few seconds on the beach.

A flame thrower team crawled within striking distance of a grass hut on the edge of the tree line. Their objective was to silence the machine gun. A blast of liquid, volatile napalm burned the thatch from the structure, revealing a concrete bunker. The occupants inside were baked quicker than microwave.

Two Phantoms with speed up to sixteen hundred miles per hour just barely topped the trees as they screamed along parallel to the beach. They veered off into the jungle, lifting their noses and kicking loose two five-hundred-pound napalm pods less than a hundred yards from our four-hundred-man assault team. On impact, the entire landing team (minus a few) got up and charged the tree line. We screamed and yelled as we swept across the sand into the jungle. The air strike had given us the necessary split seconds to get off the beach. Our yells were met by screams from several flaming Vietcong running our way. Machine guns relieved their pain. The bodies dropped, to burn for days.

It was difficult to keep our interval in the dense jungle with a cross wind carrying heavy black smoke. M Company had to penetrate the heaviest part of the Vietcong beach defense, and paid for it heavily with many wounded and the loss of their company commander. L Company was lucky, with only a few casualties. No one in Third Platoon was hit. We passed smoldering concrete bunkers and jumped over trench lines, their bottoms and parapets littered with expended brass.

Daniels remained behind the squad, working hard at keeping the interval and making sure no one got lost. We rounded up a few prisoners, some badly injured. Angry troops were restrained by Daniels and myself from an occasional butt stroke or kicking of prisoners. I could not tolerate the abuse of helpless or injured prisoners. All of them were bound with comm wire and gagged, then sent to the rear. From the rumors we had heard, they were as good as dead already. ARVN interrogators employed ingenious methods to get them to talk. They would take several of them aloft in a chopper, arbitrarily toss one out of the hatch, and then start the interrogation with the rest of them. Or they would fasten hot wires or heat tabs to the prisoners' testicles.

The sun disappeared as though nightfall were coming. There was occasional sniper fire up and down the line, and the return of machine-gun fire. The professor and I were trying to decide how to break through a solid wall of vines when an AK-47 opened up. I flew through the air and landed behind some rocks. I looked back in confusion. The professor had not taken cover.

"Professor, get down!"

He went down to his knees. His eyes were fixed ahead. He momentarily braced himself with his rifle butt. His head slowly tilted back and he looked up into the tree tops where a tiny ray of sunlight shone down. He said "Oggie" almost under his breath and fell over frontward.

Another burst of rounds slammed into the rock. One exploded, sending a piece of shrapnel into my left forearm. I crawled over to the professor, turned him over, and laid his head in my lap as I checked the jugular for a pulse. I checked the wrists and then the breathing. I checked the chest for a heartbeat and found a hole. Just a tiny hole; the bleeding could have been stopped with a band-aid. I took off his helmet. His hair felt soft, warm, and strange.

There would be no more fighting over who had to eat the ham and lima beans, no more sharing peaches, no more late-night multiplication drills. He would not get to know how well his student would do on the GED Test. There would not be any college basketball star or proud junior high school teacher. The fires of Watts would burn out and be replaced by just a single candle.

Now was the time to cry, but there weren't any tears. With forefinger and thumb, I gently closed the shades of an empty dwelling. Elgin Walter Johnson the Second did not live in there anymore.

"Goddamn it!" I yelled as loud as I could with every muscle of my body. I replaced his helmet and laid him back gently on the ground. I headed into the jungle screaming, *"You sons of bitches! You bastards!"*

When I came to my senses, I found myself tangled in vines, exhausted and lost. In my childish frenzy, I had placed myself in the hands of the enemy. My breathing and the blood pounding in my ears sounded like they were coming over a public address system amplified a hundred times.

In its dreadful silence, the jungle harbors death just as darkness plays host to evil. The thought of dying had been entertained a great deal the last few months, but the thought of dying alone added a new dimension, a congenital frailty never to be overcome from womb to tomb. Why are we preoccupied with our physical fate after death? If I dropped on the jungle floor and it grew over me, I would vanish without a trace, to rot for thousands of years on a loosely charted part of the planet. It would be excavated by an urban renewal project, creating a wrinkle in future paleontology. This species is not indigenous to this area.

While fighting a losing battle with the jungle, I stopped breathing from time to time to try to detect sounds from other living things. I wasn't aware of which direction I had begun in, since in my carelessness I had probably stopped and headed in several different directions. The sun was nowhere to be seen. I slung my cannon, which would be useless in such close quarters, and drew my forty-five. By brilliant deduction, a course of action was set: follow my nose. Again, the dreadful silence made me feel and sound like a massive, exasperated prehistoric animal trying to sneak across the ground covered with dry autumn leaves.

With five thousand Marines and probably an equal number of Vietcong in the area, I was bound to run into someone. On the other hand, I could stumble around out here for a month. As I trampled along as silently as a baby rhino, I eased but did not preoccupy my mind by switching back and forth from the Twenty-Third Psalm to my multiplication tables. I was all the way up to my eights. The professor would have been proud. Eight times nine equals . . .

Automatic M-2 carbines opened up from different directions in front of me, and I got my answer. The high-pitched crack of the rounds sounded like they were point-blank. The concentration of rounds coming in was so heavy that it seemed like volley after volley of buckshot. The ground around me began to come apart in a blur of dust, while vines, branches, and leaves splintered and disintegrated into a flying mulch before my eyes. I had just been sucked into a wheat combine, and the blades had not yet reduced me to ground round, medium lean. It took forever to get to the ground.

I sprang toward an impression in the jungle floor at the base of a large banana palm. I tried to flatten out and become invisible like a chameleon that hadn't learned what buttons to push to get the right color. I could not believe that I was not hit.

I was more concerned with my head than the rest of my body. I began to curse my helmet, and nearly took it off because it restricted me from pushing my head further down into the soft soil. Ostriches are my kind of people. My face was butted tightly against the base of the banana palm that was more like a house plant than a tree. More false security. Rounds passed through its soft, wet cortex like a sponge. Rounds blew through the opposite side of the stalk just inches from my face, blinding me with spattering juice. At this point, I would have traded a hundred acres of banana palms for just one douglas fir. Dust and debris continued to fly around me. I did not have the courage to lift my head and look around me to see where they were.

I finally got up a thread of courage (or stupidity) and spotted a puff of smoke coming from the top of a large Japanese-style ambush. They had tied themselves in trees and waited for prey to come along. There was another one up there somewhere, but I could not spot him. Easy prey came along, so why didn't they hit it?

This was no time for multiplication tables; the Twenty-Third Psalm might be in order.

They should have had me with the first volley, but any second their luck was going to change. If I got up and ran, even a chimpanzee couldn't miss. If I lay there, I would be dead for sure. I caught myself giving up and wanting to go to sleep just so the fear would go away and I would wake up in a nicer place.

"Yea, though I walk through the valley of the shadow of death, I will fear no evil."

I started to get angry with their incompetence. "You stupid bastards, I've changed my mind. You can't have me!"

In what seemed like one single movement, I was up and in full stride out of my grave. I lowered my head and galloped ahead in a straight line through the greenery like a flatfooted ostrich in full charge. I had once seen an ill-fated event much like this before from the grandstands. The object of the event is to get out of the starting blocks and get to the tape before the starter shoots you in the back. No gold, no silver, and hopefully no lead.

I was so busy and noisy crashing through the brush that I didn't know if they were still firing or not. I was still moving and wasn't leaking anywhere unnaturally; but with luck and preseverance, I would probably stumble right into their main base camp, and they would have me for lunch.

After falling down a dozen or more times I stayed down, exhausted and unable to breathe. I lay on my back and gagged for air. Another machine gun opened up, strafing the jungle overhead, then another and another. So much fire power erupted that the entire jungle overhead began to break off and fall on me. I was right! My luck had led me to the entire Vietcong regiment. How could I be so stupid? If I got out of this one, I'd better turn myself over to the doc.

Wait a minute! The lull in the firing came at familiar time intervals. Those were M-14s with only twenty rounds to each magazine. I had single-handedly found the lost brigade!

I screamed and yelled. "Cease fire! Cease fire! This is PFC Ogden from L Company! Cease fire!"

I got the answer I had anticipated. "What in the fuck are you doing out there?"

I didn't have a short, concise explanation, so I said nothing. I decided to stay put and let them come to me. There's always a trigger-happy hunter who never gets the word. I sat in the brush and waited, like a small runaway child just barely walking age. I tried to assess the events of the day.

Who is this silly, errant, twentieth-century Cervantes character who stumbles blindly but nobly from one intense ambush to another, unharmed, unblemished, in and out of the jaws of the dragon, to avenge the death of a friend named Socrates? He becomes more weary, the sword becomes heavier; the armor of his spirit has tarnished and nearly rusted away. The impossible dreams and ideals have faded. There will be no more restraining combat-crazed school kids from stomping and battering prisoners. There will be no more prisoners, if I can help it!

CHAPTER TWENTY-THREE

Our specific objective was to push the trapped enemy toward a river on the south while another company crossed the river and delta to form a blocking force from the north. At the same time, three other companies were landed by helicopter in the paddies at the backside of the peninsula to the west.

The skirmish line had slowed down because of huge hedgerows and light jungle. At calculated intervals, an invisible freight train would pass overhead and blow in the jungle a good distance ahead of us. Sometimes the six-inch artillery shells fell short, sending back stray chunks of twisted steel weighing as much as two or three pounds, able to sever a good-sized tree like a meat cleaver through a spongy house plant. We hit the deck when the Northern Pacific came in, just in case.

It's impossible to imagine being in a war with an enemy that had naval gun power or jet fighters and bombers hounding you every second, and you had no place to go. Thank God they didn't.

Reports came in that the enemy had attempted to scale a ridge line en masse and were observed by our forward artillery observer. They were right out in the open when our big guns had wiped them out—a sure sign of panic. Just when we thought the North Vietnamese regulars were going to be a piece of cake, they opened up on us from a good-sized hill that lay in front of us. We again hit the deck as machine-gun fire walloped the ground around us.

We waited for Sergeant Nick's command to assault. When it came, we charged up the hill, our fingers going numb on the trigger. The only way for men to survive out in the open in a frontal assault is to gain firing superiority, throwing up a wall of lead so intense that the enemy does not have the opportunity to aim, squeeze, and plink us off from their cover. Keep their heads down and they're ineffective.

The squad leaders remained behind their squads, barking orders to keep the interval and keep moving out, making sure each man, fire team, and squad was abreast of the other. We attacked the objective running and yelling. Balls of smoke blew from every weapon at an incredible rate, the only way we could survive the most dangerous of offensive tactics, facing a concealed enemy while traveling over open ground uphill.

I could see the enemy when they changed positions or got up to run. They had tied brush to themselves for concealment. The frontal attack was working perfectly, in fact, until a hairline fracture in the personality cracked like the sharp, crisp snap of a deadly carbine—

Sergeant Nick began yelling and screaming, ordering us to cease fire, the most moronic and abominable mistake he had ever made in his life. There is only one other thing he could have done that would have been equally mindless: he could have opened up and shot us all in the back.

He continued to yell. All three squad leaders yelled in defiance, afraid for the lives of the men and themselves. He continued to scream till his voice cracked.

"Cease fire and conserve ammo!"

The platoon was loaded with ammo—enough for weeks. But it was too late; erratic orders were penetrating regimented minds. The firing drifted off and the pace slowed down.

As expected, fire from the hilltop picked up. For an instant we stood around like confused offensive linemen in the midst of a broken play. Two men from Anderson's squad dropped like sacks of wheat. They hit the ground almost simultaneously, stone dead. I, and several men around me, hit the ground equally as hard, but alive and without a scratch.

The Swede was several yards to my left. He dropped his canteen and bent over to pick it up. A round entered his shoulder inside his collar bone and blew up the small of his back. I crawled toward him. He was white. His eyes bulged, crossed, and tried to focus. He shook, and then died.

He had been a nice guy. Although I was openly reluctant, he had tried to take me under his wing. To pass some of the long hot days on the runway, he had taken on the tedious, arduous task of teaching me chess. We both had an innate aching and longing for music of any kind. He enjoyed my miserable rendition of Pat Boone, and asked me to sing him to sleep every night. If I would have allowed another friend, he would have been it.

There were three dead. The rest of us were pinned down midway to the objective. But there was no organized effort to continue our assault, though walking brush continued to aim, breathe, and squeeze, keeping a vexed hold on our mobility and effectiveness. We kept firing—but more discriminately, and not in such heavy volume—concentrating on where we had last seen movement.

Burnett and his squad had found cover in the low brush on the right flank. He and two of his men were standing up behind a large clump of green. I felt like yelling over to them just to hear myself yell. But I didn't have the energy. Besides, I was sure that they didn't want to be bothered with the dumb cliché "one round will get you all!" They appeared to be lounging in the shade, seemingly unconcerned, with enemy only a hundred yards away. I blinked, and the three of them disappeared in a puff of blue and red smoke. The clap of the explosion sounded like a massive hand grenade. The bodies flew through the air in slow motion, like Hollywood dummies, in three different directions. One body opened up and came apart with a splash of blood and flesh that turned partially into a vapor. As the sun reflected through the volatile scene, it took on a ghostly hue of pale rose. As the bodies reached the apex of their flight they crashed to the ground, smoldering.

Someone began to yell: *"Incoming! Incoming!"*

Heavy firing came from Second Platoon, which was tied in on the left flank. They had advanced further than we had, and had wrapped around the left side of the objective. It sounded like they were assaulting from the other side. Our part of the deal had gone sour. I wondered why no on had cracked and shot our psychotic leader right where he stood.

When the objective was secured, we took up the grim task of wrapping bodies in ponchos. I found a helmet in the grass with a head still in it. The body was ten feet away. I didn't know his name. I was intrigued, if not entranced, with the fact that there was no blood on the unmarred face. Big blue eyes continued to blink with a lost gaze of confusion about what had just happened. The forehead continued to perspire, framed in damp, matted blond hair. The bottom lip quivered. I knew that it was dead, but I turned away before it spoke . . . before it started asking stupid questions, or for help. I pointed to it for the corpsman to find.

Second Platoon had taken the hill, putting the Vietcong on the run, brush and all. We learned that it was a 60mm mortar that had landed on Burnett and his men. It was one of our own from Second Platoon. They said they had thought they were Vietcong. It was a likely story. Burnett and his friends were only about twenty yards from my position, and we were out in the open. No wonder. It was the same leader who had stepped up behind a gutshot Vietcong on the runway, laying his pistol to the back of the head and blowing it all over himself.

We set up a perimeter around our self-inflicted

carnage and waited for the crosstown bus to cart them to the morgue. For the first time since I'd landed on Red Beach in Danang, I was experiencing a new fear: not the gut-grabbing, heart-stopping terror; it was an all-consuming fear that lay at the base of the brain like a termite. A subtle, bleak depression of hopelessness. We all felt the morale get chewed up along with the spirit, digested and laid to waste, because of so much needless death within a few minutes time. We were faced for the first time, I think, with the stark reality of how dispensable we were and how vulnerable we were by entrusting our lives into the hands of idiots. Gosh, sir, I'm sure sorry. That was a terrible mistake. I'll get it right the next time. Besides, boot camp is cranking them out as fast as we can kill them. We sure ain't gonna run short, are we, sir?

In the meantime, choppers were flying continuously, laden with wounded and dead. Bodies were stacked in the back of trucks five or six deep. There is a lab in Danang that works around the clock, placing bodies in large plastic bags and keeping them refrigerated, as though they were being shipped to Safeway instead of mom.

As we watched them stack the unfortunates aboard the chopper, a thin curtain of darkness and mourning covered the day like a great hand had turned down the rheostat in the sun several clicks.

It was nearly dark when we dropped in our tracks, scraping out a nesting place in the soft jungle earth and crawling in. We washed our C-rations down cold.

I shared the radio watch with Daniels. I took the first watch. I was so exhausted that if I had gone to sleep and then awakened, it would have been impossible to stay awake. As I listened to the lifeless, empty hiss of the radio, I thought of the Vietcong slithering through the jungle, grinning like lizards, like Geronimo's band in the movies. Never getting thirsty or hungry or tired, having no horses and running great distances, no guns, able to creep up behind a wide-awake cowboy and cut his throat. Good communications, and the advantage of fighting in their own backyard . . . Geronimo, considered the greatest military tactician the world has ever known. And still he lost every battle on the screen. Incredible.

My eyelids were so heavy that it took every muscle in my body to keep them from slamming shut. My head began to nod. I found a short stick and tapped myself on the skull to stay alive. It had been a very rough day in too many ways. I tried to peel away the scabs from a dull brain and think of something more pleasant.

Days, weeks, or months no longer held any significance. Life was reduced to intense intervals of minutes and seconds. A five-minute rest; a three-second pull on the canteen; a ten-minute meal; a thirty-second flashback to something homey and pleasant; a shorter flashback to death; a brief, cool breeze; a piece of shade and one could almost forget the anguish of the preceding hours. Even a bowel movement was deemed as a moment of peacefulness, momentarily cutting out the ambient, chaotic world, a moment becoming less frequent because of a lack of fresh food.

The enemy had pulled back so rapidly that we could

not keep up with them. Through more dense jungle, then down into the open sandy hills, sparsely covered with low brush and densely populated with pungee sticks that glistened in the sun and pointed in our direction like porcupine quills.

I seemed to be more exhausted than the troops around me. I must have burned up a lot of energy running through the jungle alone like a mindless idiot. No signs of heat exhaustion that had knocked me down before, but I was hurting bad.

For a moment I fantasized a dirty, sharply jagged pungee stick penetrating deep into a meaty calf, or a sniper's round finding a clean exit after entering a shoulder instead of merely nicking me in the arm. It was only my left arm. I wished they had blown it off; then they couldn't make me participate any longer in this maddening game. The big bird could come and rescue me. I would live to go home and die of cancer, old age, or on the freeway, like it should be.

This boyish man recently turned nineteen had never had a checking account, never learned to drive a car, never held a part-time job that paid more than seventy-five cents an hour, had never felt sex with someone loved or someone liked, or just some nice girl who lived in the neighborhood.

I would gladly give an arm to stand in my mother's kitchen sipping a tall glass of pure, cold Northwest water while watching her fuss over a steaming batch of rhubarb jelly while we happily chatted with enthusiasm, planning my future.

CHAPTER TWENTY-FOUR

As we continued the pursuit there was more and more incredible evidence of a one-sided battle. There were craters in the area big enough to park a truck in, left by the ten-inch naval gunfire or five-hundred-pound bombs dropped by Phantoms. Chunks of dense jungle had literally disappeared, leaving smoldering earth from yesterday's concentrated bombing.

Third Platoon sent a message they had found a lot of bodies. The message stiffened the alert, since partially alive enemy are still dangerous due to booby traps or possum. Why not? They had used every other desperate jungle tactic.

The company slowed down to a creep. Everyone was on edge, waiting to jump some half-charred soul who had survived the bombing.

Part of my concentration and tension was diverted to Sergeant Nick. I wondered if he had any guilt, and how many of us he would get killed today. I was not

271

certain about the others, but my morale was so low that he would never again blunder and jeopardize a single life. He had earned my respect and fear, just as the enemy had. I would never let him out of my sight.

As we continued forward, more bodies and more evidence of bombing was found.

"I think we're headed to where the main event took place," Corporal Daniels commented.

The rest of us silently agreed. The air was filled with the familiar scent of burning napalm and sulphur. It was also laced with the sweet acidic scent of burnt protein. The scent itself was not repugnant, only the thought.

The sun had found its favorite perch and rested on the backs of our necks and shoulders. There was an inordinate amount of flies and other insects hosting this garbage dump of dead trees and bodies.

Even in the face of the great victory, counting the bodies became boring. Viewing death was a curious and intriguing thing at first, but no more. As a kid I had felt terrible during slaughtering season, and ran and hid; but now I felt almost smug and arrogant: better these little pathetic bastards than me.

The company came to a halt at the edge of a huge clearing.

"Jesus Christ!" someone exclaimed slowly.

A chunk of jungle the size of two football fields was missing. It looked like a logging company had moved in, taken the choice lumber, then burned and plowed up the rest with a number of D-9 Caterpillars. There were bodies and pieces of bodies strewn everywhere, some hanging from surviving trees.

Sergeant Mick barked some short commands. The three squads deployed along the edge of Armageddon. We held our weapons at the ready should anyone mysteriously return from the dead.

Every square inch of the territory I scanned was a new revelation in horror, like the indiscriminating brain playing old newsreels of the cleanup of Nazi concentration camps. Several yards to my left front, a completely burnt corpse clutched its bosom as though it were cold. A tiny light flickered inside the skull through the eye socket. The flesh was burned away from the mouth, and it grinned like a lifeless jack-o'-lantern.

It struck a cord. This wasn't real, it was a giant mural. A cynical, surrealistic depiction of man's hatred of man, so detailed that it transcended the immediate imagination. Hope for the future was already dead in the present.

The partially charred corpse of a pregnant woman lay against some rocks. Grass, weeds, and brush had been burned away, and it looked as though she had climbed next to the rocks as a last resort. A burned-away blouse revealed a tiny unblemished foot protruding from a rupture in the side of her abdomen.

It was still. Welcome to the new world somewhere between earth and hell.

When input to the brain becomes too intense or too complex, the entire system shifts a gear, and the index cards are reshuffled and reprogrammed superficially to a different level. The overused dog-eared cards are bundled up and carried to the back, and a crisp new set of cards are popped into the hopper. A whole new program and set of values are initiated, based very loosely on the previous one.

The idea of a thirty-minute lunch break was not disturbing in the midst of this human garbage dump. Picnicking at a community cremation? Maybe Aldous Huxley would have understood. It was just a job; better them than us. Maybe we'd find more after lunch. The programming system works fine unless one of the cards gets jammed and mutilated within the system. Pass the salt, please!

There was mumbling and mild dissension when it was learned that the company was moving out and heading in another direction on a new assignment; there would be no pawing through the ashes to look for souvenirs. The ever-sought-after souvenir was the fighting man's only personal, tangible evidence that he had, indeed, endured the horrendous nightmare. As the years passed the old cards were again bundled up and stacked in the rear of the warehouse, and sometimes inadvertently labeled "fantasy." The souvenir sometimes acts as the key to the warehouse, since most of the men do not want to forget the horrors of death, dying, and destruction that are part of combat. This syndrome can be a practical mechanism in later years in appreciating one's life, when it was so nearly taken in the past.

I was aware of the subtle changes in my mental state, or lack of mental articulation. Complex issues and problems were becoming too simplified. There was a gleam of hope in the fact that I was aware of these changes. The fight to remain alive was one problem; the fight to remain human was quite another. I needed a letter from earth badly.

Wonderful thoughts of home and the faces of people became all too hazy. I labored to fill my head with positive thoughts. Fond memories were trying to get a carnival going under my steel pot. Starting with the most primitive needs, I was standing in my mother's kitchen in front of the sink, drinking as much sheer ice-water as I could hold, and purposefully wasting a lot of it for the pure thrill. And a feminine creature and ice cream are near the top of the list.

CHAPTER TWENTY-FIVE

I stepped out of the cab and gave the Kamikazi driver too many yen. They drove as though their lives depended upon it, instead of their livelihood. Their passengers' lives were depending on it, for sure.

A soft, unimposing rain fell on the bamboo-wood framed, corrugated-tin-roof village outside Camp Hanson Marine Base. I hiked the collar of my green raingear issue to keep the starch of my crisp khakis from running down the furrow in my back.

A mixture of mild sewage and Oriental and American rock music permeated the air along the dirt main street. It was still early evening, and there were only a few local villagers strolling the street while a few shopkeepers closed up. Several MPs strolled slowly down the other side of the street. I instinctively reached up to see if I had remembered my tie, and if my cover was on my head properly. I believed the horror stories of MPs in Okinawa. They would crack your head open for being slightly out of uniform.

At a quick glance one could tell that this bustling metropolis was not hurting for bars or pawn shops. Knowing my ex-fire team too well, I headed for the biggest, noisiest club on the strip called—what else—The Coconut Grove. The Beatles were banging out one of their latest through an antique jukebox as I stepped through the door.

"Hey Oggie, over here!"

It was Red, bouncing a plump young Naisan on his lap. Grinning Charlie was doing the swing with a pretty, short girl, in a pretty, short skirt with an inordinately large bosom, who was long on swing. Ed was also on the dance floor doing some outrageous improvisation, somewhere between Kabuki and the Twist. Richard the III was in the corner involved in tense conversation about Chicago or "Let's Make a Deal." All the girls seemed quite young except for the fat, leathery mama-san behind the bar.

"Oggie, get over here. I want to introduce you to my fiancee. This is Suko, and her sister is dancing with The Horn. Oggie here, when he was our leader, was an asshole; but now he's pretty cool!"

She took her hand from the top of his sweaty head and gave me a little wave. I smiled politely and waved back with two fingers. I picked up the highball glass half full of what looked like Hawaiian Punch and took a sniff.

"What are you apes drinking, anyway?"

"Whatever it is, it's working."

I took a sip; it was incredibly mild and sweet.

"Sloe gin, man, the greatest stuff in the world. Let me order you one."

"No thanks, pardner. I think I'll order something else."

I had been adequately warned about this stuff before. It went down like fruit punch and kicked like a plough horse. It was popular among beginning guzzlers. I walked over to the bar and ordered a beer from a character created by Al Capp.

As I turned from the bar and took a pull on the long-necked bottle, Charlie grinned and waved. He attempted to sling his little bushy partner between his legs and bring her back to her feet. With both of them a little short on technique, she landed solidly on her rear end on the floor, bringing him down on top of her. They rolled and laughed. They were hanging on each other, still in hysterics, as they approached.

"How you doing, buddy? I want you to meet Kico. Kico, this is my old buddy, Oggie."

"Charlie, you're a regular Fred Astaire."

"How is the working party?"

"Oh, as wonderful as ever."

"Them bastards are never going to give you any slack, are they?"

"It doesn't look like it. Not for awhile, anyway."

"That's Kico's sister over there picking fleas off of Bo Bo. Let me buy you a drink. I'm glad you could get out, anyway." He turned and called for the mama-san. "What are you drinking?"

"Beer."

"Give me a beer and a JB and water, Mama."

"I see you don't drink cough syrup like the rest."

"No-siree, JB is almost the best there is."

I was already feeling the first beer as Charlie dragged his little bundle of joy back onto the dance floor. As I looked around "The Longbranch," Miss Kitty was pouring four more sloe gins at the bar. I noticed the posters covering nearly every square foot of each wall. United Airlines, Air Canada, the skyline of Manhattan, and a lake in Oregon. That's close to home. The Beatles, Robert Mitchum, and the Flintstones were nailed to the ceiling. Mickey Mouse was irreverently tacked over the men's room door. Then there was the king, Elvis. He was not my king, but my God. Whoever hung all that stuff together must have been a sadist.

I punched a couple of slow Elvis tunes and Charlie's little Miss Bust eased the homesick pangs by rhythmically trying to etch a hot pattern on my chest through her Maidenform bra. The little girls were completely caught up in the western culture with their teeny skirts and frilly blouses, and with us in our starched khakis the atmosphere was somewhere between a junior high school hijinks and a scene out of "From Here to Eternity."

I forgot these were working girls. They were cute, squeaky-clean, and smelled of imaginary lotus blossoms.

I eased around the dance floor to "Love Me Tender." My new partner was not quite as pretty as the others, but she seemed to work harder at the game. She smiled more, batted her eyes more, and held me tighter, as though I might run away. When we turned with the music she rotated her hips slightly to make sure I knew she was there. Her warm breath from make-believe sighs worked on my rusty, forgotten thermostat.

I pretended I was being romanced. I was both delighted and terrified of being dragged away and romped to death. It was becoming embarrassing. The girls in Tijuana are more businesslike. They just grab you by the crotch: "Wanna go, Joe?"

We made another turn and I watched the negotiations around the room intensify; more petting, kissing, rubbing, and eye-batting. The guzzling of a whole one-and-a-half beers crept up on me, combined with waltzing around in circles, and I inadvertently stepped on a dainty foot. She let out a little yelp and stomped away to the bar. Obviously the illusion of business, or romance, had been broken.

I grinned at myself. It is better to have lost at love than never to have loved at all. Remembering a self-styled wit who had told me I wouldn't be able to make out in a whorehouse with a sack full of quarters, I grinned and swaggered over to the bar like Mitchum would have and ordered another beer. My ex-partner was already working on a couple of marines from another outfit.

I had tipped up the last of my beer when a girl walked in from the back room. My stomach did a flip for a moment and my mind forgot whether I was inhaling or exhaling. Some foam from the beer went up my nose, and I nearly sneezed the back of my head out.

She walked over to some tables opposite the bar and sat down. Spiked heels were connected to lovely little legs that were partially covered by a very short dark skirt. She also wore a pink sleeveless blouse with ruffles down the front. She began to play a game with some little pieces that resembled dominoes. Sensing me staring, she looked up and smiled.

I needed another beer. I really didn't but I did. Holding my breath, I hoped one of the other goons wouldn't move in before I got another bottle of courage down. That can't be on the menu, I thought to myself. It's too small, too young, and too gorgeous. I'm gonna burn in hell for my thoughts. Touch that stuff, buddy boy, and her sisters here will claw your eyes out. She had to be at least two years younger than them, or maybe even more. What was I worrying about? I had just turned eighteen years old a few months ago. What's a few months?

I took a couple more pulls on my bottle for courage, straightened my tie, pawed at my almost-nonexistent hair, then got off the stool and walked toward her. I walked in too straight a line and was too polite—a dead give-away for a drunk.

"May I sit?"

She looked up and smiled again. "Of course."

I melted into the chair opposite her. I took another drink from my crutch and asked the all-important question: "Do you work here?"

"Yes!" she replied with enthusiasm.

I felt a great rush come to all my nerve endings. I must be getting drunk. My face felt flushed and I kept both hands on my bottle to disguise nervousness. The thought of even touching such a lovely creature sent a shiver through my whole body. All kinds of primitive erotica raced through my mind.

She brought me back to my senses. "Would you like to learn the game?"

"I'm not very good at games," I replied weakly.

"That's all right. It's an easy game. It is a most ancient game."

I was surprised; it was very much like dominoes. Dots were replaced with characters with a very detailed and intricate design of animals, birds, plants, and patterns. It took a keen eye, good graphic ability, and a special awareness. The object of the game was to detect the flaw in the pattern or character of each tile. Only the tiles that were absolutely identical could be joined.

My enthusiasm for the game was not forthcoming. My entranced, beer-fogged brain was playing another game similar, but life-sized. And from my vantage point, there were no flaws, only exquisite perfection of beauty in the most profound sense of the word. She was an exotic Oriental creature so striking that it transcended the imagination.

She again brought me back from my euphoric, childlike rapture.

"What's your name?"

"You speak very good English."

"You speak very good English also."

We both giggled. I had drunk myself past courage and well into silly.

"Richard, Rich, or Dick." I gestured with my finger. "Never Richie, Ricky, or Dicky."

We giggled again. Then my giggle quickly faded. As

she bent over to pick up a tile that had fallen on the floor, volumes of long straight hair fell down from her shoulders and closely shrouded her face. A tiny, delicate ear protruded from the dark, rich sheen as she grasped the tile. I marveled at the small, youthful but determined breasts that softly caressed the pink material. My stomach flipped again. She was no child.

Self-awareness, doubt, and insecurity crept in beside the alcohol. The beast began to grow hair and the nose on a tongue-tied Cyrano began to grow.

We grinned and staggered out, hanging onto each other as we crawled into the Kamikaze cab and headed for the base. Everyone laughed and yapped about the fun we'd had. About the girls and how much they had to drink. I sat by the window in a bemused state of mind, staring out into the darkness and watching the cardboard village go by.

"Oggie, why didn't you lay that cute little thing you had tonight? She sure was something. I don't think I've ever seen a whore looking like that."

Little Kobi was just a figment of my imagination. I was dizzier than a bat, and hung on to keep my head from banging on the side of the cab.

At two o'clock the next afternoon I walked briskly through the streets of the cardboard village and found, to my amusement, that in the daylight it wasn't cardboard at all. My brain was still a mold of Jello that was much too aware of each stride. My whole body was slightly off time from the beer which collectively couldn't have amounted to more than four bottles. I managed to do the impossible: whistle and grin at the same time.

I had a date. I was hung over, but I still had a date. Somehow, last night, before the world managed to take a ride without me, I had asked Kobi for a date. A real date, not a five-minute wrestle. A dinner maybe, a walk in the park if they had one, and maybe something else.

Was it possible? A relationship with a working girl? She didn't seem to fit the mold. Maybe because of her age she was only allowed to hustle drinks, or maybe she was just there to be looked at. Why did I waste time playing silly games and trying to drink myself into a coma? Why dinner and all the pretense? Why was I beating around the bush? She was just a bar girl.

I stepped through the door of the Coconut Grove with composed anticipation. I just knew I was gonna be stood up. She had said it would be easier to meet here, as it was her day off.

My eyes had to adjust from the bright sunlight. Then I saw her sitting in the same booth where I had left her.

She smiled. "Hi, Richie-san!"

"Hello, Kobi-san. Shall we go?"

She slipped from behind the table and clicked across the floor in gold-colored high heels and a short, bright-red pleated skirt.

"How is your head, Richie-san? You were funny last night."

"My head is perfect," I lied. "Not much in there to hurt. The air gets a little stale sometimes."

She gave me a puzzled look and continued ahead of

me. I was drawn to an interesting gold bracelet on her upper arm. It was a cobra wrapped around her arm three or more times with little ruby eyes. A teenage dragon lady, I thought. Her whole outfit was a bit garish for my taste for a Saturday afternoon. I would have preferred dirty tennis shoes and cut-off jeans.

As she glided toward the door with me in tow, her lovely behind rolled ever so slightly and smoothly. My stomach flipped again. It's not the wrapper but what's in the package.

As we headed down the street she shortened her hold on me and took me by the arm.

"I know a good place. Good saki and good food."

"I've heard of saki, but I've never tried it."

We stopped at a sidewalk stand and I bought her some flowers. She giggled and kept sticking her nose into the bouquet. They looked like some kind of fruit blossoms.

This part of the village was even more shabby than the rest. It was hastily and crudely slapped together. A typical commercial phenomenon that flourishes near any U.S. military facility throughout the world. I was amazed by how well the Kamikaze cabs and bicycles were getting along on the same street with no traffic signs, no rules and regulations that were noticeable or practiced to any degree.

I got yanked into a side door where a dark, sweet, pungent aroma of cooking dominated the darkness. My eyes were still adjusting as we sat at a table and chairs made of wicker in the center of the restaurant. I glanced around quickly at the drab, empty restaurant.

Then my eyes never left her. It could have been a cave and I still would have felt a marvelous glow. Her big, lovely brown eyes danced and glistened.

A tiny, frail old man with just one tooth waited on us. I ordered abalone chow mein; that sounded exotic enough. She ordered something in Japanese.

I wasn't hungry. My body was anguished between hangover and wanting her. My last chance for two weeks. I had duty the next weekend. Also, we could ship out at any time.

Our ancient waiter brought us two tiny glasses of saki. It was hot. We saluted each other, giggled, and sipped. It went down smoothly, but it had an indistinguishable taste. Another sip of the saki and my whole body felt a nice, warm glow. It seemed to settle my stomach, and my appetite came back. Just a case of nerves. A combat marine terrified by a tiny little girl.

Dinner was finally served and it all looked delicious. Hers was a little more green than mine, but other than that they were the same. Hot tea and cookies were served.

"Where do you live, Kobi?"

"Just around the corner."

I nearly bit my tongue when I bit down on a piece of abalone that had the consistency of sautéed basketball but tasted great.

How convenient, I thought. Now all I have to do is get up the guts.

"Where do you live, Richie-san?"

"Seattle, Washington."

"I know where that is. It's straight across. Are you

lonely for home?"

"Yes, I guess so."

"Do you have a girlfriend?"

"Not any more."

"What happened?"

"She got married."

We finished our dinner and a lot of small talk. My mind wasn't really on conversation; it was around the corner in a dimly lit bedroom. The saki seemed to act like a potion.

"Kobi, can we go to your house?" I asked with an almost merciless approach.

"Sure," she smiled.

I squeezed her tiny wasp waist firmly, almost afraid of crushing her like a clumsy child with a kitten. We kissed. Hard mouths wide open, trying to smother each other as tongues danced, teased, and darted back and forth. I slipped both palms down onto her behind and pulled her to me, nearly lifting her off the bedroom floor. She responded immediately by arching her back and rotating her hips slowly.

We relaxed. I bent and kissed her ear close to her throat, and felt the dampness of sweet perspiration from the close stuffiness of the bedroom and the invisible fire we were building. I slipped both hands up under her bra and found the snap hidden by some lace. I slipped a clumsy fingernail under it and it popped. As her bra peeled away my hand followed the smooth curvature of her rib cage. Her small breast nearly filled my hand, surprisingly. It was firm and her nipple so erect it tickled my palm. She shivered when I opened my hand and kissed the nipple.

She took off her shoes and stepped back, then threw her hair forward and pulled her blouse up over her head. With a slip of a hidden button her skirt fell to the floor. I pulled her close again and kissed her hard. She was breathing steadily, audibly, deeply, and her eyes were almost closed. There was a musky, sweet, pungent scent distinctly her own.

I picked her up and laid her on the bed with a devilish smile and two thumbs. She slipped her black lace panties down, revealing a dark bush that could have been hidden by a single silver dollar. I had forgotten to breathe, and my stomach and heart were beyond flipping. She slowly moved her hips invitingly. Her heat building and my nerves frayed, I finally found her and her secret. She sucked in a quivering breath, and as she convulsed slightly and arched her back, I was going crazy.

We were both terribly inexperienced. I panicked, thinking I might lose it before we began. Then we settled down to a rhythm that I could be safe with as little baby sounds came from deep in her throat. Her tiny, powerful hips and thighs helped deepen a strong, heavy beat.

Her eyes rolled wildly in the dim room as if in panic. She rolled her head from side to side and the squeak of spring and slap of flesh quickened. Her moaning and near-whimpering were contagious. We held each other in panic like two children in a high, scary place. She began to move under me in great, forceful lunges, then she let out a clawing screech that scared the hell out of me. Finally she let go and relaxed. She was breathing very hard with her eyes closed. She smiled, and I knew it had been good.

My own body began to quake, and with great compassion and consideration she gave me a few more helpful lunges. I hung onto her, nearly breaking her. Then it came with such force that it left me momentarily paralyzed from the waist down.

She cuddled beside me and I looked into those child-woman eyes. Okinawa would never be the same. In fact, afternoons anywhere would never be the same again.

"Richie-san, you must have forgot. Two dollars, please!"

CHAPTER TWENTY-SIX

To all appearances the first North Vietnamese regiment was completely gutted, but no animal circled or cornered gives up or quits. The more desperate it becomes the more dangerous it is. Humans are no exception. It is a very chancy business to drop your weapon and surrender, only to be shot by one of your comrades or be blown away by a hysterical marine whose twisted philosophy is to not take prisoners. Then there is the gruesome reality of interrogation and torture by the South Vietnamese army. An appendage of the red war machine was dead or dying quickly, but dangerous nerve endings still spasmed out of desperation.

A convoy of amtracks loaded with fresh supplies made a wrong turn and got left in dense jungle without proper cover and support. They fought to the last man. Command had pushed the giant breadboxes too far.

The squad was spared out in a circle in the light jungle waiting for the squad leaders to return. We tinkered with weapons and discussed among ourselves how much ass-kicking we were doing, like halftime at a football game. We all agreed that the special team deserved the Heisman Trophy.

Daniels came rattling and huffing through the jungle from the direction of the CP. He unslung his M-14, dropped to his knees, and called us around. He could hardly catch his breath.

"There's a chopper down about three miles from here to the north, and our squad's been elected to get to it before you-know-who. There's gonna be a chopper waiting for us about a mile down the beach. The beach is only two hundred yards in that direction." He pointed with his rifle.

I was completely and thoroughly confused. I thought the beach was the other way, but I had forgotten this was a jagged peninsula.

"Okay. The fastest way for us to get our chopper and get to the downed one is for the company to use the beach. When we move out we're gonna spread out at five-yard intervals and run like hell."

"A whole company running down the beach? That's crazy!" Anderson yelled.

"Don't I know it," Daniels said. "Move out."

Two days ago, we had fought like hell to get out of the water onto the beach and into the jungle; now we were running down the beach like it was Malibu. When we got to the edge of the jungle, everyone was reluctant to hit the white sand again.

It was like standing at the hatch of a plane waiting to take your first or second jump.

When we finally got on the beach we were at a full gallop. An entire company huffing and puffing, taking John Wayne's beach again.

I was so tired when the inevitable happened that it seemed like it had taken ten times longer to find cover than usual. It took four more strides than usual to find a depression in the sand instead of dropping like a rock. I would have been left up on the top of a small sand dune with no cover. The smart thing would have been to drop in place and dig like hell.

I was so exhausted that I no longer cared; what was going to happen, was going to happen. Funny how the pop of a round hitting the soft sand and a bit landing in my face changed my mind. You skinny, greasy, mindless little bastards, you're not getting me!

The entire company crawled on its belly closer to the jungle's edge for as much cover as we could find. There were probably no more than four or five guys out there keeping a whole company at bay. We were wasting our ammo on enemy we couldn't see, and with the sea at our backs we had no place to go. I smelled another Silver Star for somebody.

I kept my head down and my face practically buried in the sand. I dropped a few M-79 rounds in their direction and fantasized squashing someone.

After about forty-five minutes of company sunbathing, the cavalry came. A little slow at two-and-a-half times the speed of sound. A Phantom dropped altitude and leveled off before it trimmed the tree line. It made an empty pass to see where the bad guys were in relationship to the good guys, then turned out over the water. We could tell by the color of the pod on its underbelly that he was packing five hundred pounds of our favorite apple jelly.

As he made his turn to straighten out and make the second run, the entire beach looked like it had been invaded by a massive colony of giant sea turtles. Hyperkinetic sea turtles that threw sand every which way and finally dug a hole like they were irreparably late for one of Mother's Nature's deadlines.

I scratched and flayed with both hands and feet. We all prayed that the hot jelly was on target. I could hear the Phantom screaming toward us. I raised my head from the sand like a busy gopher. It was frightening; he was flying so close to the jungle that the wings were nipping off branches and small tree tops.

I felt the air and ground shock of everything evaporating in the target area, then felt the heat on the back of my hands and neck. As far as I could tell, they were right on target. At least there was nothing burning on the beach.

The Phantom made another turn and came back, flying low over the water just off the beach. He tipped his wings in a show of victory and "glad to be of service." We cheered him and waved.

The jungle burned, and to our surprise two of Ho Chi Minh's finest strolled out of it with their hands in the air. Out of reflex, Corporal Daniels gave the order not to shoot. A couple of men stepped out and herded them in at rifle point and forced them to spread-eagle on their bellies to check for weapons and ID.

I couldn't get over how small, young, and frightened they were as they lay in the sand in their sawed-off black pajamas. I wasn't afraid of them and I didn't feel superior toward them. Although I knew they had killed a lot of marines, I still had empathy for them. They were terrified. I knew, as did they, that they were living dead. They would probably die at the hands of some rear-echelon liaison punk who had never seen combat but could tell the folks back home he had seen the enemy and did what was right.

We stood around them, waiting for the company commander to show up and give us orders on what to do with them. We still had a mission.

One of the prisoners made a sign for some water. I took out my canteen and put it to his mouth. Without the slightest warning, Simms stepped up and gave the other one a butt stroke on the head. Corporal Anderson and I grabbed him and threw him to the ground.

"They're prisoners of war, asshole!" I yelled. "Nobody's gonna maltreat them." I looked around at a lot of faces and made my point perfectly clear. "Take your goddamn frustrations out on the gooks that are out there, still armed and able to kill you."

Still down in the sand on his back, Simms growled like a cornered alley cat almost under his breath. "I'll get even with you, Oggie Doggie. I don't know who in the hell you think you are."

I stepped closer to him and bent over so he wouldn't miss a syllable, and smiled. "Any time you want to learn another lesson in manners, just let me know."

When I stood up and turned around, Anderson had lit up a cigarette for both prisoners. Peeling the hide of a five-year-old child with a sharp knife just to make him scream could hardly be equated with butt-stroking a bound prisoner; but I, or we, were fighting for that tiny shred of morality, that tiny particle of humanity.

After our unexpected beach party and barbecue we were all grinning again. Maybe it was the cool breeze blowing in from the hatch, or the fact that we didn't have to hump the sand or the jungle for awhile. I sat directly across from the hatch and the door gunner, and watched the jungle go by at about a thousand feet. There were no flak gear aboard the chopper. We were too tired to sit on our helmets to keep our asses from getting shot off, and too tired to look up at the top of the fuselage for spots of sunlight that appeared magically.

Corporal Daniels was sitting to my right. He put his helmet to mine, cupped his mouth in his hand, and yelled over the roar of the engines. "I'm going to put you up for lance corporal again. You deserve it."

I smiled and gave him a thumbs-up of appreciation. I was grateful he was trying. Back at the air base I had marched down to the CP to take the test and had scored in the upper ten percent of the entire battalion, but Sergeant Nick had rejected it. I didn't care much; I was getting short. I only had weeks to go in this hellhole anyway.

I kept having nightmares that red tape would keep me here for the duration of the war. There were no more rumors of enormous extensions, but I was nervous just the same because of my short time left. I had learned to live with and accept the dangers of combat, and had helped others to do the same. Inside, I had grown up, but I had also grown old. Outwardly, I kept up the front of having my guts well enough intact to get the job done, but inwardly I was becoming old and senile. I had been in Vietnam longer than anyone here. My odds were being used up. The idea of having only a few weeks to go had reduced me to a terrified old man of nineteen years. My fantasies had really started to bother me. I believed the Vietcong had stepped up the program to get me personally before I went home. I had embarrassed them by getting away from them too many times.

The door gunner was searching and traversing the ground below. I thought again how neat it would be to have his job and not have to hump the ground. He flew back to safety every night.

Then daydreaming turned to shock and horror right before my eyes. With a blink of an eye the gunner had been blown backward away from his gun. He hung upside down, dangling from his seat strap. Blood gushed from the center of his chest like a restricted garden hose. We looked on, helpless with horror. He flopped in spasms, and blood gushed up the side of the fuselage and ran down the deck. Still in shock, I watched some fool along the bench pick up his boots so they wouldn't get dirty. We looked at each other, still stunned.

I came to my senses and undid my seat strap, stood up, and unfastened the gunner, letting his body slide gently to the deck. We were flying naked, without any armaments. My next movements didn't seem to be coming from any constructive thought, but were mechanical movements. While I was on my hands and knees with the gunner, Daniels had taken position at the M-60, opened it up, and let it do its thing.

I took off my helmet, threw it on the deck, and slipped the gunner's helmet off his head. The rest of the squad was squeezing toward the hatch, opening up the M-14s. Any little thing to add to our survival. No one could see a thing—just fire like hell.

I placed the flyer's communications helmet on my head, bent the mouthpiece back into place in front of my lips, and with the other hand traced the lines from the helmet that had the male plug at the end. I found the female plug on the wall of the fuselage and shoved the male plug into it.

The ammo belt on the M-60 was running dangerously low. I patted somebody on the shoulder, and he looked up. It was Simms. I pointed to a can of ammo underneath a seat and he knew what I meant. He scrambled for it.

"Skipper, this is PFC Ogden. Your crew chief is dead. What do you want us to do?"

"Oh, no!" There was a pause.

He rattled off orders fast. "Ogden, our ETA is about forty seconds. We're going into a hot LZ. You stay aboard and man the gun and radio. I want every man out in three seconds. We're gonna make a bounce landing and that's all. Repeat, I want every man out in three seconds."

I relayed the message to Daniels, who let me take his place at the gun. He screamed orders to the squad.

The chopper hit the ground hard and bounced, knocking everybody down, but they scrambled and jumped. I helped Daniels shove men out. He hit the ground on his belly last and rolled over and gave me "thumbs up."

I yelled into the mike. "They're out. Let's go, sir." Good-bye, fellows. Keep your asses down.

The engines screamed and we lifted off immediately. I leaned on the trigger. I was having a lot of trouble staying on the seat. I was too short, so I crawled up on my knees. I kept firing aft along the tail, trying to keep our group in sight so I wouldn't hit any of them.

A huge whapping sound shook the entire bird like a giant machete had taken several whacks at it, leaving gaping holes in the fuselage. A shiver went through me. I held my bowels while sweat poured from under the helmet, blinding me. Then I found myself laughing out loud like an idiot. This was the job I had wanted so badly. My knees kept slipping off the seat as the ship began to vibrate even more.

We had gained some altitude and it looked like we might be out of danger. But just when I thought there was a glimmer of hope, the engine began to miss badly. Black smoke passed the fuselage and some drifted in, filling the inside compartment. All hope went out the hatch when the engine quit completely. A strange calm came over me and I took my finger off the trigger.

A solemn voice came over the radio. "What's your name again back there?"

"Ogden, sir."

"Well, Ogden, it's just you and me. The captain bought it, and we're going down. I'm gonna autorotate to give us some help."

He was going to turn the rotor blades loose on the shaft so they would spin by themselves and give us some lift and help with the impact.

"This is Lieutenant Torres. You did a hell of a job back there, partner. If we get out of this I wanna buy you a beer."

"Thanks, lieutenant. Now it's your turn. Give her hell."

I didn't feel like talking any more, but the silence was eerie this high in the sky. I disengaged the wires from the wall. The only thing I could think of was to crawl up into the tail section. I couldn't believe how calm and relaxed I was; I just wanted a place to lay down. Going in at such a steep angle, I knew there was no hope. I had to pull myself along the deck, grabbing onto the struts that held up the benches.

I reached the tiny end of the tail section and curled up into a ball. It was silent except for the wind rushing past the hatch. I closed my eyes. The nightmare was going to be over. It wouldn't hurt any more.

I was the tiny four-year-old child who walked away from home and got lost out in the bus intersection and was nearly hit by cars several times before I was finally rescued and brought back home. I was back in my room, safe under the blankets. No more horror, no more anguish, no more fear. Peace at last.

I woke up to some bright lights on a table of sheets. Standing over me was a clean, smiling face connected to a body wrapped in a white smock which was dotted with faded bloodstains.

"Welcome back to the world. We thought you were going to sleep all the way through it and get paid, too."

I had one hell of a headache. "What happened?"

"Oh, you just got a little bump on your head. But that's pretty good, considering you got shot out of the sky like a turkey. You crashed in a helicopter and were overlooked by a Vietcong patrol. Fortunately, you were found by one of our patrols. During the impact, the tail section broke off and sailed away while you were napping, and landed some distance from the wreckage."

He kept grinning.

"Ever think of going into the air wing? You came down without a scratch and only a bump on the head. That's more than I can say for the rest of them. Incidentally, you have been pulled from the game and sent to the showers. You will probably be home for Christmas."

I smiled back as it began to register.

"Keep smiling and I'll put you back in the game. They're hurting for smiling faces."

I didn't ask further about the Vietcong patrol.

I had lost so much weight that I looked like a young

Frank Sinatra in a Santa Claus suit in my dress greens. I had a window seat in a 707 as it sat on the runway in Danang. There were so many different emotions going through my head. I was dizzy and my stomach was turning, only this time for joy. But I was still scared. A thousand Vietcong could break through the jungle toward the plane at any second. How come we were not moving?

My heart leaped when we began to roll. A pretty stewardess tapped me on the shoulder to get my attention.

"Please fasten your seat belt."

She was a brunette with big blue eyes and lovely round cheeks on both ends. Whoever put us in such quarters with such sweet-smelling loveliness when we were right out of the jungle was an unwitting sadist.

The plane began to pick up speed, and I watched the last glimpses of hell race by the window. As the plane lifted off the runway, my knuckles went white helping it up over the jungle. I kept pulling harder on the armrest until my arms shook from the strain. Although I had great confidence in this 707, which was made at home, there could still be little bastards down there in the jungle with rockets that could bring it down.

When we were high over the jungle out of range, I realized I was still trying to help the plane. My eyes clouded up and tears ran down my cheeks, dripping off my chin onto my tie.

My eyes were still out of focus with tears when I looked across the aisle and saw the professor smiling . . a ghost that will haunt me for the rest of my life.

HORRIFYING TRUE CRIME
FROM PINNACLE BOOKS

A World of Eerie Suspense
Awaits in Novels by Noel Hynd